I0627676

Endings &
Empathy

ENDINGS AND EMPATHY (Amplifier 6)
Copyright © 2023 Meghan Ciana Doidge
Published by Old Man in the CrossWalk Productions 2023
Salt Spring Island, BC, Canada
www.oldmaninthecrosswalk.com

All rights reserved under International and Pan-American
Copyright Conventions. No part of this book may be
produced in any form or by any electronic or mechanical
means, including information storage and retrieval systems,
without permission in writing from the author, except by
reviewer, who may quote brief passages in a review.

This is a work of fiction. All names, characters,
places, objects, and incidents herein are the products
of the author's imagination or are used fictitiously.
Any resemblance to actual things, events, locales, or
persons living or dead is entirely coincidental.

Library and Archives Canada
Doidge, Meghan Ciana, 1973—
Endings and Empathy/Meghan Ciana Doidge—
PAPERBACK EDITION

Cover design by: Gene Mollica Studios
Models: Devon Ericksen & Jonathan Cannaux
Oracle card by Elizabeth Mackey Graphic Design

ISBN 978-1-989571-68-2

THE AMPLIFIER SERIES: BOOK 6

MEGHAN CIANA DOIDGE

Published by Old Man in the CrossWalk Productions
Salt Spring Island, BC, Canada

www.madebymeghan.ca

Endings and Empathy is the sixth and final book in the Amplifier series, which is set in the same universe as the Dowser, Oracle, Reconstructionist, Archivist, and Misfits of the Adept Universe series. While it is not necessary to read all six series, **in order to avoid spoilers** the ideal reading order of the Adept Universe is as follows:

More books in the Archivist and Misfits series to follow. Reading list doesn't include the shorter stories interspersed throughout all of the main series, but more information can be found at www.madebymeghan.ca

For Michael
I would walk into certain death if it meant
I got to be with you on the other side.

AUTHOR'S NOTE

Endings and Empathy is the sixth and final book in the Amplifier Series, which is set in the same universe as the Dowser, Oracle, Reconstructionist, Archivist, and Misfits of the Adept Universe series.

Sunflower

FREEDOM

WITH TWO OF THE FIVE COMPROMISED, I HAD NO choice but to go on the offensive. Hiding out—even if I was pretty much in plain sight these days—in the tiny corner of peace we'd carved for ourselves in the Pacific Northwest was no longer an option.

But the person or persons responsible for dragging me away from the life I'd fought to build, to protect? Well, they would regret every moment that I had to divert my attention toward them and away from what I truly wanted. They would regret forcing me to once again become the coldhearted, sociopathic, genetically constructed magical abomination they'd bred and trained me to be.

The Collective was already done.

I'd destroyed them more than eight years ago.

But apparently, some of those who'd survived now needed a reminder of their demise.

When it was done, I would walk away with everything that was mine to have and to hold. And what I couldn't outright destroy? I would absorb or claim for myself.

Because Emma Johnson was stronger than Amp5 had ever been.

ONE

THE DARK-HAIRED SORCERER SWATHED IN BLACK TAC-
tical gear at my side ran his hand down my spine—or
as much of it as he could reach while I was wearing
my dual blades sheathed across my back. His con-
flicting emotions filtered through to me even as I
peered through the magically enhanced binoculars I
had trained on a tiny, rocky island in the middle of
nowhere.

Literally, nowhere.

Loaded into a heavily armored, magically fortified helicopter, we were hovering over what was
practically the midway point between the Barents
Sea and the Norwegian Sea, the southern extents of
the Arctic Ocean. Though technically, we were off the
northern coast of Norway, we'd left that coast behind
two hours ago. I couldn't see even a shadow of the
mainland, not even with the enhanced binoculars.

Five days had passed since we'd been sent the first
text message from Samantha and Daniel's kidnapper,

and the sorcerer who'd all but shackled himself to my side was still angry. At the situation, yes. But also at me specifically. That didn't stop him from reaching out, though, or touching me tenderly in the very brief moments we'd grabbed on our way to finding—and hopefully liberating—my blood-bound teammates.

Aiden had his own pair of binoculars. They cut without difficulty through the gloom of the cloudy night—which wasn't actual night, because the sun never set in this part of the world in June. But they also somehow highlighted magic, picking up the energy that emanated from the magically inclined as well as magical constructs, then tagging that energy in a medium shade of blue that was slightly lighter than the color of Aiden's power.

It was closing in on 3:00 a.m. Despite the cloaking on the helicopter and the clouds obscuring the midnight sun, we'd waited until early morning to further minimize our visibility.

Even heavily cloaked in cloud, the sun sliding along the horizon, while never rising or setting, unsettled me. Not that I would ever admit that out loud. We'd been moving too quickly and crossing too many borders to do more than snatch a nap here or there, completely ignoring time zones as we passed through. So I blamed the jet lag for the disconcertion, then ignored it.

To my left, Christopher was outfitted in cool-weather tactical gear like Aiden and me, though with fewer pockets than the sorcerer. He wasn't bothering to keep watch out his side of the helicopter. His magic was a constant low-grade hum on my upper spine while he shuffled his oracle cards and called out quiet commands to our ground team of two over the comms. Mostly, though, he had been content to allow that team to implement the plan it had taken us three days to cobble together, as they navigated their way to the island, then into the research station that occupied the site's northern tip.

According to our intel, nine nonmagicals occupied the entirety of Bear Island. Researchers. But I had tuned out what exactly they were researching on a barren rock of an island in the Arctic Ocean, more interested in how we were planning to get them out of our way.

Mark Calhoun—sorcerer, weapons specialist, and former Collective team leader—was flying the helicopter. Keeping us low and moving as slowly as possible without actually crashing into the ocean below so we could keep an eye on the island coastline.

The binoculars were Becca Jackson's handiwork. The demolitions expert was one half of our two-person initial infiltration team. Since she'd been assigned to guard me by the Collective more than ten years ago, Becca had further honed her secondary sorcerer abilities with tech. She and Mark still specialized in covert ops, usually working with Daniel. They'd already been waiting to meet up with Fish and Samantha somewhere in Europe when Christopher had contacted them about the extraction mission. The helicopter, the binoculars, and most of the other gear we'd collected had been supplied or sourced by Becca and Mark.

The second half of the infiltration team was Khalid Azar, Aiden's middle half-brother. Though Kader had forced his magically sensitive son through training befitting a combat-grade sorcerer, it turned out that Khalid was also an extraction specialist for the Azar cabal.

On our initial approach to the island, Becca and Khalid had dropped out of the copter, carrying just enough air to get them to the shore underwater with the help of some magical propulsion. They'd dumped their tanks and other protective gear before surfacing, and were in the process of scaling the cliffside to the research station.

But the station wasn't our primary goal.

We simply needed its currently occupied helipad to land, and as a base for the next stage of the extraction.

Breaking into the magically cloaked fortress hidden on the far point of the island was our ultimate goal. And after that—extracting our teammates with minimal... disturbance.

And yes, I wasn't at all surprised that Samantha and Daniel's kidnapper had decided they needed a fortress to hold them.

The island was shaped like an arrowhead. It was also covered in craggy rock formations and magical sensors, prohibiting landing elsewhere. Undetected, at least.

I would have just walked in through the front doors alone. Or maybe I'd have brought Christopher to back me. Had I gotten my way.

I hadn't gotten my way.

Because apparently, I didn't get to have my way on missions in quite the same way as I'd enjoyed for the first twenty-one years of my life. Before I'd loved. Before I'd had a life to protect, beyond simply keeping Christopher and Paisley tucked away from the world.

The Collective had maintained the ancient fortress on Bear Island as a base for years. Since long before our generation had been first mixed in a tube. Our intel suggested that sections of the external structure dated back to the eleventh century. As with the intel regarding the research station, though, I had quickly tuned out the reasons that the Collective had maintained such a base, on an island so remote and so northern that no trees punctuated its craggy rock.

I was far more interested in the current facts and how those defined our mission parameters. Such as the fact that the fortress was invisible to satellites, invisible to anyone without magical sight. If any mundane—such as the scientists who occupied the research station—were to wander too close, the spells embedded into the site's rocky foundations would urge them to turn away.

Just like the compound in which the Five had been housed for the first twenty-one years of our lives. The compound we'd destroyed on the way out.

His attention fixed through the binoculars, watching now as Becca and Khalid crested the edge of the cliff, Aiden pressed his free hand firmly against my lower back again. Offering me comfort that I hadn't even known I needed. Again. Even though he was still ridiculously incensed at me.

I had made a lot of compromises over the last five days. I'd bent to Aiden and Christopher's insistence on putting together an extraction team instead of just taking the clairvoyant and heading off to Daniel and Samantha's last known location. I'd flown into London instead of Moscow. First, waiting for the other team members to join us—Christopher had insisted on Calhoun and Becca, and Aiden had called in Khalid. Then waiting for all the intel we needed to gather and sift through.

And then, instead of coming straight to Bear Island, where all that intel pointed, I'd flown with the rest of the extraction team into Oslo. Once in Norway, the equipment we'd needed had been obtained through Mark's and Becca's channels. Then it had been magically fortified even further by the sorcerers, specific to our mission parameters.

A long list of compromises. But it was the one compromise that I had refused to make that had Aiden still spitting mad. Specifically, leaving Opal at home under Kader Azar's protection. Chenda, the Mystic of the Golden Peninsula, had also insisted on staying with the young witch.

I knew the dream walker would have been safe on the property, tucked behind Aiden's wards with his sister Ocean, and with Paisley—even though the demon dog was still recovering from the torture Mercury Dunkirk had inflicted upon her. Safe from attack, at least. Though it was possible that luring me off the property was the kidnapper's ultimate goal.

But I also knew that if the dream walker decided to follow us, she would have found it exceedingly difficult to slip away from Kader Azar. Or Chenda, for that matter.

Opal hadn't protested the arrangement, but Aiden had gone ballistic.

I'd never seen him so angry.

Not at me, at least.

Kader and Chenda had been my backup plan. Originally, I'd suggested that the dark sorcerer stay with Opal himself. That had been met with a silent but pointed refusal that made it feel as though a physical wall had been erected between us, cutting through all the invisible bonds that tied us together. Even now, even without picking up his emotions empathically, I still felt as if those bonds that tied me to Aiden were muted on some fundamental level.

Well, fundamental to me. In some nebulous, purely emotion-based way. But knowing the feeling was irrational didn't ease that continual awareness.

Through the binoculars, I watched the blue-limned outlines of Becca and Khalid breach the station and enter the building. They would maintain radio silence until the second stage of their mission was concluded.

Keeping back far enough from the cliff face that the spelled binoculars were a necessity rather than a convenience, Calhoun slowly circled us around the other side of the island, heading toward the point of the arrowhead and the fortress.

As best we'd been able to piece together through the intelligence we'd gathered—and from Christopher's visions—the kidnapper had held my two blood-bound teammates for over seven days now. It was likely that I was about to be facing off against one of the last two members of the Collective who had previously been unidentified, either Lindiwe Fourie or Kai Win. According to Kader and confirmed by Chenda.

I wouldn't have thought it possible for either the nullifier or the telekinetic to be held by anyone for that long—even a member of the Collective's inner circle. Not without outright killing them. And together?

That was almost unbelievable.

Members of the Collective were powerful even as individuals, yes. But something else had to have occurred, some factor that led or contributed to two of the Five being overwhelmed, then completely locked down. Something we didn't yet know.

Something hidden to Christopher's sight still lingered along the edges of all of this… situation.

While Becca and Khalid slipped through the station and triggered an emergency scenario dire enough that it would get all the nonmagical occupants off the island, the rest of us surveyed the magically cloaked fortress as we swept past in the helicopter. It was our fifth circuit since our arrival, and I still hadn't seen any evidence of the kind of destruction that Samantha could achieve without even being pissed off.

And a kidnapped Samantha? Well, she'd be seriously pissed. As would Daniel.

"They aren't dead," Christopher murmured.

"Can you see them now?" Aiden asked sharply.

The clairvoyant hadn't experienced clear sight of either Fish or Samantha for days now. And I was staring via binoculars at the reason why. I had absolutely no doubt that the original Collective would have woven protections against all kinds of magic into the wards encasing the fortress—including against the focused intent of a clairvoyant. Though it was unlikely that the wards would have been tuned to block Christopher specifically. Not unless the kidnapper had access to his DNA. And even then, it would have needed to be a recent sample.

Because my acceptance of the power riled up in me by the immortal entity that was the Hallowed had stretched my reach— even as that power was still woefully untested—I now needed to actively avoid continually amplifying Christopher through our mutual blood tattoos. And something about accepting the Hallowed-riled power had all but demanded that I also accept the blood bonds that had been forced upon me just shy of my fifteenth birthday. That acceptance had somehow given Christopher's sight, and his other magic, a boost as well.

But we hadn't had any time to properly assess any of it yet.

Christopher flicked three cards into the air before him. "I see clearly enough, sorcerer," he said mildly.

Aiden's hand flexed on my back, his magic completely primed. As it had been since we'd left the property. Since we'd left Opal with his father.

We had traced Daniel and Samantha as far as possible via magically manipulated tech—which is to say, with the help of a sorcerer skilled in such things, overseen by Isa Azar, who was currently based out of Dubai. That tech had traced the pair to the outskirts of Moscow, then found local footage of the team who had been tracking Samantha. As well as evidence that the local coven was in the midst of cleaning up the telekinetic's reaction to being attacked and ultimately taken.

Samantha had collapsed an entire apartment building. A fairly mild reaction for the telekinetic when under threat, which meant that she'd been worried about something. Best guess? Protecting Daniel.

Or she'd been wary of killing her attackers.

Because even though the stills the tech had pulled from the Moscow footage were grainy, they were clear enough for Kader, backed up by Chenda, to confirm that somehow, four of the five members of Gen 4 had come back from the dead—though it appeared that only three had survived Samantha's wrath.

The resurrection of the generation who'd been bred before the Five had incensed Kader. The generation who the sorcerer Azar had outright indicated to me had 'failed' during our first actual meal together. Hence the loosening of his tongue on the subject.

Or maybe I just hadn't been all that inclined to ask questions of the architect of the Collective before losing Samantha and Daniel.

Apparently, Gen 4 had been held in stasis for the last twenty or so years. Tucked away in the depths of a fortress. Far, far off the coast of Norway.

They should have remained there, tucked away from the havoc they could cause if not properly contained. Hence Kader's pissiness. Though it was rather clear even to me that he was more peeved about a member of the Collective operating behind his back rather than showing concern for the welfare of those he'd had a hand in breeding and raising, if not outright creating.

If Samantha had known who she'd been facing off against, she might have hesitated to murder members of the generation of genetically constructed super soldiers who had preceded us through the Collective's test tubes.

The experiments who were presumably the genesis of a portion of our own genetics.

We'd found no other connection to the fortress, and had no confirmation that the Gen 4s would return to that location. But we'd also had no other leads in London, where the next taunting text message from the kidnapper had arrived while we were readying for our flight to Oslo.

As with the first message, I'd ignored it. But the Azar tech sorcerer hadn't.

The thing about the members of the Collective? They were all generally of an older vintage, even if they didn't look it. And as such, they could be just a little bit clumsy when interacting with the modern world, with cellphones and text messages. And, more specifically given the fortress's remote location, with the satellite linkups those text messages were being routed through.

Isa's tech had the location confirmed within two hours of my receiving the demand that I 'turn myself over to guarantee the release of my teammates.'

Only an idiot would have believed that anyone would let Adepts of the power level of Daniel and Samantha go, even if I did agree to their terms.

Only an idiot would sacrifice herself when she could just as easily retrieve her team members and neutralize their kidnapper.

I wasn't that kind of idiot.

I also wasn't a hero, willing to walk into uncertainty unarmed and uninformed, just on the off chance I was dealing with a principled kidnapper. Even if I hadn't known I was facing off against a member of the Collective—for whom principles weren't even a fleeting thought—I wouldn't have traded myself for my teammates.

My headphones crackled. Then Khalid said over comms, "And they're off." His accent carried only hints of his French-influenced childhood. Or more accurately, given who his father was, his childhood training.

The helicopter picked up speed as Calhoun whipped us around again to the other end of the island, just in time to see a second, much larger helicopter taking off from the research station's landing pad. Had we been closer, I presumed we would have been able to hear an evacuation alarm.

Calhoun simply waited for the nonmagicals evacuating their station to get over deep water. Then he swung our helicopter over the landing pad, just as the red warning lights encircling the pad snuffed out—courtesy of Becca, no doubt.

Leaving the binoculars behind, I jumped through the side door of the copter with the blades still whirling overhead. Aiden was just behind on my right, and Christopher on my left. We marched to the craggy drop on the far side of the pad, with the station at our backs.

Calhoun exited behind us, instantly circling the helicopter and setting runes to keep it obscured from casual observation. Anyone sight-sensitive to magic would still be able to see it, but we didn't plan on lingering.

I gazed across the barren, mist-shrouded, gray-on-gray landscape to where I knew the fortress sat perched above the ocean. Exiting the station, Becca joined us. Her passage was magically silenced, though her own sorcerer magic was bright and robust to my senses. Khalid strode alongside her, carrying his no-less-powerful magic far more muted. Both were clothed in the black tactical gear they'd worn under the dry-suit scuba gear they'd shed. Becca's dark-blond hair was damp, curling around her neck.

Deeply tanned and dark eyed, the Azar sorcerer didn't bother pausing to confirm or reiterate the next stage of the extraction mission. Instead, he slipped like a shadow over the edge of the landing pad, making his way down the sharp, craggy incline without dislodging a single rock or second-guessing a single foot- or hand-hold. Then he set off across the rocky ground.

The overly-magic-sensitive, combat-grade sorcerer hadn't been smoking whatever he took to dampen his senses since he'd joined us in London. I had promised to drain Khalid's power as part of his payment for the mission, so that he would get a reprieve from the continual onslaught of that magical sensitivity. But in the meantime, each opportunity he had to physically distance himself from the rest of us, he had done so.

I itched to follow him. To ghost his footsteps through all the magical traps that lay between me and the confrontation to come.

I itched to pull my blades and cut through any-thing—magic or people—that stood between me and Samantha and Daniel.

I wanted to be home, not perched on a barren island in the Arctic Ocean. But disabling those traps and plotting our course into the fortress was Khalid's part of the mission.

And… I was also done. With the killing. With allowing any member of the Collective to force my hand.

So I waited instead of charging ahead. I waited, hopefully for the last time, as Christopher stepped away to sit on a nearby outcropping, dangling his legs and shuffling his oracle cards with his face lifted to the eerily half-lit sky. I waited as Aiden and Becca set out the runed spell that they'd been working on since they'd met up in London. I waited while Khalid slipped ahead to survey the fortress on foot.

I knew we needed a better sense of the defenses we were about to breach. That I needed a sense of what sort of force stood in my way. Though I had no doubt that once I stepped through the outer wards that encased the fortress, I'd have no problem finding Samantha and Fish.

The blood tattoos etched into my skin would lead me directly to my kidnapped teammates.

And even more importantly, I was fairly certain I now possessed the ability, the focus, to amplify my blood-bound teammates from afar. I just hadn't been able to truly test my newly acquired reach, for fear of continually overloading Christopher.

Aiden straightened from a crouch, a series of runed markers spread across the rock before him now. Then, clasping his hands before his chest, he murmured a quick series of commands in that language he spoke that was unique to the Azar cabal. With a well of magic gathered between his cupped palms, he gestured forward. Elbows still bent, he parted his hands to the sides in a sweeping gesture. Then with his forefingers, middle fingers, and thumb extended, his ring and little fingers curled into his palms, he created a wide frame with his arms.

A dark-blue shimmer of magic bloomed before him, then stretched into a hovering image about the size of our flat-screen TV. Through that magical view screen, the fortress appeared, tiny and distant, along with Khalid moving steadily overland toward it. It was as if Aiden had triggered a remote camera and was now projecting its viewpoint in front of us, except with magic, not tech and electricity.

"Nice," Becca murmured as Aiden made another gesture and the viewer zoomed in on the fortress, bringing it fully into view. "We're up and running," she added for the benefit of Khalid on the move and Calhoun still working to cloak the helicopter. Her voice echoed more over the comms unit in my right ear than coming through in person.

The two sorcerers stepped back from Aiden's magical viewfinder. Becca circled around to stand with Christopher on my left as the clairvoyant joined us, and Aiden stepped back to my right.

I quickly scanned everything I could see of the fortress and its now magically highlighted defenses through Aiden's view screen, picking up even more detail than I'd been able to see through the binoculars from the air.

"One main entrance, as we thought. Heavily reinforced…" I could see that the layers of warding thickened around the edges of the main doors, making what should have been the most vulnerable part of the fortress more difficult to breach. "The darker blue squares?" I gestured to the top edge of one of the stone ramparts. "Defensive spells?"

"Yes, likely remotely triggered," Aiden said, clipped and formal. As he had been for most of the last five days.

That was fine—both the tone and the info were understandable given the circumstances. We had already known we weren't going in through the front door. But depending on the state we found Samantha and Daniel in, we might have to use those doors as our egress.

There was no road or trail leading to or from the fortress. Maybe there had been once, centuries ago. Or perhaps whoever had originally built the structure came and went by magical means. Or even by boat. The entire island was one huge cliff, though, just jutting out of the water. So unless there was a docking bay carved into the far cliffside—and only accessible at low tide, since we hadn't sighted it—boat access seemed unlikely.

Knowing that breaking through the front might take too long, it was clear that we might need to land the helicopter within the courtyard of the fortress. Or that Calhoun would need to hover over us and drop down a line. That in turn made it clear that the outer wards were going to have to come down. And that it might be better for someone to stay behind with Calhoun, guarding our exit from outside in order to facilitate that exit.

I didn't bother mentioning any of that, though. I'd already been voted down enough over the past few days to severely test my patience.

Nothing I was looking at now changed the next stage of the extraction plan. We would go through the cliffside wall on the far side of the fortress, where no one would expect the site to be breached. Just as soon as Khalid confirmed that stage of the mission was a go.

Granted, I couldn't have even planned to sneak in if I hadn't let Aiden and Christopher talk me into involving Mark, Becca, and Khalid. I would have had to walk right through the main doors, cutting through the magic that sealed them and likely taking a lot of hits, even with Aiden shielding me.

Shielding us.

'Us' was why the sorcerer now stood at my side when I'd wanted him to stay with Opal. And unfortunately, even the fact that Aiden was currently at my side hadn't quelled the ongoing argument over that. I couldn't remember when anyone else in my life had ever had the fortitude to fight with me, almost continually, for five days straight. Even Samantha didn't do that. She just sulked while I ignored her, until eventually she had to give in, give up.

My phone buzzed against my leg, tapped into the satellite link on the helicopter. I had tuned out the specifics, but Aiden had made sure all our phones were connected that way, making use of Becca's expertise with the tech. I refused to be out of touch for one moment longer than necessary.

I stepped back, Becca instantly filling my spot. She and Christopher began tracking and timing all the magical signatures shifting within the fortress, gesturing to each other and nodding. They were really only confirming the plan we'd laid out in advance, but could now factor in the number of guards and the amount of magical munitions on site—at least those they could currently see and count. Because even though Aiden's brilliant spell could see through the fortress's first layer of stone behind the boundary wards, we'd be going in mostly blind beyond that.

"We have to market this, sorcerer," Becca murmured, nodding to the view screen. "You'll be a millionaire in a matter of months."

Aiden offered the other sorcerer a tight smile, stepping back with me as I tugged my phone out of my thigh pocket. I glanced at the screen, even though only one person could have been, would have been, calling me.

Opal.

Right on time.

Aiden had her checking in every eight hours and sending text updates every two.

My dark sorcerer pressed against me, shoulder to shoulder, tugging one of his copper rings off a finger and flicking it into a spin in his open palm. A silence spell domed over us. We could still hear what was happening around us, but no one could listen in.

I answered the call, accepting a video link and already smiling in anticipation.

Then I blinked at the screen, not quite certain what I was seeing. Bright-blue plastic… with flowers? The perspective shifted… an edge… sunlight glistening off water… and something green and leafy floating on top…

Aiden chuckled.

Then I caught sight of light-brown skin… a knee? Then a shoulder. A vibrant-pink tank top—and a demon dog flashing her teeth in the direction of the phone. Half of Opal's face appeared on-screen as the little witch leaned on Paisley's shoulder, then held the phone above the both of them.

"Wading pool," Aiden murmured, somehow sensing my confusion. As he always seemed to be able to do, livid with me or not.

"Emma!" Opal cried, utterly delighted—utterly delightful—as she was every time she called. "Aiden! Where are you?"

Though it was 6:00 p.m. and just before dinner in BC, Lake Cowichan was still sunny and bright. "On location," I said. "And where are you?"

Opal pouted playfully. I wasn't keeping secrets. I just didn't want to burden my little witch with too much detail. She didn't need any extra strife in her life.

"We're having a restorative soak." She shifted, and water sloshed around on her end. "To help Paisley heal. Chenda taught me how to mix this one after she got the fresh ginseng she special ordered. We're going to try to root some and plant it in the garden." Opal lifted a leather-bound, rune-covered book into view. "Don't worry. I'm also doing my homework."

Aiden flinched beside me. But before he could explain the reaction, a voice murmured something in the background.

Opal nodded to someone off-screen, then spoke as if relaying information. "Grandfather taught me a waterproofing rune."

That didn't ease the tension radiating from Aiden.

"Say hi!" Opal crowed. Then she lifted the phone over her head and angled it so it showed the back patio of the house—on which Kader Azar was sitting in the shade and reading. Wearing one of his beige summer-weight suits, the elder Azar lifted his hand in the barest of waves, not bothering to look up from his book.

Aiden swore quietly under his breath. Energy shifted across the copper rings on each of his fingers, lightly reverberating against the invisible sound barrier bubble surrounding us.

I gave him a look.

He huffed and reined in the power display. My magic might not have affected technology, but his did.

Opal reframed her face on the phone, settling back with her head on Paisley's shoulder. This close up, I could still see the scarring crisscrossing the demon dog's gray-blue pelt, including a concentrated ring around her neck. Mercury Dunkirk's attempt to compel Paisley had done some serious damage. Even after five days, the demon dog's inherent healing power was still trying to counter the aftereffects of that vicious, repeated assault.

And now suddenly I was the one struggling to keep my anger out of my expression.

Opal was glancing between Aiden and me, her smile quieter but still curving her lips, that same joy was still visible in her bright-blue eyes. Her dark-brown, gold-and-silver-streaked curls stirred in a light breeze.

"Soon, then?" she asked.

I nodded. "We should be home to you by tomorrow."

Opal's gaze flicked to Aiden. "And then you'll stop being mad, right?"

Aiden huffed. "I'm not mad at you."

Opal's eyes narrowed in disbelief.

"I am simply mad at the disruption of our life together," Aiden said, offering the little witch a tight smile.

"That's how life works," Opal said, on the edge of testy. She looked at me. "Four and a half years. Then I'll be strong enough not to be left behind."

That was an ongoing conversation as well. And only with Opal and Aiden did I not seem to mind repeating myself.

"What are you doing today?" I asked gently.

Opal hit me with another narrow-eyed gaze, and I could feel Aiden stifling a smile under the onslaught of her playfully dramatic discontent as much as I was. "Being bored."

I laughed quietly. "Really? Being tutored by two ancient Adepts is boring?"

I heard another murmur in Opal's background.

The dream walker grinned. "Grandfather says he's only seventy-seven. Middle-aged for an Azar sorcerer."

I rolled my eyes.

Opal giggled quietly, then she said thoughtfully, "I've learned more in the last four days than I learned in the entire semester of first-year herbology. And Chenda isn't even a practicing witch."

Chenda, aka the Mystic of the Golden Peninsula, was some sort of mind mage. More than a simple telepath but not as powerful as Bee. I had a feeling that the former member of the Collective, who had claimed to be Christopher's mother in a more direct fashion than simply being one of the Adepts whose DNA was in all the Five, was trying to bond with Opal via the care and feeding of the demon dog.

The dream walker wasn't so easily wooed. But Paisley wouldn't remotely mind the attention.

"But I've still learned more," Opal added in a rush. "From you, Aiden, about spells and runes."

"It's not a competition," Aiden said gently.

My comms earpiece crackled lightly. Then Khalid said, "Confirm that the exterior guard are rotating on a ten-minute interval."

"Confirmed," Becca murmured back.

"Be ready to move in behind me," Khalid said. "On my mark."

"We have your back," the demolitions expert concurred.

The comms went silent.

Opal's wide eyes flicked between me and Aiden, reading our expressions. Then she settled her gaze on me and swallowed. "You have to go?"

I nodded. "Aiden will text you the moment we're clear and heading back to you. We'll move as quickly as possible."

Opal nodded a little frantically. "Be stealthy. Grandfather says it's better for you to move slowly, and that I should expect radio silence after this call, but it doesn't mean anything is wrong."

"He's correct," Aiden said begrudgingly.

"I love you," I said.

"I know." The little witch angled the phone to include Paisley's head again. "We love you back."

Paisley dropped her mouth open in a wide, toothy grin. Then with a flick of her forked blue tongue, she licked the phone right out of Opal's hand.

I caught a cut-off squeal, a splash, then a shot of the submerged halves of Paisley and Opal. Then the call dropped.

Aiden sighed heavily. "I just replaced that phone."

Tucking my own phone back in my pocket, I leaned into the dark-haired sorcerer, lifting up on my toes to brush a light kiss across his lips. He had shaved the short beard he'd been sporting, but it was steadily growing back.

He slipped his free hand into my hair, whispering across my own lips, "Emma…" Then he deepened the kiss.

I curved into him, my hands splayed across his chest. Just enjoying the contact, the simmer of desire building between us.

Aiden broke the kiss but not the embrace. He sighed against my temple, then slipped the copper ring back on his finger with his arms still loosely wrapped around me.

The silence spell dissipated with a quiet snap, but we stood loosely embraced for a moment longer, holding on to the happiness bequeathed to us from Opal's phone call.

"I love you too, my dark sorcerer," I murmured. Then I sucked lightly on his lower lip. "Wanting you to be the one to protect Opal was only because—"

"I know," he growled quietly, trading kisses with me. "I would have asked the same, except I know that

Samantha and Daniel are important to you. To your family."

"Well," I drawled playfully, "it's more that I'm tired of the Collective trying to screw with me."

"Right, amplifier," he said, teasingly doubtful. "Which is why two of the main members of that nefarious Collective are sipping tea on our back porch, watching over our daughter and our Paisley as we speak."

There were a lot of 'ours' in that statement. A lot of claiming. Enough that all I could do was just smile at my sorcerer, my Aiden, because anything I said wouldn't be enough.

"Divide and conquer," Christopher said quietly, stepping back to join us. The white of his magic shimmered faintly in his light-gray eyes, as if it was aware but not fully awoken. "Plus they kept us contained for twenty-one years. Opal doesn't stand a chance of manipulating either of them."

"She is not manipulative!" I snapped, forgetting to moderate my voice.

Christopher raised his hands. "Sneaky! I meant sneaky."

I narrowed my eyes at him. "She listens. She understands."

Christopher snorted. "Opal listens to you. And to you alone."

I lifted my chin. "And I don't try to cage her."

Aiden was grinning at me.

Christopher just shook his head. Then he revealed three oracle cards that he'd pulled from his deck. He held them in a spread in one hand, faces outward. The remainder of the deck was tucked in his other hand.

Finally.

"The reading has settled?" Aiden asked quietly while I tried to figure out what insight the cards brought to our current mission.

Arranged in the clairvoyant's hand, the Chrysanthemum card, paired with the Balance intention, and the Sunflower card, paired with the Freedom intention, flanked the Rosemary card.

The Destiny card.

The first two cards were tucked behind the third, the arrangement not fanned out or spread evenly.

Something that felt a lot like anxiety churned low in my stomach. I ignored it. "Was the grouping intentional, or…"

"That's the way the cards landed in my hand. Five times," Christopher said quietly, his gaze pinned to me.

Aiden glanced between Christopher and me. "What am I not seeing?"

Neither of us answered. I was still trying to sort out the implications without Christopher dictating them to me first. And the clairvoyant wanted to see my reaction before he tried to convince me I was wrong. At least that had been our previous dynamic.

But something had shifted for me internally when I'd accepted the Hallowed's powers. Like a kernel, a spark of… belief. Even so, I wasn't going to let Christopher use me. I wasn't going to willingly wear blinders, and not demand that he decipher the reading in a rational manner.

"Balance, Destiny, Freedom," Aiden prompted. "That's a solid, positive reading."

Christopher nodded, still watching me. "Chrysanthemum. Truth, honesty, and protection paired with justice, responsibility, and reason."

"That's Emma," Aiden said, getting a bit testy.

"If she accepts," Christopher said without heat.

Aiden looked at me questioningly.

"Destiny," I finally spat. "The Rosemary card has ascendancy over the other two in this reading. If you believe in that sort of thing."

"Hard not to believe it when it's wielded by a clairvoyant," Aiden murmured gently.

"Everyone has their own... preconceptions," I said, more than a little peeved at what felt like a gigantic shove in a direction I didn't want to go. I could accept the power I wielded. I could accept the people bound to me, whether or not I'd originally chosen those bonds for myself. But I wasn't going to be pushed around by the clairvoyant's fanatical belief in fate and destiny.

Christopher laughed quietly. Then he shuffled the three cards back into the main deck. Unseen energy writhed around his hands as he shuffled once more. Then he flicked three random cards out from the deck. Borne on magic, the cards hovered in the air for a moment in a loose arc. Rosemary—the Destiny card—was slightly higher than the other two.

We all stared at the still-hovering cards.

"It's a clean reading," Christopher said with a shrug. Then he gathered and tucked all the cards away in his upper pocket, as if he felt no need to look further.

The clairvoyant stepped back to join Becca. The demolitions expert was collecting the runed markers the sorcerers had used to anchor the magical view screen, all the while listening to our conversation.

Aiden raised an eyebrow in my direction.

"I regret giving him the cards," I said sourly.

My dark sorcerer chuckled doubtfully.

I sighed. Heavily. "According to Christopher's cards, all I have to do is remember my responsibilities, mete out justice, and accept my destiny."

"To… achieve what? The mission?" Aiden frowned, putting it all together himself. "To… gain your freedom?" He shook his head, correcting himself. "To bring about change and free the others."

"Sure. Something like that," I said.

Aiden glanced at Christopher, whose back was to us—deliberately, I thought—and narrowed his eyes. "Destiny."

"Yeah, the clairvoyant is a big believer."

"Enough to…" Aiden trailed off.

"Enough to throw me in front of a death curse." I hadn't bothered lowering my voice. Christopher's shoulders stiffened, but he didn't turn around.

"More than once?" Aiden asked in a whisper.

I met his bright-blue-eyed gaze, not having to touch him to know that concern had momentarily over-taken his seething anger at the situation, at me. "No."

Aiden nodded, but didn't look truly relieved.

And neither was I.

But the time for distrusting Christopher's motives had passed. I had allowed Kader and Chenda to sign a personal copy of Opal's adoption papers. At the dream walker's bidding, of course. And if I could accept their presence in my life, I had no rational reason not to forgive—and forget—Christopher's ill-conceived past deeds.

Becca tucked the runed markers from the view screen into her jacket pocket. The sorcerers had indicated that the markers should be usable three times in total before they ran out of magic. The view screen spell wasn't something that Aiden could renew easily while in enemy territory. And he hadn't had enough time to fully fortify his newly acquired tactical gear either, so his pockets held all the premade spells he'd have access to for the next stage of the mission—no reaching through to pluck items from his fortified safe at home. I wasn't actually sure if he would have been able to reach them from this distance anyway.

"We need to work on a more mobile version," Becca muttered softly to Aiden as she stepped up to join us.

The dark-haired sorcerer didn't answer, glancing back over his shoulder instead. Calhoun had gotten the helicopter cloaked and was crossing toward us. He would be staying with the copter, monitoring our progress. If and when we needed it, he'd bring transport to us.

I opened my mouth and almost asked Aiden to stay as backup as well. It was a legitimate request. A regular mission would have had more than one support team member. Calhoun could fly and could operate any and all weapons with deadly accuracy. But we weren't going to need the weapons specialist's kind of support until after we had Samantha and Daniel, specifically during our exit. I knew enough about extraction missions to know that the chances of getting in and out undetected were infinitesimal.

Aiden caught my gaze. Then he smiled at me tightly.

I closed my mouth on my request, keeping the impulse to protect him to myself. Again.

As the main extraction team, Becca, Christopher, and I needed a shield specialist, especially if Daniel was compromised once we found him. Plus the plan we were currently running had been suggested, torn apart, then set two days before. Khalid, the extraction specialist, would scout ahead, then cover our backs after entry. Becca, the demolitions and tech expert, would keep us moving forward no matter what obstacles we hit. Christopher, the clairvoyant, would make certain we were heading in the right direction and that nothing snuck up on us. And Aiden would be there to shield and protect us all.

And me? I would be held in reserve, amplifying the others as needed until something came up that demanded my sort of attention.

Hopefully without me pulling my blades.

I had already killed in the name of the Collective for far too long.

"Your path is laid," Khalid said over comms. "Watch your step."

Christopher pulled a black knit hat over his white-blond hair. Aiden double-checked his pockets.

Becca tightened the straps of her black backpack, murmuring over comms, "We're headed your way, K."

I stepped forward with the others at my back, following the path I'd watched Khalid take across the barren landscape.

DEPLOYING AIDEN'S VIEW SCREEN LET US CONFIRM that the point of possible entry Khalid had tagged on the far side of the fortress was indeed as vacant as we'd hypothesized. It was the farthest point away from the main entrance, with only a thin stone ledge as a foothold against the sheer drop down into the icy ocean depths. So with our destination set, we had silently skirted the fortress with only the light of the gloomy sky to aid our passage.

Given the muted sound of the surf pounding against the sheer rock wall below, it was far enough down that a tumble off the mist-shrouded cliff would have killed even me had I slipped along the narrow ledge. And the magically fortified stone wall that rose to eight meters or more along the sides of the fortress—and to easily eighteen meters at the rear—

offered little in the way of handholds to reach the patrolled rampart walkway above.

To go in covertly while seeking minimal losses, we had deliberately selected this most unlikely insertion point. Choosing what should have been an impossible entrance into a subbasement level carved directly into the rock and the cliff face. An impossible entrance for other teams.

But not for us.

Aiden, Becca, Christopher, and I met up with Khalid, then clung under the sorcerers' minimal shielding at the rear of the fortress while the guards paced their timed circuit above us. Though we were at risk of being spotted, throwing more magic around might draw even more attention.

The heavily armed guards, outfitted more like mercenaries than uniformed troops, passed above us, oblivious. I couldn't feel any magic from them or the weapons they carried, but that wasn't unusual given the boundary wards between us.

Tucked between Khalid and me, Becca taped a rectangle just slightly taller than herself onto the side of the fortress. Her silver duct tape was etched in black marker runes. The demolitions expert splayed her fingers across the runed tape at shoulder height. Then without further ceremony, she whispered a phrase heavy with magic and intent under her breath.

The runes marked along the duct-taped rectangle ignited with her medium-blue magic. Then within that perimeter, the meter-thick stone barring our entry—along with the magical wards covering it—just disintegrated.

The massive mound of stone dust left behind flowed down and outward, covering the ground to the height of Becca's upper calves. With another whisper of power from her, it was whisked away off the cliff, caught in the wind to sprinkle into the ocean far below.

Khalid and Aiden both grunted, completely impressed.

I had always admired efficiency over flash. But Becca had managed both with one spell. And the years of experience it took to create and cast that spell, of course.

The sorcerer, swaying on her feet and pale even under the cloudy, half-lit sky, tucked closer to me, clearing the short passageway she'd carved into the fortress for us.

Khalid slipped into that narrow passage, so silent that I wouldn't have even known he was moving if I hadn't been able to feel his magic—a low hum that I knew would let him continually obscure cameras and other tech.

Yes, all our exclusive talents had been laid out in detail while crafting the extraction plan. It was the only way to do what we wanted to do with this small a team—and with minimal casualties.

Becca slipped her hand into mine, panting quietly from the exertion of her efficient and impressive breach. I amplified her, gently filling her depleted reserves with my power. Unfortunately, I could only amplify her magic. I wasn't a healer. Even if she completely drained herself again, Becca could handle maybe one or two more full top-ups from me. Then she'd need to sleep—or to outright crash.

I could amplify the other four who made us the Five over and over, for days if needed. I might even be able to amplify Aiden that way now, as his tolerance for my power had been steadily built up through living together daily and delectable sex.

"Nice spell work, Becca," Aiden murmured over comms. He was pressed against the wall on the other side of the passageway, Christopher beside him.

Becca raised her arm, noting the countdown on her watch.

Two more minutes until a guard crossed the rampart walkway overhead again. In the gloom, they might still miss us clinging to the wall. But if they were magically sensitive, they might now feel the breach Becca had sliced through the wards, even as narrow as it was when factored into the entirety of the protections coating the fortress.

One minute.

Becca freed her other hand from mine.

Thirty seconds.

Khalid's voice came over comms. "Clear."

Aiden stepped into the passage Becca had cut through the stone, followed by Christopher.

Fifteen seconds.

Becca followed.

I kept as close as I could to the demolitions expert without stepping on her, then pressed myself against the magically smooth stone wall. Becca shimmied past me a step, then paused to erect a temporary shield over the hole in the wards. She couldn't actually mimic the magic of those outer wards—but she could harmonize with it. Still, if the last members of the Collective, or whoever else had commandeered the Bear Island compound, had someone on guard as magically sensitive as Khalid, even a well-sealed breach would be discovered.

That was why Becca now placed runed sensors at the opening before she crossed by me a second time to join the rest of the team waiting in the room beyond.

The space we stepped into was large and dark, enough so that it took me a moment to realize what I was looking at. Wood-slat flooring spread wall to wall, slightly springy underfoot and marked and marred by magic. No windows. The concrete-reinforced walls were also cracked and worn by years of magical back-lash. Barely discernible dormant runes were etched across every flat surface, including around and across the only exit—a pair of heavy-duty metal double doors.

"Practice space," Christopher said grimly. His expression was tight. He had almost died in spaces like this one—multiple times—in the first twenty-one years of our lives.

Once, during a dual training session when we were around sixteen, he'd been told to whisper the wrong prompt in my ear. It had taken me completely draining multiple healers—also at the Collective's behest—just to function again. And I had been resoundingly taught by our handlers that my instincts were occasionally more trustworthy than the clairvoyant blood bound to me.

Magic flared in Christopher's eyes as his sight showed him something, presumably related to my current thoughts.

I countered whatever the clairvoyant was seeing by striding forward and claiming the space. "Perfect," I said. "The interior door will be spelled as well, easily appropriated. We can regroup back here if we get separated or injured."

Christopher's magic settled down into a low hum.

"Agreed," Khalid said, moving up on my heels.

I paused before the doors. I could slice through any magic that might have been sealing them with my blades, but we were trying to be as clandestine as possible. Until we no longer had that choice. So once again, Becca stepped forward instead.

She cocked her head to the side, then shrugged and removed the glove from her right hand. She pressed a series of seemingly dormant runes that ringed the locking mechanism. They lit up under her touch.

Multiple locks on the door clicked open.

Aiden yanked a black-leather notebook out of his right thigh pocket, then began scribbling in it furiously.

I quashed the urge to smile at him, at his need to collect and understand magic. Now wasn't the time for coy smiles or lingering glances.

"Why change it up?" Becca muttered with a shake of her head. "Same codes as Peru." Then she flashed a smug grin over her shoulder at the rest of us.

Becca and Calhoun hadn't known about the Bear Island compound before we'd homed in on it as our target. But apparently, they were still just as impacted by their time spent in the employ of the Collective as the rest of us. Of course, it was also possible that they had been stationed on Bear Island at some point—and had their minds wiped. Bee, and possibly Chenda, were capable of that level of psychic manipulation, as was just about any witch coven. But neither Christopher or I had mentioned that as a possibility to Becca or Calhoun during our strategy sessions.

"Lazy," Khalid pronounced with a disdainful sneer, pushing the door open just enough to slip into the outer hall and scout ahead of us.

"If the layout's also the same…" I murmured, catching Christopher's gaze.

He nodded. "The Gen 5 barracks were two floors below the training level. But here, they would have had to excavate into the rock when they took over the fortress."

They had done the same with the compound in Peru. Almost the entire facility had been underground. However, it had been constructed that way, not retrofitted after being originally built in the eleventh century.

"Unless they've got Samantha and Daniel in medical," I muttered. The med bays in Peru could be sealed almost as effectively as the concrete cells that had housed the Five. "That would put them only one floor down."

"We got out," my Knox murmured. To himself, not me. "Fox in Socks got us out."

Or maybe he was speaking to whatever his magic was showing him?

My comms unit crackled in my ear.

"Clear," Khalid said.

I stepped into the hall, with the others following. Both Becca and Aiden cast muted, blue-tinted light spells around our feet and just ahead of us. Except for his magic, Khalid was indistinguishable from the shadows collected around the far doors, presumably leading to the stairs.

Power fluttered across two more of the blood tattoos on my spine—T1 and T4.

Fish and Samantha were near.

Smiling grimly, I glanced back at Christopher. His answering grin was toothy in anticipation.

TWO

THE REST OF THE TRAINING LEVEL WAS SMALLER THAN it had been in the Peruvian compound in which we Five had been raised. It was also unused and locked up tight. Becca got us through the locks without blowing anything up, then Khalid dropped back to keep our exit secure. The rest of us continued forward—and up. There was no down from the training level, at least not that we'd found.

Daniel's and Samantha's blood tattoos on my upper spine remained relatively quiet, simply sending a constant, feather-light shimmer across my skin that didn't offer me any sense of their direction or location. However, that binding was enough of a pull for the clairvoyant's sight that Christopher didn't have any issue leading the way. I covered our rear, with Becca and Aiden tucked in between us.

We kept the magic use to a minimum—meaning no shields until needed. The first few cameras Becca spotted weren't actually live. They were easily disabled by pulling a few wires—and confirmed that our entry point had been a strategically sound choice.

Two floors up, Christopher kept us to the edge of what appeared to be the guard barracks. There, despite the early-morning hour, snippets of murmured conversation filtered through to the stairwell. More English-speaking mercenaries, with a variety of accents. We didn't get close enough to confirm whether or not any former Collective operatives we knew were on site. Not that very many of those had made it out of the Peruvian compound.

Neither the clairvoyant nor the blood tattoos were drawing us into the sporadically lit corridor, so we continued up to the next level.

Oddly, the magical signatures that I could sense from the occupants of the barracks, sleeping and awake, were far dimmer than I would have presumed. Becca and Mark were both powerful magic users, enough so that the Collective had partnered both of them with me on missions. So I was surprised that the fortress guards didn't emanate more robust power. Maybe they were wearing dampeners? Though with Samantha and Daniel on site, that seemed unlikely—and potentially deadly. Dampeners often worked both ways, hindering a magic user's power in addition to masking it.

Unless the magic user was as powerful as someone like Pearl Godfrey, of course. The innocuous-looking trinket that the head of the Godfrey coven wore strung around her neck—a necklace constructed by a powerful alchemist—enhanced her own ability to keep her power signature muted. It in no way stopped her from casting obscenely powerful spells.

According to Aiden, there was nothing simple about the necklace or the abilities of the alchemist who'd made it. I, however, wasn't as easily beguiled by pretty magic as my dark sorcerer was.

Christopher led us up the next set of stairs, constructed mostly of concrete and steel, even though the walls of the fortress corridors remained the same thick stone throughout. It appeared as though the Collective had simply carved rooms, corridors, and stairwells out of the depths of the ancient fortress, then connected them as needed.

Hoping to continue avoiding all contact with the fortress's occupants for as long as possible, we progressed through the compound silently, following the clairvoyant's lead. As we wound through the stone halls and stairwells, Aiden cast a secondary shield twice in anticipation of someone sensing us. The dark-haired sorcerer couldn't render us all invisible, especially not while we were moving. But he could erect a temporary barrier that blended us into our immediate surroundings. Becca disabled the now actively transmitting cameras before we passed them—'fogging them,' as she put it. I noted Aiden watching everything the demolitions expert cast as if he was dying to take even more notes.

Both sorcerers were conserving their magic and their premade spells as much as possible. In Aiden's case, pausing to sketch specific runes in the middle of a firefight wasn't an ideal scenario. And for Becca, even with me amplifying her, getting us through the wards and into the fortress had already been draining.

The longer she went without casting anything else on that scale, the more her magic would reassert itself.

Just as I was passing the closed doors leading to the next level, the barely simmering blood tattoos on my T1 and T4 vertebra stirred—my ties to Fish and Samantha.

Partway up the next run of concrete stairs, Christopher paused as the white of his sight flickered over his eyes. Taking that as confirmation of what I'd already felt, and leaving the clairvoyant to take up the rear position, I opened the unwarded, unlocked steel doors. I stepped into an annoyingly familiar hallway, its stone walls reinforced with concrete. I paused just long enough for the others to gather behind me on the landing.

Unlike the other levels of the compound, both in Peru and in the fortress so far, no secondary exit marked the far end of the corridor. Just five doors, all open. Data pads were set to the side of each door.

"Only five doors," Christopher murmured, looking over my shoulder.

I had no idea whether Samantha had dug up any more background about our specific generation. I hadn't wanted to be involved when she'd started her search, and I still didn't now. But there had been six rooms on the level that had housed us at the Peru compound, though only our five rooms had ever been occupied. It was as if when that compound had been built, perhaps after the Bear Island facility had been abandoned or decommissioned, there had been plans for the fifth generation of the Collective's super soldiers to actually be the Six.

I ignored the urge to step forward and scan the rooms. As far as I could feel, they were empty. I wasn't certain why the tattoos had momentarily drawn me to visually check them.

"Medical?" I said grimly.

Christopher nodded, stepping back without comment.

With the Bear Island fortress set up so similarly to Peru, the most secure place to house Daniel and Samantha would have been the rooms on the level stretched out before me. Rooms that had been continually upgraded as our powers had grown in the compound where we'd been bred and raised. To keep us contained, if necessary.

Rooms I'd had to break into to rescue the others over eight years ago.

Rooms I hadn't realized I never wanted to lay eyes on again. Not until I saw the facsimiles now set before me.

A cool rage unfurled in my belly.

I had walked away.

Well, I'd torn myself away. Literally obliterating everything as I left.

But now someone had figured out how to force me to return.

That someone was going to seriously regret getting my attention.

THE MODERN SEALS ON THE DOORS TO THE MEDICAL wing—possibly even newly installed by their look—proved stubborn to Becca's more subtle entry techniques. In the end, the demolitions expert muttered, "Get ready for some noise, Khalid," over the comms as a warning to the sorcerer still covering our escape route. Then she tore off the data panel and started manually manipulating wires, giving each a little spark of electricity and magic as she tied and twisted them.

"How many beyond the doors, Knox?" I asked the clairvoyant.

He settled his hand on my shoulder, and I glanced at him. The white of his magic flickered across his eyes as he tilted his head, listening to what he was seeing in his mind's eye rather than trying to hear anything in the immediate vicinity. "I'm missing some component of all of this… there's a blank spot."

"Someone moving unseen?" I met Aiden's gaze behind Christopher. He'd fallen back to cover the stairwell, which led back the way we'd come as well as farther up into the facility. The sorcerers had been placing detection runes on every doorway as we'd passed—to be collected on our way back—but that didn't guarantee that someone couldn't sneak up on us.

Christopher hadn't answered me.

I pushed.

On mission and with extra lives under my care, I had to push him, even though I preferred to not force his compliance. "A blank spot that you can't see beyond? Or a blank within what you're already seeing?"

"Sunflower," Christopher murmured, referencing one of the trio of oracle cards he kept pulling. The Sunflower card—confidence, energy, and wishes—paired with the Freedom intention—beginnings, embracing folly, and being true to yourself.

"Nope… fuck!" Becca snarled viciously, pained as she shook out her ungloved hand. Then more power boiled under both her hands, rising to tip each of her fingers with a medium-blue magical glow.

The smell of fried plastic and metal wiring filled the stairwell landing.

Interpreting an oracle card wasn't going to help us in the moment.

"Christopher," I barked. "We need a body count!"

He flinched, then dropped his hand from my shoulder and blinked rapidly.

Something was coming, something all-encompassing enough that it was swamping his sight. But all I needed to know now was if that *something* was on the other side of the door Becca was trying to crack.

"Six mercs guarding this level. Seven noncombatants," Christopher said to me. Then he tapped his ear to trigger the mic in his comms. "Three heading your way, Khalid."

I frowned. "We tripped something? Missed a camera?"

Aiden was already shaking his head. "Not with Khalid and Becca with us."

"Ready," the demolitions expert barked.

Christopher and I stepped back. Aiden, standing behind but centered between us, placed a hand on both of our shoulders. He could shield us without physical contact, but he preferred to set the spell while touching.

Becca stretched long lengths of a wide green tape around the edges of the doorway, runes etched along its length. She then ripped off and taped out an X on the door at around shoulder height.

I'd seen her use a similar spell on missions a few times many years before, but this appeared to be a refinement of that technique—with the runes still dormant. Becca dropped the now-spent roll of tape, knocking it out of the way into the corner of the landing with the side of her foot as she placed her hand on the center of the green X. She angled her body to the side, then winked at us. "Set."

"As you will, demolitions specialist Jackson," I said, grinning at her.

She laughed huskily. It was rare that any of us got to test the full extent of our magical prowess, and despite the huge output of energy, it was always intoxicating.

Even, admittedly, for me.

Aiden's magic slid across my shoulders and down my arms as he triggered one of the mobile shielding spells in two of his copper rings. Christopher would have felt the same effect beside me.

The runes on the green-taped X sparked, energy streaking out to each point, then jumping to ignite the runes on the larger expanse of tape surrounding the door. Those runes ignited in multiple directions. Power punched through concrete and steel, formidable enough that I felt the blowback through Aiden's shield.

And then Becca, with her hand still pressed to the center of the X, was somehow holding the entire metal door aloft. I'd expected it to crumple, or at least be thrown into the corridor beyond.

Where it possibly would have taken an unknown number of casualties with it.

"Elegant, sorcerer," Aiden purred, impressed.

Becca chuckled, winded. Her shoulders sagged, knees bent, as she struggled to hold the metal door aloft, still edged in the concrete that had previously framed it.

"Guns," Christopher barked.

Becca dropped the door to the floor. She stumbled to the side, but still kept her hand pressed to the X.

A rapid-fire storm of bullets impacted against the other side of the door. Or perhaps projectiles of another sort. I could feel small pings of magic from each of them as they impacted the surface of the door.

Aiden, muttering complex phrases in that arcane Azar language, fished three black marbles out of his left thigh pocket. He'd been working on the rune-scribed marbles diligently as the team had gathered to plot and plan, anticipating what we might need defensively.

He flicked the marbles forward. The tiny glass balls spun across the concrete floor, then arced around the door that Becca was still using as a shield.

A moment later, the guns on the other side of the door went silent as they jammed, followed by muttered curses and the click-and-slide of ammo magazines being exchanged. Not a knockout spell—because we didn't want to disable Samantha or Daniel any more than I suspected they already were. But something that interfered with mechanics or mechanisms for three to five minutes, as best we'd been able to test it in the short time I'd allowed us for prep.

Shuffled footsteps filtered through to us as the mercs fell back to regroup.

"You are handy, sorcerer," Christopher crooned playfully, leaning in to press an enthusiastic kiss to Aiden's stubbled cheek.

"Did you doubt it?" Aiden's tone was cool. Because he was nearly as pissed at Christopher as he was at me, for having signed off on having Kader and Chenda stay with Opal and Paisley. Leaving my dark sorcerer to fight me without any backing.

Becca began trembling. I stepped forward, even though I was already amplifying her without actually touching her. She gasped, then groaned quietly, though not in pain. No matter how hard I tried to be gentle, my amplification affected everyone just a little differently. Daniel had to struggle to focus through having my power twine through his and not get a raging hard-on in the middle of a mission. His words. That reaction wasn't exactly surprising, however. I had spent years inadvertently amplifying him every time I'd initiated sex.

Conversely, as I found out only a few months ago, I actively hurt Samantha when I amplified her.

But most Adepts reacted somewhere in between, with Becca closer to the pleasure side of things.

The demolitions specialist rallied enough to set the door gently to the side of the craggy-edged hole that now led into medical, leaving just enough room for us to step around it single file. Then she disengaged the obviously energy-draining spell she'd been using to hold it aloft.

"Thank you," I said, stepping around her. "For not killing anyone."

She nodded stiffly, dropping her hand from the door and leaning back against the stone wall of the landing. "I'm right behind you."

"I'll clear the hall first." We were going to need more doors opened, hopefully with less force.

Becca flapped her hand in loose-wristed agreement.

I stepped through the opening into a wide corridor with Christopher literally on my heels. In another echo of my childhood spent in captivity, the walls, floor, and doors of this level were encased in large sheets of a white polymer of some sort. My connection to Samantha's and Daniel's blood tattoos strengthened with every step I took into the medical wing.

Aiden's mobile shield moved with Christopher and me as the sorcerer brought up the rear. Becca had her own shielding capacity, but it wasn't likely that anyone was going to easily sneak up on any of us. Khalid was watching our backs, plus both the sorcerers and the clairvoyant were more sensitive to magic than I was.

Midway down the corridor, three mercenaries stepped out into the hall from three different rooms. Their still-useless pistols were holstered at their sides.

The merc in the lead was a sorcerer—or at least he was wielding sorcerer-constructed objects of power. I knew that because he unleashed a volley of combat-grade spells that exploded barely ten centimeters from my nose, harmlessly skittering over and off Aiden's shield.

Closing the distance between us in three quick steps, I snapped a right hook and a wallop of magic—and not the kind that made Becca groan so contentedly—to the throat of the lead merc. His light-brown eyes widened a moment before he went down. Oddly, his own magic wasn't robust enough to even tickle my senses.

Christopher took out the second-closest mercenary, while Aiden crumpled up one of his notebook spells and flicked it over our heads to hit the chest of the third. She dropped without a sound.

Christopher raised an eyebrow at me. "Working some anger out?"

I sniffed. "Aiming at my head was just rude."

Aiden chuckled, darkly delighted. I flashed him a grin.

Christopher sighed affectedly.

Then one of the barely simmering tattoos flared on my upper spine.

"Zans," Christopher murmured.

I quickly searched the pockets of the merc I'd taken down, looking for a key card or badge but finding nothing. Christopher did the same with the other two prone figures.

We tossed all the weapons we found down the hall for Becca to collect or permanently disable, not bothering to arm ourselves. The pistols would still be compromised from Aiden's jamming spell, and such weapons were unreliable in my hands anyway. My magic didn't affect tech in general. But for some reason, it didn't interact well with projectile weapons, causing them to backfire—whether actively wielded by me or just pointed in my direction. That quirk of my magic wasn't reliable enough for me to wander around unshielded, though.

Aiden collected any active runed spells the mercenaries held, frowning over each as he settled his hand on the wrist of the merc he'd just looted. "The magical signatures don't match. These spells were supplied, not made?" He shook his head, pocketing the purloined spells without further comment.

Coming up empty-handed myself, I continued up the hall, feeling the magic sparking off various unseen Adepts tucked into the rooms ahead of us. Even people who Christopher had previously deemed noncombatants might attack.

The Collective didn't hire morally upright magic users. Except Becca had just chosen to drain her reserves a second time instead of simply blasting the heavy door through the corridor and taking out anyone unfortunate to be stationed on the other side. And she was former Collective.

I pressed my hand to the nearest closed door on my right. The white polymer that appeared to coat every surface of the medical wing was likely magically resistant. And physically resilient, no doubt. The mechanically triggered med-bay doors slid into the thick walls, rather than opening inward or outward. No handles, so I couldn't punch through the wall to get them open. Not that I'd expected to be able to.

The energy quietly prickling from the blood tattoo that tied me to Samantha didn't intensify.

Using that as a barometer, I moved forward, still under Aiden's mobile shield. I had argued about being continually shielded early into the extraction, but Aiden had wanted me shielded the entire time. So I'd been forced to compromise, eventually agreeing that my dark sorcerer could start to drain his reserves only after we came under fire.

The female merc Aiden had dropped let out a gentle but extremely contented snore as I stepped over her. I smirked at him.

He shrugged. "Should keep her down for about two hours."

Better than a punch to the throat and a wallop of the nastier side of my power.

"And she'll wake better rested than she has been at any time since she took this contract," Christopher teased, though with a touch of his future sight backing the words.

I stepped across the corridor to press my hand against the next door. My blood tattoos remained quiet, but steady. Samantha and Daniel were near, but their magic wasn't active.

"They're organizing up the hall," Christopher murmured to Aiden. "Three more mercs. And I'm guessing three medical techs of some sort, plus four others." He sucked in a quiet breath, anger flickering over his face at whatever he'd just been shown by his sight. "We're going to need Becca or Samantha to torch this level. At minimum."

"Blood samples?" I asked. We'd already speculated about why the kidnapper had taken Samantha and Daniel, and why they were willing to risk holding them instead of outright killing them. Beyond taunting me into action.

Christopher grunted in agreement.

"I'll take care of it," Aiden said, slipping a copper ring off his middle finger and sliding it over the forefinger of my right hand. Thereby transferring his shielding spell to me. My power would erode the rune magic etched into the metal quickly, which was why separating had been deemed secondary protocol for this mission, even if only for a few moments.

My dark sorcerer brushed a kiss over my lips, and I nipped him lightly before he could withdraw. He shook his head at me playfully, though his expression remained dark.

I wasn't going to be teasing Aiden out of his mood until I got him home. Which was fine. Because I wasn't planning on this idiotic rescue mission taking longer than a few more minutes to complete.

Aiden nodded at Christopher, tugging more marbles out of his thigh pocket—multicolored this time. Side by side, the two of them picked up their pace down the corridor, bypassing numerous closed doors.

I crossed the hall again, placing my hand on the next door.

A tattoo on my spine flickered—the topmost binding that tied me to Daniel. Fish.

But the connection was still far weaker than I'd ever felt while within a few steps of one of the other four. Presumably the rooms had some sort of dampening properties. But if this particular med bay was holding the most powerful nullifier in the world, then there was definitely more going on than simple shielding.

Anticipating my request to get the door open, Becca stepped into the corridor from the stairwell, steady on her feet as she swiftly crossed to join me. Two of the mercenaries' guns, clearly deemed worthy of not outright destroying, were tucked into previously empty holsters on her legs.

Khalid's voice crackled through my earpiece. "All clear here."

I glanced up and over to check on Christopher and Aiden—just as magic exploded through two of the open doorways a dozen meters away.

"Give us a second," Christopher said cheerfully, replying over comms.

The clairvoyant and the dark sorcerer parted ways, crossing past each other to step into rooms farther down on either side of the hall.

Becca paused to eye the data pad built into the wall beside the door that I still had my hand pressed against. "This one?"

"Daniel," I said.

She nodded, dropping the personal shield she'd erected around herself and tucking in beside me. My shield would offer her some protection while she focused on getting me through the sealed med-bay door.

It was rare that an Adept could create mobile shields, especially ones that wouldn't falter under a few hard hits. The fact that Aiden had developed a shield that we could move in and out of, as well as cast through, was remarkable. But there had never been any doubt about my sorcerer's skill—even while he'd been slowly drained by the Hallowed, thanks to his mother. Without that constant energy drain, he'd become even more powerful just in the last few weeks, noticeably lengthening his endurance between amplifications.

Becca was rapidly tapping open what appeared to be submenus on the data-pad screen. It was a little dizzying to watch, so I glanced back up the hall.

Christopher stepped back out into the corridor, grinning madly though his sight was clear. The clairvoyant rarely got to play, to do as he willed. Or as he would most likely say, as magic willed him. He crossed to join Aiden in the other room, stepping from my sight but not my senses. His blood tattoo was a robust hum on my T3 vertebra.

I tamped down on the impulse to amplify him. And yes, I could do that just by thinking about it now. We were that tightly bound.

Which made me wonder…

I closed my eyes, blocking out the distracting sight of Becca's swift fingers flying over the data pad, and reaching for the light simmer of Daniel's magic on my spine. I tried feeding power into it, tried strengthening that connection.

It remained quiet, barely discernible.

I reached for my connection to Samantha next. Shoving power through that bond.

Nothing.

But… just as I was about to stop, I felt… a surge of feedback. An acceptance?

Becca grunted, pleased.

I opened my eyes, still feeding power to Samantha, wherever she was, as Daniel's door slid open a hand's width.

Then it got stuck.

"Shit," Becca snarled.

I grabbed the edge of the door, anchored my footing against the narrow spaces of the doorjamb on either side, and tried yanking it open.

Becca, still tucked in front of me, did the same, lining up her hands below both of mine.

We heaved, gaining another hand's width.

Then someone inside the room—their magic likely cloaked from me by the dampening properties of the med bay—grabbed Becca's wrist.

The sorcerer shrieked in pain, instantly convulsing.

Wrapping one arm around her shoulders and clasping her against me to hold her upright, I reached out and broke the wrist of the offender. A healer, at a guess. But one capable of weaponizing their power.

The Collective only hired one type of Adept. And the capacity of an Adept with the innate ability to heal for also causing pain was so rare that there wasn't another designation for them. There were those deemed black witches and dark sorcerers, but no black or dark healers. Which seemed shortsighted on the part of the Adept community.

The asshole inside the room screamed and let Becca's wrist go in favor of cradling her own. In another not-so-delightful quirk of the rules of magic—or, more specifically, in the properties that underpinned the transference of energy—healers couldn't heal themselves.

The demolitions specialist crumpled in my arms. I set her against the wall beside the door, checking her eyes.

She blinked at me, then tried to wave me off, not terribly successful at controlling her limbs. "Go, go," she slurred. "I just need a moment."

I tapped my comms earpiece. "Aiden, Becca needs you."

The dark-haired sorcerer was stepping out of a room farther up the corridor before I'd even finished my sentence, heading steadily back toward us.

Becca tapped the back of my hand lightly, reminding me that I was still touching her face. I let her go without amplifying her. I had no idea what spell the healer had hit her with, but I didn't want to inadvertently amplify its effects. And as always, the best way to figure out unknown magic was to get my hands on the perpetrator responsible for it.

Becca slid down the wall in a controlled movement, though I wasn't sure she'd be getting up on her own.

I stepped to the side as Aiden joined us, brushing my fingers across his palm as he reached for me even while crouching over Becca. He was wearing his blank expression, which usually meant he was hiding his thoughts as he sorted through them. But the emotions that filtered through from that brief touch were steady. Focused. Determined.

He pressed something into Becca's hands, then tugged his notebook out of his pocket.

"For me?" Becca said, smiling weakly. "Ah, Emma, your sorcerer is a darling."

Glancing down as I squared off with the partially open doorway, I noted the badge that Aiden had given Becca. Someone he and the clairvoyant had taken out must have had more authority than the merc guards with their lack of access cards. Likely a senior healer.

Bracing my foot against the doorjamb a second time, I angled my body in the opposite direction. Then with a single burst of pure, muscled effort, I single-handedly shoved the rest of the door back into its pocket within the wall.

Within the med bay, the not-a-true-healer was standing before some sort of domed medical-unit bed. A stasis chamber by its look, meant to keep someone medically stable—or incapacitated—long term. The healer was tiny, dark-haired, and light-brown skinned. Her hand—its wrist visibly reddened and swelling—was pressed to the control panel on the stasis chamber, while she held an injector in the other. She angled the injector toward me like she was planning on stabbing me with it if I came too near.

Daniel, easily identifiable through the upper part of the glass dome, was stiffly laid out on the bed within the stasis chamber. Unbound, his arms were tucked at his sides and punctured by three IV lines running toward the head of the chamber. He was wearing nothing but Collective-issue gray boxers—and appeared unconscious.

The only other things in the room were a cart on wheels that appeared to hold numerous injectables, and a number of monitors flush-mounted into the far wall. Our incursion into medical must have interrupted the not-a-true-healer on her graveyard-shift rounds.

The healer curled her lip at me. "All you genetic monstrosities are too stupid to even stop to think—"

I lunged across the narrow space between us, grabbing her outwardly stretched wrist with one hand and her neck with the other.

Her eyes widened, slightly delayed.

Yeah, this too-stupid monstrosity was rather quick on her feet.

The healer tried to retaliate, her power welling up wherever our skin touched. Unfortunately for her, she was the idiot in this interaction. I pulled that power from her in one long, harsh draught.

She shuddered, gasping. Tears formed at the edges of her eyes as she dropped the injector.

Holding her so tightly by the neck that her toes barely touched the ground, I guided her free hand to the control panel on the chamber holding Daniel. None too gently, I manipulated her broken wrist at the same time.

Color drained from her face, and her eyes widened, pain overriding the fear emanating through my touch-triggered empathy.

"I assume there's some sort of nice way to wake my brother?" I said, perfectly pleasantly. "Rather than me just smashing through the glass and hauling him out?"

Her words strangled by my neck hold, she garbled something in response, then tried to nod.

"Go ahead, then." I smiled. "But try to kill him, and I will snap your neck. After draining every last drop of your magic so I can heal my friend Becca. She's the one you hurt a few minutes ago."

A tsunami of pained fear poured through the empathic connection I still couldn't stop myself from making whenever I touched someone skin-to-skin. It coated my mouth unpleasantly.

The healer tried to nod again.

I freed her broken wrist and loosened my hold on her neck—just enough for her to key in some instructions on the data pad, then press her palm against it.

Nothing nefarious flashed across the screen or any of the wall monitors—at least as far as I could tell. Hopefully, a kill command, digitally triggered or not, would require a second confirmation.

The lid of the chamber clicked open but didn't automatically lift.

My comms crackled. Khalid said something garbled, then "… headed… your way…"

The connection went fuzzy, then dead.

As if it had been overridden.

Apparently, a coordinated response to our incursion was now in full force.

I glanced at the open doorway a moment before Aiden stepped into view. His expression was still blank, even as his bright-blue eyes locked to mine.

"You have two choices," I said to the healer. "Step out into the hall, heal my friend, and leave. Or I drain you down while you realize that you aren't paid enough to lose all your power for the rest of your life to a genetic monstrosity."

A shiver of relief filtered through my empathic connection with the healer before she croaked, "Healing. I choose… the healing."

"I thought so." I let her go.

She stumbled back a few steps as I watched her closely. She rubbed her throat, then wrapped her hand around her broken wrist and glanced warily between me and Aiden.

Deliberately making myself appear vulnerable, I bent to scoop up the injector she'd dropped. Making certain the needle wasn't exposed, I tossed it to Aiden. He caught it, making a show of inspecting it.

I gestured from the healer to my dark sorcerer. She stepped carefully toward him, trying to not take her gaze off me.

Aiden tucked the injector into an open front pocket with the end pointing up, leaving his hands free.

Energy flickered almost imperceptibly over my T1 vertebra just a moment before Daniel groaned. I was turning toward him when he suddenly slammed his hands up against the glass dome—hard enough to crack it and fling it back off its hydraulic hinges.

All of the Five were stronger than our regular Adept counterparts. We'd been bred with only the best of the DNA that the Collective could source while constructing, then perfecting, their monstrosities.

Along with the three IV lines still connected back into the top of the stasis chamber, Daniel was covered in sensors. Panting with the effort, he tore those connections from his skin, then swung his legs off the side of the bed. He swayed, nearly went over, and braced himself with both hands.

He finally raised his head to meet my gaze. He looked haggard, and despite the panicked display of strength, he was drained. Of energy and magic.

I shook my head at him. "I hope that was worth it. I was just giving you a moment to wake naturally."

"Next time…"—his voice was gravel—"… don't wait."

"There isn't going to be a next time."

He tried to laugh, but managed only a pained huff.

"We need to move," I said. "We don't have Samantha yet."

Daniel shook his head, not in denial but just trying to clear it. He slipped from the bed, and his legs buckled. I caught him, pressing him back against the stasis chamber.

Rather unhelpfully, he wrapped his arms around my shoulders and pressed his face into my neck. "Fox in Socks," he murmured against my skin.

Under other circumstances, I would have thought him trying to fake me out in order to claim an intimate moment—except that he was seriously heavy, even for me. I slipped my hand around to the back of his neck, pressing my palm over the blood tattoo that tied my magic to him. His own magic was the barest of whispers, possibly not even enough to amplify. At least not enough to get him functional. Thankfully, all of the Five had robust immune systems, given enough time for them to kick in.

But with Khalid's warning still crackling through my head, I was extremely aware that we'd just run out of that time.

Daniel's embrace eased enough that he could run one hand up, then down, my back, then up again to cup my neck gently. "Socks?" he asked questioningly.

Whatever drugs they'd pumped into the nullifier, they were oddly powerful. "I'm going to try amplifying you."

"You never have to ask," he murmured.

"Yes," I said stiffly, teasing a lick of my power through the blood tattoo I was still touching, and trying to tangle it with the low simmer of his own magic. "I do."

Connection achieved, I slipped more and more energy into Daniel.

He shuddered under my touch, and I withdrew slightly.

He tightened his grip on me. "No."

"There's no point in expending energy if it isn't doing anything," I snapped. "And if it's painful, then—"

"It's not painful." He raised his head a little as if he was about to whisper in my ear. Then he stiffened, looking over my shoulder. "You… brought him."

I followed his gaze, already knowing that I would see Aiden in the doorway. "Becca?" I asked the dark-haired sorcerer.

"Better. But not on her feet." Aiden's expression was intense. He traced his gaze over every location where Daniel was in contact with me, then locked eyes with the drained nullifier.

Then he smiled. All sharp teeth and deadly intent.

A lick of utter thrill ran through me at his possessiveness. Not that I would ever admit that reaction out loud. I flashed my dark sorcerer a smile.

And he smiled back.

Daniel cursed quietly, then settled his hands back on the edge of the bed, trying to take most of his weight on his own.

"Shall we try again?" I asked the nullifier.

He met my gaze. His own light-brown eyes weren't as darkly shaded as they'd been a moment before. As I said, all of the Five rebounded quickly. "Always, Emma," he murmured. And I knew he meant something different than my simply amplifying him.

I ignored whatever he was trying to imply, though, settling his arm over my shoulder. I got us moving toward the door as I continued to feed more power through our blood tattoo connection.

We made it into the hall, and Aiden helped me settle Daniel next to Becca. The demolitions expert was fiddling with the key card Aiden had given her, doing something with a host of tiny wire filaments she'd exposed across its back. "Genius…" she muttered. "I'm totally stealing this imprinting tech… the card is specifically keyed to the user…"

"Hello to you too," Daniel said, grinning tiredly at her.

Becca bumped him with her shoulder, but didn't look up from her task.

I pointed at the healer, who was pressed against the opposite wall—as far as she could get from us without actually running away. Then I pointed at Daniel.

She shook her head. "The dampener will have to wear off. I could try to rapid detox him, but… it might make things worse."

Christopher paced back down the corridor from the direction of the stairwell. He must have backtracked, likely trying to get a read on Samantha through the still-sealed med bays.

"Open the other doors," I demanded of the healer.

"I don't have the authority," she said, actually quivering. She didn't seem to know where to look, flicking her fear-widened eyes between Christopher, Aiden, Daniel, and me.

"Already asked and answered, Socks," Christopher said mildly.

"Yeah. But you're so pretty, clairvoyant," Becca cooed without looking up. "Emma gives off a more I'll-rip-out-your-heart-and-eat-it vibe without even trying."

Christopher snorted.

"That would be a highly ineffectual way to murder someone," I said stiffly.

Everyone laughed quietly. Except the healer.

Which was fine because I really hadn't been joking.

Christopher crouched by Daniel, placing his hand on the nullifier's shoulder. "Brother."

"Took you long enough," Daniel said, trying to tease, but his rough voice was still filled with pain.

"Emma would have been here days ago, but Aiden and I insisted on her having backup."

Daniel closed his eyes, pressing his head back against the wall. "Good, because—"

Christopher's head snapped suddenly toward the exit that still had a door. The white of his magic flooded his eyes, and he cursed. "Telekinetic."

"Samantha?" I asked, confused.

Christopher straightened, his gaze still trained down the corridor as he unsheathed his sword. "No."

"Got it!" Becca crowed, thrusting the modified key card in the air.

Aiden reached for the card, but Christopher shoved him back. "Behind me, sorcerer, or—"

The far exit door buckled, then tore free from its frame. Solid steel and propelled by a tsunami of magic, it advanced down the hall toward us, slowly at first and banging off the walls—seemingly with deliberate intent.

The magical signature of our attacker felt familiar. Almost as familiar as the blood tattoo that had just sparked on my spine. Samantha wasn't attacking us, but she was nearby and awake.

The healer dove into the room we'd just vacated.

Fish grabbed Becca, who was still holding up the card, and tried to throw up a shield around her. His power faltered.

Aiden's power punched across the width of the hallway, forming a shield wall rather than a mobile dome over us all, to better conserve and focus his energy. Because it was about to take a hell of a hit.

As the door shot toward us with a burst of speed, I pumped power into the remote connection I'd made with Samantha, even as I continued to filter a trickle of power to Daniel. Fish's own magic still felt so thin that I was worried I would crush it completely if I tried to amplify him any quicker.

"Gen 4," Christopher growled, his magic backing his knowledge of an attacker we hadn't even laid eyes on yet. "Telekinetic." He glanced at me, grinning even as his power whited out his eyes. "He's not as strong as Zans."

I snatched the card from Becca's still-out-stretched hand. The demolitions specialist grabbed Daniel's arm instead, then the two of them wrestled over who was protecting the other. I almost snapped orders at them, but didn't have the time.

In the Gen 4 telekinetic's powerful hold, the massive steel door had curled into a huge, crumpled ball as it ricocheted off the wall about three meters ahead. Standing centered in the corridor, Aiden thrust his hands out, palms open, shoving his shield wall forward so that it was in motion when it met the unseen telekinetic's crumpled steel projectile.

My sorcerer's shield held.

Held.

I laughed, utterly delighted at that display of magical prowess.

Aiden chuckled, darkly delighted himself. But more at my reaction than his magical abilities.

Christopher shook his head, sighing at us.

The balled-up metal door was yanked back by a thick arm of the Gen 4 telekinetic's power, already lining up for its next hit.

I bounced lightly on my toes in anticipation of the next few moments, then caught myself doing so.

"Which door, oh clairvoyant?" I asked, deliberately holding the key card in Christopher's line of sight.

"Oh, yes," he breathed. His magic snapped to me, caressing the hand I was holding aloft. "That will work." A pause, then he pointed to the wall behind me. "Three up."

Across the hall from Daniel's room, but beyond Aiden's shield wall and into the telekinetic's field of play.

"I'll need a bit more space, my sorcerer," I said, grinning.

Aiden grunted in acknowledgement. Then with another massive push of power, he shoved his shield forward a few more steps, just as it caught the next onslaught from the crumpled steel door. Not far enough.

I clucked my tongue playfully, shaking my head. "Telekinetics. Always so showy."

Christopher laughed. "Could have cut us down before we even knew they were near... well, except for me."

Smirking at the clairvoyant, I stepped up to Aiden, pressing my hand against the back of his neck and feeding him a whack of power. He groaned, more shocked than aroused. But as we had practiced over and over, he channeled everything I gave him into the shield, wrapping it around the crushed steel door. Claiming it.

Cut off from the telekinetic by Aiden's power, the massive projectile crashed to the floor. As it did, it revealed a tall, mixed-race male in tactical gear standing at the end of the hall, blinking at us.

"Don't worry, Tek4," Christopher crowed. "You're about to get used to being trounced really, really quickly."

Key card in hand, I darted forward.

The telekinetic unleashed a barrage of smaller metal projectiles.

Aiden's mobile shield snapped around me, flickering as he tried to maintain it even while keeping hold of the crumpled steel door and the separate shield wall stretched across the hall to protect the others.

The projectiles hammered against the shield encasing me.

It flickered again.

Then it died.

"Faster, Socks!" Christopher shouted.

I pressed the modified key card to the data pad, hoping it would open the door Christopher had indicated led to Samantha. And quickly.

"Duck," the clairvoyant shouted. "Spin right."

I ducked and spun with no sense of whether the card had worked. Not quickly enough, though. The telekinetic managed to clip my right shoulder with a ball bearing. It bounced off me, but hurt like hell and rendered my arm momentarily unusable.

"Stay down," Christopher barked.

I pressed against the wall, as low as I could go while still keeping my footing. I gauged my distance to the telekinetic, watching him key in on me at the same time. His expression was oddly blank. Disengaged.

He raised his hands, bits of metal spinning in the air around him.

Then the door I'd just unlocked tore free and slammed against the far wall.

Wearing only a gray tank top and panties, Samantha stepped out from another med bay.

Because she just had to show off. And simply letting the door slide open would have been a waste of such an opportunity.

Pulling the med-bay door back and holding it aloft like a shield, she grinned down at me. Her face was drained, haggard. And she'd lost too much weight. From rapid magical depletion and then having even the embers of that power suppressed and unable to replenish her.

"Took you long enough, Socks," she groused.

"That complaint has already been logged."

Samantha laughed brightly, as if actually pleased to see me. Then she glanced over her shoulder and took in everyone else with a quick sweep of her dark-eyed gaze.

"Sorcerer, shield Emma, please," Christopher murmured, grinning back at Samantha.

A moment before the Gen 4 telekinetic unleashed his next assault, Aiden managed to erect another flickering shield over me.

Samantha's attention snapped to the telekinetic. "Give me a moment. I've got a grudge to settle."

"Try not to take too long," I said. "One of our teammates is unaccounted for, and Daniel and Becca are compromised."

She huffed, playing at being put out as she centered herself in the hall. Then every projectile that the Gen 4 telekinetic was in the process of flinging our away, everything he'd already thrown except the crumpled door Aiden was still holding, rose in the air to join the med-bay door.

I straightened, easily and continually amplifying Samantha, even through the flickering shield Aiden was trying to hold around me.

She winked at me, though I knew the touch of my magic actually hurt her. And then she unleashed everything she was holding against the other telekinetic.

That telekinetic easily shielded himself from Samantha's counterattack. But I wasn't the only one with a few extra tricks that I didn't think Gen 4 had in their arsenal.

On the tail of her barrage of projectiles and the med-bay door, Samantha stepped forward... only to appear right in front of the telekinetic.

She had triggered her short-range teleportation. He stumbled back.

All the projectiles dropped to the floor, an elaborate decoy.

It took three punches for Samantha to get through the Gen 4 telekinetic's shield. Then he crumpled to the floor at her feet.

She turned back to us, taking an elaborate bow.

Christopher clapped obligingly. "Even prettier in real time," he said.

Then Samantha's eyes rolled back, and she collapsed on top of the other telekinetic. She'd burned through all my amplification and more.

Already heading for her, I flashed Christopher a disgruntled look.

He held up his hands placatingly. "I missed the collapsing part. In my defense, there is a lot of interference."

The mention of interference inspired me to tap the comms unit in my ear. Still dead. "Initiate secondary communications protocol," I said as I plucked the earpiece out of my ear, tucking it in my pocket.

The others all did the same. If whoever we were ultimately facing was sending members of Gen 4 to intercept us and possibly blocking our comms, they could just as easily tap into our communications.

Either way, though, I had successfully reclaimed my teammates. And no one was going to stop me from getting back home to my Opal.

THREE

WITH SAMANTHA BARELY ON HER FEET, AND DANIEL and Becca looking only a little better, I opted for a strategic retreat to meet up with Khalid on the way out. But first, we locked all the combatants into the med-bay rooms, including the still-unconscious Gen 4 telekinetic.

As before, none of us recognized any of the mercenaries as former Collective operatives. And as before—and still oddly—their magic was far less robust than the trainers and healers the Five had spent the first twenty-one years of our lives surrounded by. Or perhaps my own power levels had just grown that much stronger in contrast.

Christopher, Samantha, and Daniel had briefly argued among themselves about leaving the teleki-netic, with the clairvoyant wanting to drag him along with us. But since Knox admitted that he hadn't seen as much in our future, Samantha mocked him for being sentimental. Daniel was just overall angry at being attacked and kidnapped.

Under my direction, Aiden and Becca sealed the rooms, and we left before the other three had reached any sort of consensus.

With our presence most definitely marked by whoever was running the facility, we didn't have time to chat.

And yes, if Samantha and Daniel had been at full power? I might have considered confronting their kidnapper. But that would have to wait. Mostly until I had Aiden secured.

But I didn't mention that part out loud.

My dark sorcerer was currently in the lead and ready to shield us as we headed for the stairwell, then retraced our route. He held his hand slightly raised, the runes on his copper rings the brightest thing on the dark stairs. Proper light sources would draw attention, and the runes he had triggered amplified his sense for other magic, both spells and people.

"What were you trying to tell me?" I asked Daniel to my right, not understanding why I was suddenly feeling more anxious, specifically about Aiden's safety, while heading out of the facility than I had been heading in.

The nullifier was on his feet, but barely. Becca was on my left, her magic and energy having recovered much more quickly.

"Before the telekinetic showed up," I added. "That we're up against Gen 4?"

Daniel grimaced, glancing back at Samantha. Our telekinetic had drained herself so thoroughly that it was going to take multiple applications of amplification to get her fully functional. She was currently upright only because she was draped over Christopher's shoulder.

"You tell her," she said to Daniel. Then she snarled wearily. "I'm still too pissed."

"Bee." Daniel sighed. "It's Bee and the Collective's Chemist, working together, who took us. To lure you here."

"No," Christopher said sharply. "That's not possible."

"It's Bee, Knox," Samantha said. Then she softened her tone. "I'm sorry."

"Who else did you think could have taken us both down?" Daniel muttered.

Christopher shook his head vehemently. His magic lashed out over all of us, pulsing around my tattoos as if seeking the truth in those blood bindings. "No, not Bee. I would have seen her. She can't block me."

"She wears this suit…" But Samantha trailed off, distracted as Aiden's head snapped to the side.

Without a word, the dark-haired sorcerer darted into a dark, stone-walled corridor that we hadn't bothered fully investigating on our way up to the medical wing.

As one, we picked up our pace, dashing after him. But he'd gone only a half-dozen steps before stopping to lean over someone crumpled against the wall.

I slowed, casting my gaze around but sensing nothing. I could function fairly well in near dark, but even I needed some sort of light source to see more than a meter ahead.

Aiden grabbed the shoulder of the sprawled person. And for the briefest of moments, I thought I felt a flutter across the tattoo nestled between Knox's vibrant energy and Daniel's low ebb along my spine.

My T2 vertebra. Bee.

The sensation abated as quickly as it had come, and I decided it was simply Daniel's mention of Bee that had drawn my attention to our dormant blood connection.

Aiden rolled the body over—all loose limbs and lolling head. For a brief moment, I thought he'd found his brother. But it wasn't Khalid.

The male in tactical gear crumpled on the floor was lighter skinned and slighter than Khalid. In the dark, I couldn't see any obvious wounds, but I also couldn't see if the mercenary was breathing or not.

Aiden glanced sharply to his left.

Khalid appeared seemingly from out of nowhere, leaning heavily against an open doorway a few steps up and across the corridor. He'd manage to hide himself from all our senses—even Aiden's. Impressive, if not slightly disconcerting. Of course, anyone else that well shielded who'd wanted to attack us would have had to move or cast a spell, and neither of those options would have caught me unaware.

"Bastard would have had me," Khalid said. He wiped his nose, which appeared to be steadily bleeding. "I could feel him boring into my mind. Then he just dropped, like someone flipped a kill switch."

I glanced at Samantha. "Are they linked? Gen 4? Is this their telepath? Maybe he went down when you took out the telekinetic."

She shook her head grimly. "Bee. Bee is piloting them. That's definitely the telepath, Tel4. And it was probably Bee's kill switch. Embedded, maybe?" She glanced at Daniel, but he'd keyed in on Khalid. Perceiving him as the immediate threat, no doubt.

When he wasn't drained, Fish was the most magically sensitive of us all. Khalid's impressive ability to mask his presence had to be bothering the nullifier.

Samantha huffed at Daniel, then continued, "Maybe Bee embedded something in their minds to stop Gen 4 from murdering people? Or to shut them down before they do irreparable harm?"

"No, no," Christopher said. Then he just repeated himself, over and over. "No… no… she wouldn't… she couldn't…"

"You don't have the monopoly on betrayal, Knox," Samantha said darkly.

"What the fuck does that mean?" Daniel asked, proving he was listening at least.

The telekinetic ignored the nullifier. Apparently, she hadn't shared all the sordid details of Chenda's return. Specifically, how Christopher had thrown me in front of a death curse so he could have an extended chat with the Mystic of the Golden Peninsula.

"He's still alive," Aiden said, straightening at the telepath's side. "Leave him?"

I nodded, stepping forward and reaching for Khalid.

He shook his head at me, then nodded toward Aiden. "A few healing runes first. Otherwise, Emma's magic will just be wasted."

Aiden tugged out his notebook even while crossing to Khalid and slinging his brother's arm across his shoulder.

Christopher was still shaking his head. His magic had completely obscured his eyes. He reached for me when I looked his way, abandoning Samantha, who had to hold herself upright against the wall with one hand.

I let the clairvoyant grab my hands, to anchor his magic in the blood bonds that tied us together through life. And possibly into death.

"Don't leave us, Socks," he murmured. His grip was tight. A sliver of his panic and confusion filtered empathically through to me. "Don't do it."

"I'm not going anywhere," I said mildly, aware I was speaking to his magic more than him. "I made a decision. I'm here, and I'm—"

Daniel clamped his hand on Christopher's shoulder, and a flicker of his nullifying magic flowed over the clairvoyant. Even not in contact with it directly, it was shockingly cold.

Christopher jerked, stumbling to the side. I held him steady.

"Touch him again," I snarled in Daniel's face, "and I'll leave you behind."

"There you are," he murmured, leaning closer and scanning my face. "I'd been worried your sorcerer had made you all soft and gooey."

"You're about to become gooey," Samantha muttered caustically.

Christopher blinked, gently releasing my hands. The white of his magic settled into thick rings around his light-gray irises, but he kept his gaze on me, not bothering to acknowledge Daniel.

"You haven't forgotten the protocols when working with the clairvoyant, have you, Amp5?" Daniel said mockingly. "Don't let him get caught in a loop, otherwise—"

I turned my back on Daniel.

He wanted a fight. But I had a different one in mind.

Samantha laughed sharply. Then she pushed off the wall and stretched her hand toward Khalid. "Samantha."

"Khalid."

"You Azar sorcerers are way too powerful. You should have gone down the moment the telepath had you in his mental grasp."

"Pleased to meet you as well, telekinetic," Khalid said smoothly.

"Oh, I'm not saying it like it's a bad thing…" She tilted her head thoughtfully. "How do you feel about horses?"

"Majestic creatures."

Samantha hit the extraction specialist with a blindingly bright smile. "Perfect."

Daniel swore, quiet but vicious.

"We keep moving," I barked, taking point so that Aiden could fall back to help Khalid.

"Our exit is blocked by something that feels a hell of a lot like the power trickling off your... contrary friend," Khalid said, nodding toward Daniel.

The nullifier leveled a cool look at the extraction specialist. Not that Khalid's 'trickling' comment wasn't apt. Daniel and Samantha were both still fighting through the drugs that had been pumped into them.

"I was heading for you to let you know," Khalid added.

I glanced back at Christopher, giving him a moment to contribute. I knew we could cut through whatever the Gen 4 nullifier had done to block our entrance, but doing so would expend a lot of resources that were already running thinner than I liked. Then, even if we got out of the fortress the way we'd come in, we'd still have to skirt the site, pretty much out in the open. Unless we wanted to do some cliff diving that fewer than half of us could survive.

And they knew we were here.

We weren't getting out without a fight.

The fight I wanted to be having, but was uncharacteristically avoiding. For Aiden, for Opal. For my team.

Especially if Bee was at the center of it all.

I could take Bee.

But Aiden, Becca, Khalid, and Mark couldn't.

Christopher didn't chime in with a magically directed opinion.

"We'll go out the front door," I said with a nonchalant shrug that I was mostly faking. "I only came in the back way to please the rest of you."

Samantha laughed.

Becca pulled a tiny black notebook out of her upper jacket pocket, then jotted a message within its pages. Mark Calhoun had a paired notebook, with anything written into one immediately appearing in the other. From the moment we'd gone radio silent, he would have been waiting for a message from Becca that way.

Christopher sighed then, his power flickering briefly in his eyes.

I waited another moment.

He scrubbed his hand over his face, then spoke. "I can't see why yet, but if you go out the front door, Emma, you don't end up in the same place as the rest of us."

Aiden stiffened, pausing in the process of tearing rune-scribed pages from his notebook and slapping them against the exposed skin of his brother's neck. "How so? A remotely triggered teleportation spell?"

Khalid shook his head. "Even depleted, I'd feel a spell of that magnitude. At enough of a distance for us all to avoid it."

"No," Christopher said grimly. "Bee might be hiding from me, but I can always clearly see the choices Fox in Socks makes."

"Well," I said stiffly. I hated standing around and chatting about future possibilities. "I've already made my choices." I glanced between each of the team I'd gathered—that I'd allowed to be gathered for me—lingering on Daniel, Samantha, and Christopher. Then settling on Aiden.

Each of the other members of the Five straightened under my regard. Aiden just looked at me in that way that told me I was hurting his heart somehow, but that he'd be with me to the end.

"We keep moving forward as a group until we can't move forward anymore," I said. "And then we cut our way through. Is that clear enough for you?" I asked the question of Christopher—or, more specifically, of his magic.

The clairvoyant nodded. "Crystal."

"Do I have to ask if you're with me?" I added almost mockingly.

Christopher, Samantha, and Daniel spoke with one voice. "Never."

The magic on my spine sparked brightly in three places. And Bee's tattoo fluttered—again—with a barely discernible hum. I waited a moment, but none of the other three mentioned the flickering connection to the telepath who made us four the Five, so neither did I. Not yet. Instead, I stretched my senses through those bright spots, reinforcing my connection to each of the other three. Then I sent them all a trickle of power, a slow and steady amplification.

"Calhoun is engines hot," Becca said, still scribbling in the notebook. "He'll meet us at the gates if we make it there unimpeded. Or drop into the fortress if we need cover fire once we get the outer wards down."

The helicopter was magically fortified and had been weaponized just enough for that specific scenario. However, if we picked up any other passengers on the way, most of the guns would have to be dumped to get us safely back to the mainland. Even magic had limits, and it could be burned just as easily as fuel. Especially if we were being chased.

Though very few people chased after me.

For a variety of reasons.

I was actively trying to not think about the extra passenger I might come across on my way out. I had to get the rest of my battered team to safety. That came first. Especially Aiden.

Opal needed Aiden almost as much as I did.

Khalid grinned, looking suddenly and abruptly charming even with the runed notebook pages stuck to his neck. He looked more like Aiden than my dark sorcerer did himself at that moment. "I haven't seen you in action yet, Emma. I'm not going anywhere."

"Careful what you wish for, sorcerer," Samantha groused. "You see Emma move? You run the other direction, friend or foe."

"It's true," Becca said earnestly.

Done with the talking, I stepped through to take lead, trailing my fingers across Aiden's hand as I did so. His fingers twined through mine for a brief moment. Then he tossed another crumpled page from his notebook slightly ahead of me.

Dark-blue magic sparked, then spread along the edges of the wall, stretching about two meters ahead before fading into the dark corridor.

"Witch spell?" Khalid asked in a murmur behind me. The magical outline faded as we passed, even as it continued to stretch out before us.

"Combined," Aiden said stiffly. "If I have it calibrated correctly, it should lead us toward open air."

"Brilliant."

"As long as there aren't any large windows up ahead," Daniel muttered caustically.

I moved steadily forward, not bothering with stealth anymore for the same reason that Aiden had lit us a pathway. Our presence was already known, our entrance point discovered and fortified against our using it again as an exit. Presumably with more mercs, along with the Gen 4 nullifier, waiting for our retreat.

I was fully aware that we might even have been allowed to rescue Daniel and Samantha as a way to erode our own defenses and to burden us with compromised teammates.

Whoever had masterminded the kidnapping of the two either knew me very well. Or not at all.

I had a strong, distinct feeling it was both. Because it was two masterminds we were dealing with. Both of whom were about to be seriously disappointed.

When forced to play games, I did so by my own rules.

AIDEN'S SPELL LED US TRUE, LEADING US STEADILY through the huge fortress. As we climbed along a steady upward trajectory, the corridors and stairwells narrowed, and the floors and stairs became rough-hewn stone interrupted by more-modern doorways that we left unexplored. It quickly became clear that only certain sections of the original structure had been adapted to fit the Collective's needs.

Aiden and Khalid simply disabled each potential side route we passed, so that no one could attack us from more than two directions—ahead and behind. Becca needed time and more amplification to regain the rest of her strength, so we held her in reserve, in anticipation of anything that might need to be blown up in our very near future.

Samantha had thought I was being funny when I'd given Becca her orders, but Christopher hadn't laughed. I could feel the clairvoyant's gaze on my back, almost as if the blood tattoo on my T3 vertebra was weighed down with his lingering trepidation.

I shoved the feeling and the thought that accompanied it away—the idea that I really wasn't going to like whatever the clairvoyant was seeing of my near future. I wasn't going to die. I knew that even without Christopher saying anything. Killing me, or even attempting to do so, would waste all the effort the kidnappers had put in to secure Samantha and Daniel. To get my attention.

As the connection between me and Bee flickered with a staticky energy that was seriously annoying, I knew it wasn't just the machinations of the telepath that we were traversing.

If she'd needed it, Bee could have just asked for help. She could have contacted me through Christopher at any time.

So either she was completely compromised and in need of rescue. Or she'd gone all the way rogue.

And if she had gone rogue? A masterful telepath who could kill with a single thought? Who could play with people like puppets? Who Samantha claimed was already controlling some of the fourth generation of the Collective's super soldiers?

Then I was likely the only one who could take her down.

At least before the guardian dragons got involved.

I shelved all those thoughts—knowing that I would react in the moment like I always did—as Khalid got the final door open between us and what appeared to be a cavernous entranceway, aka the main access point into the fortress.

I paused on the threshold, aware that whoever was in control here could have allowed us to move in this very direction. The stone walls were unadorned. The plain stone floor stretched between us and two steel-reinforced, arched double doors that looked a lot like the entrance to a castle. Which was what we were standing in, as it happened.

Directly ahead, a massive staircase shaped of smoother stone swept up through the middle of the grand foyer, rising to interior ramparts that ringed the entire space.

Most people would have just called it a walkway. But I knew what I was looking at. I knew why this setup would have been deemed suitable by the members of the Collective when they'd chosen the fortress as a base.

"Kill box," Samantha muttered from over my shoulder.

Exactly. I glanced to Aiden on my right.

"Coated in magic," he said grimly, meaning he couldn't pick up any specifics. Just that we were either walking into a trap or about to set off defensive measures.

That was what I'd presumed, even if I couldn't feel the magic myself.

"We move along the wall toward the door," I said quietly. I would have preferred to cut directly through the space, but Aiden, Christopher, and I were the only ones not still slowly recovering. The wall at our backs would stop anyone from sneaking up on us.

I stepped forward before anyone could argue or protest.

The cool sensation of Aiden's shield slipped over me. Khalid, tucked within the same shield just behind his brother, held what looked like platinum ingots in both hands. Combat-grade spells, by their feel.

"Try not to kill anyone," I muttered.

He nodded.

Behind our protected bubble, Daniel and Becca were holding dual shields over themselves, Christopher, and Samantha. I'd never seen those two dual cast before, but it was a smart choice with neither of them at full capacity.

Not a single spell triggered. No one appeared.

Until we were halfway to the door.

A niche of some sort—perhaps a walled-off hallway—opened to my left. And in crossing by it, I triggered some sort of electrical net. Aiden's shield instantly clamped tighter around me. But even through its protection, I could feel the cool sting of distinctly familiar magic.

Nullifying power trying to quell Aiden's shield.

The others instantly took up defensive positions around me. Khalid's magic sparked.

"No," I said quietly. "Don't waste your energy." I glanced over at Aiden. "Same with you."

He grimaced, but stopped trying to shield me.

The magical net instantly sank into my skin, freezing me in place.

"What the fuck, Socks?" Daniel growled. "We don't have time for you to—"

I reached for the rope of energy that still stretched between the nullifier and me, and I tugged. Hard.

Daniel jerked forward, almost losing his footing.

Yes, I had been continually amplifying him. And now I was using that same bond—the one that had been forced under my skin and embedded into bone and muscle and nerves without my permission—to take a chunk of Daniel's nullifying magic for myself.

I visualized allowing that power—flowing from Daniel to me—to spread out from my T1 vertebra, across my shoulders and down my body.

Daniel swayed on his feet. His incredulous expression turned dark.

The net fell away, countered by the very magic that had been used to construct it.

Both Christopher and Samantha leveled scathing looks at Daniel. As with the nullifying cages Silver Pine had used to hold Christopher and Aiden, Fish had been selling his wares to members of the Collective. Again.

Giving him the benefit of the doubt, he presumably hadn't known it.

"It never would have held you," the nullifier snarled.

I turned my attention toward the main doors. Aiden stepped in front of me, hands held at the ready and copper rings glowing. I touched the back of his neck, indulging in the warmth of his skin to shake off the remaining chill of Daniel's power. My dark sorcerer reached back to caress my wrist, and I allowed myself to amplify him. Pretending it was for his and the mission's benefit, and not because I wanted a reminder of the connection between us that I had forged by choice.

Khalid stepped into the niche, checking it for other spells. He grunted twice, impressed. Then, with a flicker of power, he disabled something. Presumably defensive spells set to be remotely triggered, rather than automatically as with Fish's net.

"Been selling things to the wrong people again?" Samantha asked Daniel mockingly, never one to let such slights go.

"Give me a list of the right people, Zans," Daniel snarled. "Since it's all of your bank accounts I keep topped up with my nullifying tech."

'Tech' was an interesting way to describe the cages—and now the nets and traps—that Daniel traded in.

"I pay my own way, asshole," Samantha said snippily.

"You better hope Socks doesn't regret yanking that chunk of power from me," Daniel muttered darkly.

"She's feeding it back to you right now."

And I was. No matter how pissed I might have been—because that net had been far too well hidden from Aiden's and Khalid's senses and could have seriously hurt them or Becca—I didn't need Daniel incapacitated.

Behind me now, Christopher stopped walking. So abruptly that Samantha ran into him, swearing. He slowly pivoted to look over at the massive staircase looming up and behind us.

It was still empty.

The tattoo on my T2 vertebra flickered. Again.

"Bee?" Christopher called out, sounding young and unsure. His magic was at a low simmer, not enough to be swamping his mind. He wasn't seeing things. Or at least no more than he continually saw things.

We all paused, carefully scanning the space around us.

Becca went down first. So quickly that Daniel barely broke her fall.

Then, even shielded, Khalid dropped.

Aiden managed to grab his brother, but then pain was etched across his own face, and he stumbled.

Anger sliced through me, hot and vicious. At the cowardly sneak attack. At the selected targets—taking out those deemed weakest instead of confronting me directly.

"Pathetic," I snarled in the direction of the still-seemingly-empty staircase, already stepping forward, crossing out of Aiden's shield, even against the desperately clawing thoughts I was actively ignoring that told me to grab the sorcerer and run.

Run far, far away from what Bee could destroy with a single malignant thought.

The clairvoyant stepped up with me as Daniel tried to stretch his shields to encompass the rest of the team. I pinned my gaze to the point on the stairs where Christopher was fixated.

"No!" I snarled. Magic was laced through the command.

Aiden gasped behind me. In relief, I thought.

The tattoo on my spine flickered again. But this time, I could feel that energy resolve into a sharp blade. It sliced through the air, aimed over my shoulder and straight toward Aiden.

Another telepathic assault. And the reason I could feel it was because I was intimately connected to its wielder.

I unleashed my power—all of it—and wings of white energy threaded through with strokes of gray exploded across my back, snapping out from between my blood tattoos and my shoulder blades.

"Holy fucking wings!" Samantha shouted.

The telepathic spell aimed for Aiden hit my right wing. I absorbed it with only the briefest thought.

Then I reached out a thick tendril of power—power I was still learning to wield like a weapon without skin-to-skin contact. But I didn't need more training to know it would home eagerly in on my target. Because my DNA was branded into her skin. She couldn't have blocked me if she'd tried.

I speared the asshole trying to take down my dark sorcerer, right through the back of her neck. Specifically, her T1 vertebra.

That asshole stumbled on the stone of the stairs. Then the shield she'd somehow managed to erect so expertly that even my mind hadn't detected it flickered and died.

A petite figure wearing pink hard-shell combat armor appeared partway up the stairs. Her face was fully masked, and she wore a domed helmet. It took her a moment to counter my assault.

But only because I let her think I'd lost hold of her.

"Get them out," I commanded coolly over my shoulder. "Get to Calhoun."

"But…!" Samantha started to cry out.

I gave her a look.

She shut her mouth, bent down, and heaved Becca over her shoulder. His expression murderous, Daniel crossed to do the same with Khalid. Aiden was on his feet, but barely.

They ran for the doors.

"I told you what would happen if you made Emma come for us," Samantha called back. Her tone was tinged with regret.

Aiden's magic bloomed behind me as his power pummeled the arched steel doors. They were magically sealed. Becca was still unconscious. As was Khalid.

I deliberately placed myself between the uber-powerful telepath and the rest of my team, wings spread so that I occupied as much space as possible. Completely unleashed, my power roiled around me, but I left it undirected. For now.

"Bee…" Christopher whispered quietly, standing tucked up behind me. Not near enough to brush against my wings, but close enough that I could easily pick up the emotions rolling off him—stronger even than the press of his own power. "Why?"

Concern and confusion. Wounded?

Christopher was devastated.

The pink-armored figure reached up. She removed her helmet and mask, revealing familiar shoulder-length, blunt-cut yellow hair, golden skin, and light-brown eyes.

In real life, I had never seen that hair any longer than a buzz cut. But in her mindscape, where she had often invited the rest of us four, she always wore it long.

Tel5.

Bee.

Amanda Smith.

Our missing telepath wasn't missing anymore.

The tattoo that connected me to Bee flared fully on my back for the first time in over eight years, then settled into a low simmer. So the helmet had a practical purpose as well, beyond its strange aesthetics. It dampened her power. But only against detection? Or did it also restrict her own access to that power, or her reach?

Except why would Bee have handicapped herself?

"Shouldn't you know why, Cla5?" she asked dismissively. And rhetorically.

Christopher stiffened behind me. "But—"

"We don't use those designations, Amanda," I interrupted coolly. "As you should know, since you and Becca were the ones to give us the names on our passports."

The empty air two steps down and slightly to the right of Bee flickered.

Christopher settled his hand on my upper back, between the wings of energy. He tapped a finger to the left of his blood tattoo, silently calling my attention to the cloaked attacker attempting to sneak forward while Bee distracted us.

"So the only reason for you to use that designation is to upset Christopher," I continued blithely. As if I had all day to chat. As if nothing else was going on. As if the currently compromised members of our team weren't still frantically working together to get through the doors at my back.

"Coward," I spat derisively.

Amanda flinched.

The still-invisible attacker lunged forward, attempting to cover the last few meters between us.

I grabbed them by the throat—not needing to even extend an arm and hand to do so. I simply lashed out with my empathy, now weaponized as a result of whatever aspect I'd absorbed from the immortal entity that was the Hallowed. What that entity actually was, at least when not being imprisoned by the guardian dragons, I had no idea. Since my wings had first appeared, I'd wondered whether they might have been part of the Hallowed's form. But it seemed even more likely that I'd simply manifested them on my own, as an instinctive way of accepting and absorbing yet another infusion of stolen power.

I cinched a thick rope of my magic around the still-unseen attacker's neck. Using the empathic connection between us—which felt oddly blank on the other end—I then channeled one of my two primary abilities. The ability I'd been bred and born to wield.

I siphoned a whack of the attacker's magic from them.

A garbled groan.

A body thudded to the stone floor, on their knees.

I hadn't bothered to look away from Bee. Not once. A myriad of expressions flitted over her face.

While she settled on a response, I countered a wave of what felt like nullifying magic. Magic powerful enough to travel back through the rope of energy I'd cinched around my attacker's neck.

A dreadful chill ran through me.

I yanked more magic from the attacker.

They groaned again. The chill receded.

And still, I didn't drop Bee's gaze.

She took a step down, then another. Christopher unsheathed his sword.

Bee's gaze flicked to the clairvoyant. She wasn't quick enough to hide her disbelief. But then she looked back at me, pink-gloved hands clenched at her sides. "What took you so long? I've needed you for months!" Then she clamped her mouth shut quickly, as if she'd said too much.

"And I told you not to need me," I said, my tone low and deadly.

She flinched. Again.

The nullifier—another member of Gen 4, judging by their magical strength—made another attempt to break my hold. It was almost successful. Impressive, even.

It hurt.

I countered.

And oddly, it was Bee who stumbled to the side in response, slipping off a stair and almost falling.

A dark-haired, pale-skinned male with shoulders almost as broad as Daniel's appeared on his knees before me. He was wearing black tactical gear similar to my own. He'd gotten close enough that I could smell stale cigarette smoke wafting from him.

Bee straightened, her gaze now locked on the Gen 4 nullifier. Her eyes widened in concern.

And not because I was still draining him just enough to keep him on his knees.

Because she'd been in his head. And I'd broken her hold on him, hence the stumbling.

She'd been piloting him. Just as Samantha had accused her of doing.

And that degree of manipulation, even more so than her being involved in kidnapping Samantha and Daniel, even more so than dragging me across an ocean and two continents, crossed so many lines it made me utterly irate.

So when I felt Bee's magic shift, her intense gaze still on the nullifier, I stepped around and in front of him, protectively. Christopher helped him to his feet, staying slightly behind me.

Bee blinked, completely thrown. "You don't understand. He… they are—"

"How could you?" Christopher snarled. He was completely livid, in a way I wasn't certain I'd ever seen him.

Bee blinked harder, her cheeks flushing. "If you would just let me—"

"No," the clairvoyant said darkly. "He's us! He's us, and you're using him like a—"

"No, no!" Bee cried. "It's for their own good."

Christopher laughed harshly.

"That… that…" Bee backtracked. "That came out wrong."

"Is that why we're all here, Amanda?" I asked coolly. "Did you think you could subsume us as well? For your new keeper?"

Bee snarled, emanating anger and frustration now. "Are you actually going to ask me questions, Socks?"

"You don't need to be rescued," Christopher interjected. His voice cracked, causing reciprocal pain borne on emotion to shoot through my own chest. "You need an intervention. I'll leave that to Emma. She'll be kinder than the rest of us."

With the mute and mostly drained nullifier partially slung over his shoulder, the clairvoyant started for the door.

"Don't be ridiculous," Bee snapped. "He's not stable! He'll hurt you, and he'll regret it."

Christopher snorted dismissively. "He belongs to Emma now. He'll never need you in his head again."

That was an untested supposition, and an emotionally generated declaration on Christopher's part. But the nullifier certainly wasn't going to be accidentally hurting anyone in the next few minutes.

Amanda looked at me, incredulous. "What does Knox mean?"

Behind me, Aiden and Daniel finally got the door open. I actually felt the moment my dark sorcerer glanced over to me.

I took a casual step back. Bee wasn't going to let me go without a fight. I actually wasn't certain why she hadn't attacked my mind already, but assumed it was because she was stalling. Not because she didn't think she could hold me. She almost certainly thought she could.

She was stalling because reinforcements were on their way.

That was the problem with remote facilities, whether in the jungle or on an island. Backup took too long to arrive. Most fights between Adepts of the power level of the Five were over in minutes, if not seconds.

With me amplifying her, Samantha could have dropped the entire front of the stone fortress on Bee's head.

I reabsorbed my wings as I turned my back on one of the most powerful telepaths in the world. A telepath I couldn't fully block because she was blood-bonded to me.

I lowered my newly discovered defenses, and I turned away.

For the implied insult, yes. But even more so to express a clear message—we were leaving her behind. Plus, I wanted to get this fight over with before more of my team could be hurt.

Samantha was already through the door with Becca and Khalid. Both appeared to have recovered enough from Bee's mental assault to be walking under their own power.

Daniel lingered. His gaze was riveted to Bee as he spoke to me. "Wheels down in five minutes."

Aiden met my gaze.

I smiled. "I'm right behind you." My dark sorcerer nodded.

"You don't think you're actually walking away," Bee said mildly.

I kept moving, slow and steady.

"It's just that easy for you," she snapped, stalking down the stairs. She would need even footing to engage with me.

"You've abused my trust, Amanda," I said, slowly turning back to face her. Keeping the now-open door at my back, and the wide entrance of the foyer between us. "You've abused all of us. Siding with the enemy. Hiding in that suit like a coward instead of just telling us that you'd made that choice."

She clenched her fists, still steadily closing the space between us—and still not mentally attacking me.

I figured something out then. "You need skin-to-skin contact?" I asked mockingly.

Her jaw tensed, but she didn't slow.

I unzipped my tactical jacket, tossing it to the side. I stripped off my black T-shirt and pulled my hair around my shoulder in one sweep, exposing the blood tattoos on my back.

Her step hitched.

I spread my now-bare arms, standing clad just in a tank top, pants, and boots. "Why settle for skin when you can access the blood that binds us?"

Bee's eyes flicked over me.

I hadn't drawn my blades.

She got within reach.

I didn't shift my stance.

She reached over my shoulder.

I locked my gaze to her light-brown eyes as I whispered, "Everyone will know, Bee. That you attacked me instead of letting me get the others to safety. You'll never be our sister, not ever again."

"I can show you," she said stiffly. "I can make you see."

"Doubtful," I murmured, turning to whisper against her ear. "But either way, the other three will never forgive you."

She wrapped her hand around my neck, angling her fingers to touch the tattoo on my T2 vertebra. To touch her blood and DNA encased under my skin, anchored to bone and nerves.

"I can make you see," she whispered again, fear and doubt filtering through our empathic connection.

"You can try."

So she did.

FOUR

I WOKE UP IN A HOTEL ROOM. OR MAYBE, GIVEN THE view out the window of parked cars, a motel room. It was decorated in shades of sun-worn orange, which should have been ugly. But after being surrounded by gray-on-gray my entire life, it was actually a visual relief.

The warmth laced through the breeze filtering past yellow-tinted curtains informed me that I'd slept through the cool of the morning. An oppressive ache in my head and a thick halo of fuzziness edged my vision, even after I'd brushed away the stringy blonde hair that had stuck to my sleep-crusted face, telling me why I'd slept.

I was alone.

I had distinct memories of a rushed, heated coupling in a back alley that smelled of jasmine, barbecued meat, cumin, and onions. I'd been with a beautiful brown-skinned, brown-eyed boy barely old enough to buy me the caipirinhas that I had oh-so-willingly chugged as soon as I laid eyes on him.

He'd been tall enough that he'd had to hoist me up and press me against the adobe brick wall. With no magic to mitigate the rough sex I'd enthusiastically encouraged, I had little doubt that the general soreness I was wallowing in came with bruising all over my back. Though my naturally golden-tanned skin had only darkened further after spending months under the hot sun, I'd have to avoid sleeveless dresses for a few days.

Afterward, when he'd gone to get us another round of drinks, I slipped away through the crowd in the bar, my limbs loose from the orgasms, the alcohol, the heat—relaxed in a way I never really was. At least not for any extended period of time. That relaxation hadn't even lasted long enough to bring him back to the motel room I'd planned on abandoning in the morning either way, for more sedate, lingering sex. The kind of sex I'd never actually indulged in, even if it was thoughts of kissing for hours and gentle caresses that fueled my own fantasies.

Simple… companionship. Maybe even an actual exchange of words, thoughts, ideas, memories… curled up against the warmth of a lover… basking in the moments in between.

No.

I was alone.

As I had been for almost a year. With not even a shimmer from the blood tattoos embedded into my upper spine to keep me company.

Though three days before, when I'd arrived in Rio de Janeiro, Brazil, I'd felt a flicker from those bonds that confirmed two things. One of the others who made us the Five was near. And Socks hadn't actually drained all of my magic when she'd implemented the Amplifier Protocol and destroyed the compound in which we'd been created and trained to be killers.

That act had freed us from the clutches of the Collective.

I just hadn't realized how lonely freedom was going to be.

We Five weren't supposed to meet up, ever again. Socks had issued that as her final order—our formal discharge and severance.

But Samantha had reached out via the email addresses that Becca had hastily set up for us all, that information tucked in with the money and passports that she, Flynn, and Calhoun had cobbled together. According to Samantha, Socks's email account hadn't been activated. So I wouldn't have been at all surprised if she didn't even know that the rest of us had planned to remain connected, even tentatively. Christopher, aka my Knox, would have kept that from the amplifier who'd held our fate in the palm of her hand, then had ordered us all away.

Ordered us to stay away.

Really, Bee?

As if called forth by my thoughts of her, an achingly familiar voice murmured through my mind.

This is what you wanted to show me? Sex, hangovers, and feeling sorry for yourself?

I blinked. The room, the view outside the window, hazed over completely. And I remembered…

I remembered where I really was, what I was really doing.

I needed to focus… I needed to not think about *her*. Thinking about her would allow her to disrupt my hold on her mind.

But why was I back in this moment? I had carefully curated the series of mindscapes I'd planned for her. All designed to trigger her empathy, to force her to help me.

No one forces me to do anything, that familiar voice said. Sounding more amused than angry.

Amused was bad.

Amused meant she was indulging me.

I had seen those white-and-gray wings simmering with energy. I had no idea what they indicated about the power the amplifier now wielded, but—

I squeezed my eyes shut, focusing on solidifying the room and the memory that my subconscious had pulled me—us—into. Socks was supposed to be standing here with me, at my side. I tried to grab onto her energy, to firm my hold and pull her through instead of her simply riding my thoughts.

What had happened in this moment that made me subconsciously want to show it to Socks? Why had my mind brought me here instead of forward to what I'd wanted her to see?

I opened my eyes. The motel room had solidified around me, the bed firming enough that I could feel the scratchy sheets against my bare skin.

I sat up, crossing to the window and looking out. The sun was high overhead, as I'd expected.

My magic had come back, had started to reassert itself.

That was it.

That was this day.

The day that all my hopes of living a normal life—ignoring that I was doing anything but living at that point—crumbled.

This was the final moment—waking up hungover with my body, heart, and soul aching—before my magic started to come back.

I had taken a shower, grabbed my already-packed backpack, and headed on foot into the blistering heat to the place I'd rented for the next three months.

On the way to my next temporary home, someone had brushed against me. I was completely unshielded. Incapable of shielding myself, because magic was like any other muscle, and not using it for over a year came with massive ramifications.

I had ended up in a back alley, hunched against a rough, stuccoed wall at the rear of a restaurant, with an older, darkly tanned woman in a grease-stained floral apron pressing cold towels to the back of my neck.

Antonia was witch born and had thought she'd known what I was. She had dragged me away from the busy street, away from the foot traffic and all the wide-open minds. She'd been careful not to touch me skin-to-skin, fed me coxinha. And when my magic had ebbed enough to allow me to function again, she'd had her grandson, Paulo, escort me to my new rental.

Later on, after my first job with Fish—and feeling utterly contaminated by what that job had required me to do—I'd sent Antonia enough money to retire on. She'd kept cooking, but bought the restaurant. For her grandchildren to inherit.

I had visited Antonia and her peaceful-minded, strong-limbed, smooth-skinned grandson three to four times a year after that, actually maintaining a small apartment in Rio myself. Buying furniture and hand-painted dishes and art and clothing… so much color and warmth in a city filled with music and laughter.

That grandson, Paulo, had fallen madly in love—love at first sight, it seemed—and gotten married two years ago.

And while watching him dance with his bride. Watching through a spelled telescope I'd stolen from Fish, even though I'd been invited to the wedding, my magic had started degrading. My control had splintered, and my power… my abilities…

… expanded.

A heavy sigh echoed through my mind.

Not my own.

I clenched my hands and held onto *her*. I visualized cinching her mind in a vise grip. I tried to force the two of us through this unfortunate pit stop.

But though I meant to push forward, I tumbled us farther back, into the past.

I HAD TAKEN SOCKS'S FINAL COMMAND LITERALLY, heading south from the Collective's compound in Peru.

Even though Mark and Becca would have checked all our vehicles thoroughly before escaping themselves in the wake of the Five utterly destroying the compound, I was aware that the black SUV I'd taken might have had embedded trackers that I had no idea how to counter. I sold it in Santiago, Chile, to a sorcerer who didn't ask questions, but who paid very well for armored transport that could hold up to being driven—for a while, at least—by someone magically inclined.

Even with my magic drained, effectively nonexistent, I still read as an Adept of some kind to his senses. But the sorcerer didn't ask, and I didn't tell. I had assumed at the time that it was the blood tattoos embedded into the top four of my thoracic vertebrae that he'd picked up on.

The fact that those bindings still held fast was what initially warned me that my magic wasn't completely gone.

I had felt like I was running that entire first year. And not from my keepers, not from the Collective. But from everything embedded into my very DNA. Running, trying to avoid the moment when that power would reassert itself. The moment when my mind would no longer solely belong to me.

The Chilean sorcerer tracked me down in Puerto Montt a month later. Apparently, he had decided he wanted to keep me along with the SUV.

I probably shouldn't have had sex with him— my first lover after Fish, even though it had always been Knox I'd ached to visit in the deep of night. The sorcerer had been the first lover who didn't dampen my power, chilling me more than skin deep, because there was no magic in me to quell. His skin had been smooth over hard muscles, his hands warm. And just his breath against my neck was practically orgasmic.

To make one more attempt to woo me to his side, he'd brought his brothers as backup. He had tried to ask nicely, so he wasn't a complete idiot.

Unfortunately for him, I didn't have to destroy his mind or even manipulate him to extricate—

Enough. Socks's voice snapped through my mind.

I lost my hold on her. Enough that I could suddenly feel the uneven stone of the fortress under my feet, the warmth of her pale skin under my palm, and the fluttering of the blood tattoo—my blood embedded under her skin—against my fingers.

I speared another blade of magic into that binding, reinforcing my connection. And this time, when I closed my eyes, I took her with me to where I'd wanted to start in the first place.

Two years ago… on a rooftop in Rio de Janeiro. Watching a man I might have loved—if I'd known how to love—gazing at his bride with utter devotion.

I had needed Emma's help.

You could have called.

No, I snarled in my own mind. You wouldn't have answered. You'd made that clear. You turned away Fish. You chose—

How did you know? Emma mused. *Weren't you off sulking somewhere and avoiding Fish at the time?*

You always have to be convinced, I insisted.

So convince me, telepath, she whispered. *Quickly, now.*

I felt it then.

I realized then. I realized why she'd let me touch her.

I put that together with what Samantha had said, about Emma finding a loophole in what we'd thought the blood tattoos meant for us all. We had long believed, because of the bindings the Collective had forced upon us, that the death of one of us might mean the death of all of us.

Power was pouring through from Emma to me, riding the connection I'd made to pull her mind into mine. It wasn't pure amplification. And she wasn't draining me. Not yet.

It was something very... very different...

"The wings," I whispered.

Yes.

"You can kill me," I whispered.

Don't make me, Bee.

I squeezed my eyes shut in the physical world and pulled us all the way into the memory I'd wanted to access. Socks first had to understand the why. And then I'd have to make her care about that why, not just dismiss it.

And then we could rescue the boy.

The boy?

Her murmur was so quiet that I knew I was now deeply embedded enough in her mind to pick up her stray thoughts.

I smiled.

I had her attention.

At last.

I WAS ON A ROOFTOP. THE HEAT WAS MUTED BY THE comforting dark of the night, and the air was so fragrant. A multitude of luscious flowers and bushes had seemingly all conspired to bloom at the same time, to help celebrate the wedding.

A small blessing, Antonia would have called it. But I didn't doubt that the local coven had a hand in that blessing. Through the handheld telescope that magically cut through the distance and darkness between us, I could see the older witch who had rescued me all those years ago, when my power had reasserted itself and tried to crack my mind open. Across the street in an open-air plaza, Antonia was gazing at her grandson, Paulo, as he swayed his bride gently around the dance floor, smiling and deeply delighted.

Tall enough to tower over her—as he towered over me—Paulo leaned closer to whisper in his bride's ear. She flushed prettily, her fingers teasing the smooth skin of his neck, a deeply tanned brown against the white collar of his embroidered wedding shirt.

Something terrible yawned open in my stomach. A fierce rush of some emotion I'd never felt before flashed through me.

One moment, I was on that rooftop. And in the next…

I was no longer peering through the telescope, I was…

I blinked, staring up at Paulo's face, seeing the shards of lighter brown within the deeper warm-brown of his eyes. His hand pressed to the side of my waist, then he twirled me away from him… my skirts swirling around my knees…

I was… dancing?

I'd never danced—

No.

Panic streaked through me.

I could still feel my own body, but I'd slipped so far into the bride's mind that for a moment, I'd gotten lost within her.

I'd been her.

Paulo twirled me back into his arms, tucking me against his body. His touch was gentle, though his erection was a hard length against my belly.

Desire flooded through me in a heady flush, instantly dampening my panties. I pressed my free hand to his chest…

There were no extra voices in this mind. The bride's mind.

I opened my senses wide, so that I could feel almost-dormant magic within this body. Witch magic.

"But no telepathy," I murmured.

Paulo stiffened in my arms. Then he asked me a question that I didn't quite catch, and not because I didn't speak Spanish.

Because… I'd spoken out loud.

I wasn't just inadvertently piloting his bride.

I was her.

And anchored within her, I got the distinct impression that I could…

I could stay…

I could have this life.

Could I… could I… snatch her body?

Paulo murmured, his concern and confusion hitting me clearer than his words.

"This is wrong," the-me-who-was-also-her blurted. I yanked free from his arms, stumbling back as I realized that this body didn't move properly. It was clumsy and slow, weak. I twisted my ankle, harshly. I was wearing high heels. I never wore…

The other wedding guests were all looking at me. At us. My new husband reached for me but didn't touch me, pain from my ankle radiating up my leg.

I pressed my hands to my head.

And for just a moment, I thought…

I thought I was trapped.

Trapped within the bride's mind. Within Mariana's mind. And yes, though I'd been refusing to acknowledge it, I had seen her name etched across the invitation… with the long list of her family members who were giving her away.

I was trapped more thoroughly than I'd ever been before.

Stuck.

Stealing her life… would I just snuff her out? If I couldn't pull free?

Then I was suddenly back on the rooftop, sprawled on my back, arms and legs all twisted as if I'd been thrashing them, as if I'd been seizing. The star-speckled sky came into focus.

My face was wet, my hair at my temples was damp… I was crying?

Weeping silently, I… grieved? Grieved for the life I'd just lost.

The life I could have had if I'd stayed with Paulo. If I wasn't who I was. If I wasn't one of the Five.

A genetically constructed… aberration.

The life… the life…

The life I could still take.

I was that powerful.

I could subsume Mariana. I could live her life, love her husband, maybe even wield her all-but-dormant witch magic. What would happen to my body? Bee's body?

Could I—

I shoved the thought away. I didn't need to figure it out. It was wrong. Just wrong. Not a problem to solve, not a muscle to stretch. To see if I could, if I could be—

I forced myself to roll over, to peer over the edge of the roof again. Paulo was running his hand down Mariana's arm, smiling gently down at her. She was shaking her head, touching her temples.

A headache, I could almost hear her saying. Just a headache.

What would have happened to Mariana had I stayed? Had I abandoned my body on this rooftop and taken over her life…

No one should be able to do what I already could do.

But this new ability, this was—

Footsteps. Behind me.

I rolled over, already grabbing for the mind approaching me. But my power slid off her consciousness...

I blinked up at her as she crossed to the edge of the roof, standing in full view of the street, of the open plaza below, of the wedding and the guests...

A light breeze stirred her long, dark-red hair, the color vibrant even under the night sky. She took a deep, thoughtful breath.

"You always were skilled, Bee," she murmured. "At these..."—she flicked her fingers—"... mindscapes."

I squeezed my eyes shut, realizing that I'd gotten lost in my own memory again. I had pulled the others of the Five into alternate realities within my own consciousness before, dragging their minds into spaces of my own construction. But I'd never tried to force one of them into an actual memory.

"I..." I cleared my throat, forcing myself to sit up. My limbs, my body, were still out of sync, haunted by the memory of momentarily being someone else. Not just controlling them or seeding their mind, but actually being someone else...

"This is where I broke," I whispered.

Emma—or more specifically, the projection of Emma's consciousness—shrugged. "We're all broken."

She turned and walked away.

Just like that.

Just like she always did.

I watched her go. Emma never changed any aspect of herself when within one of my mindscapes.

She always appeared exactly as she was in the present moment.

I glanced down at myself, already knowing that instead of the dark clothing I had worn that night on the rooftop, I'd be wearing…

I frowned down at the sunflowers on my sundress. Why would I have put myself in a dress I'd never owned? I liked color, yes, but not prints.

"Oracle card," Emma said over her shoulder, utterly dismissive. She was perched on the curbed edge of the roof, peering down into a well of darkness that hadn't been there a moment ago.

I scrambled to my feet. "You can't just walk away."

"I have a life and people I love to get back to, Bee. I'm not interested in your games."

"This isn't a game. This is my… this is me. And I need you to—"

Emma stepped off the roof.

She just dropped.

I lunged forward, even as the mindscape shuddered around me, then literally tore apart.

Too powerful. I had a moment to form that thought.

Socks was too powerful for me to hold.

I let loose everything I normally tried to hold at bay. All the magic that made me an abomination.

Stone momentarily firmed beneath my feet. And even as my mind still arrowed for Socks's consciousness, I quickly stripped as much of the armor I wore in the physical world as possible. I needed access to everything I had.

I kept pouring out my power, holding nothing back.

I felt the touch of a half-dozen minds, then a dozen. Each far more welcoming than the mind I needed to control, if only for just one more moment.

I could own all of them.

I could be any one of them.

I shoved away the impulse to latch onto one of those, reaching for the mind nearest to me. It was so bright, pulsing with power. I wrapped it in my own magic and forced it to comply.

BEE, WEARING MODIFIED TACTICAL GEAR AND WITH her yellow hair pulled back in a high ponytail, walked up a white-polymer-walled corridor. Any guard or medical personnel who stepped into the hall at her approach tumbled bonelessly to the floor. She turned to look over her shoulder for a moment, directly at me.

Frowning deeply, she slowly slid her katana out of the sheath she wore across her back. She was wearing something over her head. A circlet of some sort that widened across her forehead. More tech than jewelry.

Bee continued up the corridor, turning her back to me though she held her katana at the ready. She couldn't see me.

Nor could she see the version of herself in the sunflower sundress standing to my left.

"Finally," sunflower-dress Bee said.

She had yanked me so hard into the mindscape in which we stood that my brain felt like it was bleeding. The blood tattoo that bound me to her burned as though on fire.

If Bee had a better grasp on me—had I been more willing to walk alongside her through her mind—I wouldn't have been able to feel any pain.

Up ahead, memory Bee crouched beside the white-coated figure she'd just felled without a single touch. Some sort of technician. Pulling off her glove, she pressed her first two fingers to the figure's temple, then tilted her head, listening.

"I thought you didn't like doing that," I said pointedly.

"I'm not wiping her brain," sunflower-dress Bee said stiffly. "I'm gathering information."

She wanted me to ask. Ask where we were and why she was showing me these things. Instead, just to piss her off, I said, "There's something wrong with your magic."

"I've been trying to tell you that," she snapped.

I laughed harshly. "No."

I tapped her in the center of her forehead, moving so quickly that she didn't see me coming.

She flinched.

Nothing, and no one, should have been able to move through Bee's mind in any way she didn't want them to move. Not even me.

"Why are you wearing a dampener? Here, it's that circlet. But in real life, it's that stupid pink suit and helmet. I'd thought at first it was to stretch your range, but it's meant to quell it."

"I just showed you why."

"You're scared of your own power."

"You're the one hiding out on a farm in the middle of nowhere."

I didn't bother responding to that. Bee had never been willfully ignorant. She knew I had taken on the responsibility for keeping Christopher sane, for keeping Paisley… well, alive.

"I'm sorry," she murmured, presumably skimming my thoughts. "I do know."

"The more you hold me," I said darkly, "the easier it will be to break you so completely that you'll never be able to function again."

Bee blinked at me, truly aghast. "You… you don't have that power."

"No," I said, grinning that smile that usually made its recipients flinch. "But you do." I reached for her shoulder.

She stumbled back from me.

I let my hand drop back to my side. I could break Bee's hold. I'd almost broken Chenda when she'd tried to hold me, when she'd forced me to relive my own memories. But this was different…

Bee was scared.

It didn't remotely make up for anything she had done, but… I couldn't break her mind in retribution.

So I would wait just a little longer. I could feel the power pouring from her, and what it was taking for her just to hold me. She would need only to weaken a little more to lose that hold.

Beside me, Bee squared her shoulders, lifting her chin. "Come with me."

She strode forward in the wake of her memory self. That other Bee stepped more purposefully now, as if she'd gleaned whatever she needed to know from the tech. A key card purloined from the pocket of the white coat allowed her easy passage through the next two sets of doors.

I recognized where we were, then—the Collective's Bear Island fortress. The medical wing.

"So I have you to thank for the security system being extra locked down," I said.

At my side, Bee didn't answer. She picked up her pace, jogging for two or three steps, and then... then...

The white-paneled walls and doorways rushed past in a blur until we were standing in a completely different room.

Bee had just fast-forwarded her own memory.

"Nasty," I spat, my mind reeling as the distortion slowly eased.

She snorted, but her attention was on her memory self.

Four stasis chambers, identical to the one that had held Daniel, were arrayed side by side in the large room. A series of monitors were set on the far wall, and were attached by various cables to the head of each chamber.

The wall to our immediate right was lined with computer workstations. Medical equipment of some sort was tucked in the far corner as well.

The former occupants of the workstations were slumped on the ground, having fallen out of their chairs. Memory Bee appeared to be trying to find something on one of the computers. She grew more and more frustrated as she moved from the first station to the next, then the next.

"Why are you here alone?" I asked. "You aren't a tech."

She didn't answer me. Ignoring her other self, she'd moved closer to the nearest stasis chamber, peering into it. "I didn't know which one was the telepath."

She'd dropped all communication with the other three that made us the Five. She'd sought out and somehow found where the Collective had housed Gen 4. And she'd broken in. Looking for answers to how to fix her slowly degrading mind.

"Why not ask Daniel and Samantha to back you on this mission?" The same question, asked in a different way.

Bee looked at me. "I didn't know," she whispered. "The Collective killed Gen 4's amplifier, thinking she was the cause of the… instability. She wasn't."

"They aren't tied like we are," I said, filling in the blanks. "No blood tattoos."

"No empathy…" Bee murmured so quietly that it might have been only a whisper in my mind. "No empathy constantly filtering in over the first twenty-one years of their lives. No way to know that they'd truly become monsters." She cocked her head to one side. "There's a peace in not knowing, I suppose."

Memory Bee got frustrated by her inability to find what she was looking for on the computers—presumably which chamber held the telepath. A telepath she thought might have answers to the metamorphosis of her own powers. She marched over to fiddle with the controls on the nearest chamber instead, standing side by side with sunflower-dress Bee.

"So you woke them all up."

"Yes."

"And then you realized that they couldn't function," I snapped. "That they had to be continually controlled."

"Yes."

"But you didn't put them back."

She looked at me. "Would you have?"

"I wouldn't have been here in the first place."

She laughed harshly. "No, you wouldn't."

"That doesn't justify your actions."

"What would you have done, had I come to you? You told me not to need you."

Memory Bee started triggering the sequences to wake the four remaining members of Gen 4.

Livid, I spun away from her, getting far enough to cross through the door.

The hall did that distorted rushing thing around me again.

I lost my footing. I lost my sense of space.

I was a moment away from releasing my own power in a flood that I knew would shake Bee's hold on my mind. But then I landed hard on my knees, with hands gripping my shoulders, pressing me down.

My limbs were weak, my head fuzzy.

I was in Bee's mind again.

She was being held—likely drugged—against her will.

And there… peeking around a doorway as if he knew he shouldn't have been spying… behind the dark-skinned, smooth-haired woman wearing a white coat and looming over Bee…

The Chemist, a voice helpfully supplied. Bee's voice. In my mind, even as I rode her memory.

The Chemist was pressing something against the skin of Bee's neck. My neck. It was cold, and she was actively weaving magic into it as she smiled… and smiled… and smiled… with deadened eyes. That magic stung, then seared itself into my neck. Bee's neck.

The young boy peered around the door, watching. Watching. Everything.

Two sets of hands were holding Bee down—holding me down—and two other figures were standing woodenly to each side. Gen 4. They'd already been compromised by the Chemist—which I knew because Bee knew. The Chemist had occasionally woken one or more of them when she had need of them.

But Gen 4 would be far, far more useful to the Chemist with Bee to control them.

Heavy within my mind—the memory that wasn't my own—Bee forced my gaze past the Chemist, watching the boy as he eased his hold on the door and slipped silently away.

Warm-brown skin, medium-brown hair… maybe three or four years old?

He had bright emerald-green eyes.

Fox in Socks's eyes…

Bee's realization, not my own.

Sixth generation, the telepath whispered across my mind.

I wrenched myself free from the memory, from her hold.

I was tired of being played, of being manipulated.

I lashed out with my power.

I flared my wings.

And found myself on my knees on the cold stone floor of the fortress's kill-box entranceway, panting and exhausted.

Sprawled before me, Bee barely managed to prop herself up on one arm. Her pink armor was arrayed around her in discarded chunks. Her eyes were bloodshot. More blood had gushed from her nose, over her chin, and down her neck.

My gaze fell to the tiny skin colored patch anchored there, visible now as it was rimmed in blood. Fixed above her carotid artery. The Chemist's fail-safe, woven into her skin. Yet I still didn't feel even a flicker of empathy for my blood-bound sister.

She had made her choices, just as I'd made mine.

FIVE

THE NOISE OF AN ONGOING BATTLE FILTERED THROUGH to me. My head still swimming, I cranked my neck to the side, noting that a protective barrier—shimmering with the dark blue of Aiden's magic—had been sealed over the now-open arched steel exterior doors. My dark sorcerer had secured my back so that I couldn't be locked within or hit by any of the magic I could feel exploding just beyond the doors, even as he attempted to press forward and get our team to safe ground.

I tried to get up, but stumbled and fell on my knees again. Moving more by intention and willpower than command over my limbs, I got my feet underneath me, then paused while I crouched to snag my jacket off the floor. It was layered with as many protective spells as Aiden had been able to adhere to it, plus no doubt more than one tracking rune.

Shrugging it on, I straightened with deliberation, feeling my stolen self-healing ability already flooding through my system to correct any imbalance

I'd suffered while wrenching my mind away from Bee's thankfully weak grasp.

I pivoted, heading out the open doorway and into what I presumed was the inner courtyard of the fortress.

"Socks!" Bee shouted weakly after me. She couldn't get her legs under her. "If you won't help me, you have to… at least take Gen 4, hide them… and the boy! The boy!"

I picked up my pace. I couldn't see what was going on beyond the doorway. I pulled my comms earpiece out of my pocket and shoved it in my ear, but it was still dead. Or the rest of the team was operating under radio silence.

I couldn't spare any more time for Bee's games, her mental manipulations.

Ultimately, if she was a danger to those I loved, if her actions threatened the life I'd built, I would take her out. And I didn't have to kill her to do it.

She thought she couldn't control her power?

Well, I could take it from her. Then quickly siphon it off myself. There was no way I wanted to retain any telepathic abilities. Or Amanda could voluntarily lie down in one of the chambers within which she'd just helped a member of the Collective imprison Daniel and Samantha.

And the boy?

A Collective-bred, sixth-generation super soldier with my eyes?

Right.

I wasn't that gullible.

Bee could make me see what she wanted me to see. Everything I knew about the Collective already informed me that a boy with my eyes wouldn't have been free to hide behind doors and spy on his maker, the Chemist. Even if he was that sneaky—and granted, I'd been pretty damn sneaky at almost as young an age—that sort of sneakiness came with a wallop of raw magical talent. Magic the Chemist would have, should have, easily felt.

No. There was no boy.

Just Bee's agenda.

And I had no interest in anyone's agendas, least of all Amanda's—especially given the method she'd chosen to grab my attention.

Zipping up my jacket, I slipped through the door, passing easily through Aiden's seal and aware that the telepath had made it to her feet behind me. Pausing a step into the courtyard, it took me a moment to piece together that our evacuation plan had met with some final resistance.

Apparently, Bee had thought she could hold us with a dozen mercenaries and the remaining members of Gen 4. Even as she'd been trying to crack my mind, Amanda would have maintained control over those remaining guards, the Gen 4 telepath, and the Gen 4 telekinetic. Maybe even the Gen 4 nullifier, though I was fairly certain I'd severed their connection. But once Bee was rooted in someone's mind, she could always access those pathways. Usually more easily than when she first carved them.

Spreading out from the front of the fortress, the massive courtyard was edged with a tall stone wall replete with walkways and parapets. The center of that fortified space was open to the moody, gray-clouded sky above and filled with chaos below. Magically fueled chaos.

Piloted by Calhoun, our black helicopter hovered just overhead to my left. Its whirling blades were still magically muted. It had taken at least three hits—I could see magic still smoldering from the impact points—but showed no visible damage. Samantha was in the process of clearing a landing area, shoving the crumpled ruins of another helicopter, smoldering with dark-blue sorcerer magic, to the side with her telekinesis.

Bodies and battle debris littered the rest of the courtyard. None of my team was down. Though more than half of them weren't supporting their own weight.

Behind a barrier that appeared to be constructed out of a crumpled shipping container, a mangled, heavy, stationary gun of some sort, and flickering magic-fueled shields, the rest of my team was hunkered down between the mercs, their still mostly intact equipment, and the landing pad. Aiden was ripping pages out of his notebook, systematically moving between wounded teammates and pressing runed painkiller and healing spells to whatever exposed skin he could find.

He looked up the instant I cleared the doorway, passing through his sealing spell. His eyes blazed with the bright blue of his sorcerer magic as he checked me over, head to toe. Then he offered me a smile that was much closer to a declaration of war than an expression of joy.

I smiled back, jogging to join the others behind the barrier.

Becca, crouched before Aiden, took the opportunity to rip a page out of the dark sorcerer's rapidly diminishing notebook. She barked a command and pressed the runed page to Aiden's own neck.

Aiden blinked down at her.

Khalid, propped next to Becca, laughed warmly. "Quick study."

Becca sniffed offishly.

The Gen 4 nullifier was situated on Becca's other side. He watched me warily as I approached, his hands on full display on his knees. I ignored him, intent on my sorcerer.

Christopher waved an all-clear to Calhoun, stepping back to join Samantha, who was leaning against the far wall. No visible wounds on either of them. Aiden's shields had held, and possibly Daniel's as well. Though the nullifier's magic was still so drained that it barely registered to my senses, even through the blood tattoo that bound us.

They were all drained.

Aiden's hair stirred as Calhoun settled the helicopter on the landing pad. On the other side of the barrier, the remaining mercs shouted orders at each other, suggesting their comms were down as well. Presumably something Daniel had done—his nullifying magic could be turned against tech and electronics as well. The nullifier had probably disabled the big gun he was currently propped against, with Samantha then mangling it so it couldn't be reacquired by the merc squad.

Except shouldn't the Gen 4 telepath have been handling communications for the fortress guards? Or Bee, for that matter, if the telepath was still out of commission?

The spells that coated our transport were still flickering from the damage it had taken. Maybe Calhoun had tried to land, gotten hit, and eased off to protect our exit?

A strategic retreat. Since Samantha and Aiden appeared to have taken out any other helicopters, we couldn't get off the island without our transport.

The sound of movement from the enemy combatants started filtering in from beyond our barrier as I stepped close enough to Aiden to quickly assess him for wounds. His magic was dim. I amplified it as I gently caressed his stubbled jawline.

"Sorcerer," I murmured.

"Can we go home?" he asked gruffly.

"Yes." Aware that we had an audience, and that not all of them were friends or allies, I dropped my hand. Intent on getting our wounded to the copter, I started to step away.

Aiden cupped the back of my head and pulled me into a harsh but heady kiss. His frustration and lingering anger were clear through our automatic empathic connection. I could practically taste everything he wanted to say—everything he presumably wanted to actually yell. I answered those unvoiced frustrations, his lingering fear, by meeting his tongue with my own and funneling as much power into him as I could.

He broke the kiss. But his hand lingered, buried in my hair. His tone was measured but darkly tinted. "I'm not a fan, Emma, of leaving you behind."

"Look at it like securing my exit, sorcerer," I purred.

He huffed. "How about you just don't do it again?"

I nipped at his bottom lip, then stepped back before he could retaliate.

He shook his head, huffing a second time. Then he started drawing more runes in his notebook. There weren't many pages left, but I had no doubt that Aiden had more notebooks within easy reach even though he wasn't wearing one of his suits with the seemingly bottomless pockets.

Behind us, Daniel had made it to his feet and crossed to jump into the helicopter. Samantha was heading to me, grinning madly, though her magic was still dim.

The Gen 4 nullifier's head snapped toward the partially open doorway to the fortress a moment before Bee stepped through Aiden's sealing spell. Perhaps it wasn't designed to keep her within. Or, more likely, the tie of my blood and DNA and magic collected under her skin was enough to let her pass.

The telepath had stripped off the rest of her pink armor, revealing a white-woven under-layer body suit.

Samantha, pausing beside me, grunted dismissively. "White? Really? Somehow that's even worse than the pink."

One of the reasons we all wore similar tactical gear was to blend in with each other. It was also the same reason Christopher covered his distinctive white-blond hair—

My mind flashed back to the image of the boy that Bee had shown me. The distinctive green eyes that I'd only ever seen in a mirror before, when I even bothered looking.

I shoved the thought away, not certain whether it was actually my own. Bee was sneaky, and the pathways she'd carved into my mind during the first twenty-one years of my life were deep, no matter how quickly I healed from physical wounds.

"Socks?" Samantha murmured as if repeating herself. "Does Bee need rescuing?"

"If she wanted our help," I said, my tone harsh even to my own ears, "she should have asked." I hated being manipulated. And being played by someone I should have been able to trust was even worse.

Samantha scanned my face, then nodded curtly. She leaned down and offered Becca a hand. Aiden did the same for Khalid.

I directed my power toward the blood tattoo I could feel on Samantha. Then, as gently as possible, I twined my power through hers, just tiny threads of amplification that hopefully wouldn't hurt. But with her magic as drained as it was, with the toxin that had knocked her out and kept her down still in her system,

I was fairly certain she'd feel it even with my amplification working at a slow trickle.

Bee was attempting to make her way toward me. The Gen 4 nullifier pushed off the ground, sliding up the side of the crushed shipping container to make it to his feet.

A groan and a stir of movement beyond the section of the barrier powered by dark-blue sorcerer magic—the section nearest the exterior door—drew Bee's attention to a slight male with light-brown hair wearing tactical gear. Using Bee's mostly drained magic as reference, the male rolling to his feet but not making it upright was also a telepath. Gen 4.

He must have circled around somehow from where we'd left him behind in the hall after he tried to turn Khalid's brain into mush. Or perhaps he'd managed to pass me while I was in Bee's mindscape?

The Gen 4 nullifier pushed off the container and slowly started making his way over to Bee. Amanda had stepped through the sorcerer-fueled section of our barrier as easily as she'd crossed through the seal on the door. She was trying to get the other telepath on his feet.

Catching my gaze, she snarled, "Some help?"

Samantha turned away with Becca propped up on her shoulder. Even though she bore no visible wounds, the demolitions specialist didn't appear to be taking much of her own weight.

"I thought you were figuring it all out yourself, Tel5," Samantha said, sounding more wounded than sarcastic.

Aiden, balancing Khalid across his shoulders as well, trailed Samantha to the helicopter. Though he brushed against me as he departed to urge me to accompany him.

I did so. Except slowly, keeping my eye on the telepath and her Gen 4 puppets.

At the helicopter, Christopher paused. Then he began turning in a slow circle with his head cocked to one side. The magic in his eyes was at a low ebb, but his senses were being tweaked somehow.

I glanced back at Bee just as the Gen 4 telekinetic darted forward to take up a ready position in front of her. Tall enough to tower over both telepaths, he was steadily bleeding from a head wound.

I didn't know any of Gen 4's names. I didn't know if they even had names. But I refused to refer to them by their designations, not even in my mind.

And if that made me soft—

"Incoming!"

For one confused moment, I thought it had been Christopher who'd shouted the warning. It wasn't. It was Khalid. The sorcerer was hanging half out of the side door of the helicopter and pointing up—way up.

There was nothing overhead.

Power flared in Christopher's eyes, blazing bright enough that it whited out the top half of his face.

Shoulder to shoulder, Aiden and Daniel spun away from the side door of the helicopter, throwing up a secondary shield. Everyone on our team near the helicopter was now tucked behind it, except for me.

Then, utterly inexplicably, the clairvoyant spun and lunged back for me, as if to take a hit I couldn't even feel coming, let alone see.

"Emma!" Bee cried. "She has chemically armed magical munitions—"

Something invisible to all my senses exploded in front of Bee.

I blinked.

At first there was nothing to see…

Then another explosion… of magic.

Another blink.

Then the Gen 4 nullifier was throwing himself in front of Bee.

A third blink.

… my mind, my brain, was desperately trying to catch up to what I was seeing.

But before I could focus, the entire area around the exterior doors to the fortress went white. Completely washed out from all my senses.

The power contained in that explosion—those explosions?—shredded the sorcerers' combined barrier spell, shuddering over me and shoving me back a few steps.

The tattoo on my T2 vertebra flared… not identifying Bee, but her… her power?

Magical munitions?

Built with Bee's power?

More white exploded through the skirted courtyard. But this time, I saw the bombs as they dropped from above, a moment before impact.

Then Christopher hit me from the side and took me down, covering me with his body.

Only seconds had passed.

I lashed out with a wave of pure amplification—practically wild magic when wielded without focus—hoping to push back against the onslaught.

Everything around us went white again.

Then a blast wave hit us. Christopher and I rolled, tangled around each other, his hands cushioning my head, my arms wrapped around the back of his neck to protect it.

Then everything went still.

Terribly still.

Either my senses were all compromised or…

I shoved the second half of that thought away unexamined. Discovering that I could still move despite having my sight completely whited out, I rolled Christopher under me, keeping low so I was still shielding him.

I strained to see, to hear.

After another breath or two, a flicker of dark-blue power drew my attention to the far left.

Aiden's power.

He was still shielding the helicopter, though that shield looked weak.

We hadn't been thrown too far.

Christopher cupped my face. Power boiled from him, intensified by our skin-to-skin contact. He shuddered under the weight of whatever his sight was revealing to him.

"She can't take you, Socks," he mumbled. "She can't take you."

"Of course not," I snapped. Even with everyone else drained, and without factoring in all the other firepower we had access to—that Bee had access to—no one person could take me.

"I see you… apart," he rasped. "Alone."

"I'm never alone," I said, trying for a gentle tone even as my eyesight slowly came back. Either that or the whiteout was thinning. "You can't see yourself, Knox. You must be with me."

He exhaled shakily. Then his head snapped to the side. "They're coming… she waited… this is her end game. She's here for you, Fox in Socks. The rest of us are expendable. Bonuses. But expendable."

That got my attention. I could see the outline of the clairvoyant's face now. "How expendable?"

Christopher grimaced instead of answering. But before I could ask for more details, I heard… something…

Footfalls.

Not steps, but…

Landings. Multiple people dropping onto the ground nearby, followed by quick movement.

Though I couldn't hear any aircraft above us, the Chemist—or maybe Bee herself—had called in paratroops.

As far as I could make out, the earlier wave of strategically dropped, magically fueled bombs had destroyed the physical and magical barrier protecting my team and shielding the helicopter. Our only escape option.

I lashed out with my amplification magic, homing in on Samantha behind me though I couldn't see her. "Barrier, Zans! Now!"

All the power I was pumping into her from afar blazed out of the telekinetic. It cut through the thinning white haze enshrouding us as she flooded the immediate area and grabbed every bit of rubble and detritus she could hold. The telekinetic smashed those bits together to form a short wall in front of the helicopter—blunt but efficient.

Keeping low but still pumping power into Samantha, I gained my feet, grabbed Christopher's hand, and ran toward the helicopter.

Samantha, standing with her arms flung out and her head back, continued building the barrier with whatever she could sense nearby. Chunks of stone from the walls started coming loose.

Too much magic.

The telekinetic was channeling too much, too quickly. Not a problem she'd ever had before, not when being actively amplified by me. But she wasn't at full strength, and I could feel something degrading in the connection stretching between us…

With a grunt of effort, Aiden and Daniel stepped forward, shifting the shield they were struggling to hold so that it crested the top of Samantha's wall.

The telekinetic stumbled back, then fell to her knees.

I stopped pumping power into her, switching to amplifying Aiden and Daniel as I closed the final few steps between—

"Bee!" Christopher shouted, wrenching his hand from mine and darting back the way we'd come.

Aiden and Daniel's shield started taking fire. More magically fueled projectiles from the team of mercenaries I could sense more than see on the other side of Samantha's barrier. But these projectile spells were somehow tuned to Daniel's magic, because he grunted and fell to one knee even as he tried to keep his portion of the shield intact.

As with Samantha, I could feel the power I was pumping into the nullifier flickering... thinning... eroding?

I met Aiden's gaze.

His eyes flicked over my shoulder, tracing Christopher's progress in the opposite direction—toward Bee. My dark sorcerer grimaced and shook his head at me. Just once, but it was emphatic.

He wanted me on the helicopter.

A glance to my left confirmed that Becca and Khalid were upright enough that both could perch in the open side door of the copter, pressing their hands to its sides and fueling the compromised shield protecting our only mode of retreat.

Calhoun was still in the pilot's seat.

I went after Christopher.

Aiden swore viciously. I couldn't even pause to flash him a grin.

Bee was sobbing over a body at the edge of Samantha's barrier—as if they'd been running for cover but hadn't made it. Two of the other Gen 4s were trying to pull the telepath away and keep low to the ground at the same time. The Gen 4 telekinetic's magic sputtered, then surged, as he tried to keep what appeared to be an air shield over them.

That was a neat trick—one that Samantha would probably sell what remained of her soul to learn.

The Gen 4 telepath kept touching Bee's face, trying to call her attention to him. His own power flared with each touch.

Except Bee had been drained while attempting to hold me. And now someone she'd been psychically attached to was dead.

Closing the space between us let me identify the body Bee was mourning over. The Gen 4 nullifier. He stared sightlessly in the direction of the press of magically armed mercenaries I could feel approaching us. I couldn't see or sense what wound he'd taken, but I had no doubt that he'd put himself between that killing blow and Amanda.

Christopher scooped Bee up in his arms.

She screamed.

The Gen 4 telekinetic's shield took fire and faltered. He took a round to the chest—a flare of white that mimicked his own power and knocked him to the ground.

Then we were suddenly surrounded on three sides. The half-dozen mercs were masked, guns raised.

Bee was still screaming as Christopher spun, then simply outright ran her back to the helicopter.

Shoulder to shoulder, the Gen 4 telepath and I turned toward our attackers. The telekinetic was still immobile at our feet, possibly dead.

I flared my power, ready to drain all six mercs at once, right from where I stood. But the tendrils of my magic slid off them as they stalked toward the telepath and me, holding us between them.

I could feel their magic. I should have been able to—

A gun swung up, pointing directly at my face. The finger on the trigger tightened—

"Not her!" someone shouted from behind.

I lunged forward, grabbing the barrel and slamming the gun back into the face of my attacker. They went down.

Three more mercs suddenly dropped, making a ring of bodies around the telepath and the fallen telekinetic.

I still couldn't drain any of the mercs. They were somehow shielded against my reach.

The Gen 4 telepath's power faltered. And instead of charging forward, trying skin-to-skin contact on the mercenaries, I slammed my hand into the telepath's back, amplifying him with no time to ask for permission.

He gasped. Stumbled. Then he snapped upright and... focused. Magic I could feel but not see flooded from him.

147

Three more attackers fell under his psychic assault.

Why could his magic touch them when mine couldn't?

A merc covered by two others on either side slipped by the telepath's net, coming for me with what looked like handcuffs. Magical cuffs, apparently. Because he threw them before he was within my reach, and they homed in on me.

I countered with a wave of my power, knocking the cuffs to the side.

I tried contacting the telepath mind to mind. *Why can't I grab their magic?*

He shot a startled look my way. His eyes were crystal blue. "They aren't Adepts," he said, his attention on the next wave of mercs.

So they were magically armed but not magically inclined. And both aspects of my inherent power— amplifying and draining—only worked with magic users, not spells or magical objects.

Our opponent thought she was far too clever.

The telepath took a hit to the chest. It exploded, spreading more of that white-tinted magic over his torso.

White-tinted magic.

Our magic. Or at least the telepath's own power.

A quelling round. Though I assumed the nullifier must have been hit with something different, or had a bad reaction, because we couldn't actually be killed by our own—

The telepath went down.

The second wave of mercs pressed forward all at once, forcing me a few steps back. But then instead of attacking me—because they couldn't all rush me at once without tripping over each other, and I could easily pick them off if they weren't willing to shoot me—they grabbed the fallen telepath and telekinetic.

As quickly as they'd rushed forward, the mercenaries dragged the remaining two members of Gen 4 back across the courtyard, away from Samantha's hastily erected barrier.

Leaving me. Just like that.

I blinked. Rather idiotically. But I had never seen anyone retreat while fighting with that much of an advantage. However, before I could assess the situation and decide on a course of action, Christopher started shouting.

The clairvoyant never shouted. At least not in panic.

I spun and ran.

The air had mostly cleared from the first assault that had been meant to quell us. Except our opponent clearly didn't have access to all of our magic. Only the Gen 4s, Bee, Daniel, and Samantha.

I just had to get the others onto the helicopter while Aiden and Daniel's shield was still holding.

Christopher was shouting again, grabbing for Amanda. "Bee... Bee!" But his warning was erupting from whatever his magic was showing him, not addressing her directly.

Bee was twisting from his grasp, looking around as if she had the capacity to sense whatever the clairvoyant saw coming her way. She was on her feet but clearly dazed. Overwhelmed.

I was only a dozen meters away.

Three things happened in rapid succession.

Christopher's head snapped to the side. "Clear the barrier! No! Aiden!"

Without a moment of hesitation, Daniel heeded the clairvoyant's warning, grabbing Aiden's arm and shoving the sorcerer in the direction of the helicopter. In that same motion, he shifted his own faltering wards from the top of the barrier to shield Aiden directly.

The section of the barrier where they'd been standing exploded.

Everywhere.

I covered my head and face with both of my arms and kept running. Debris slammed against my entire right side.

Bee screamed—sharp and pained. She clutched her neck, falling to her knees as blood spurted between her fingers, instantly coating her shoulder and chest, stark against her white body suit.

Christopher grabbed her shoulders, dragging her the last few steps to the helicopter.

I went for Aiden.

Daniel had fallen too, half on top of my dark sorcerer. I rolled him off, knowing Aiden was okay as I felt his personal shield slide over me. I pressed my hands to his face, taking a brief moment to meet his bright-blue gaze before shifting to check Daniel.

The nullifier was unconscious but breathing. Not physically wounded, unless he was bleeding internally, but his power was drained. So drained that it didn't accept my amplification, not even through skin-to-skin contact.

"Bastard saved my ass!" Aiden snarled, clearly displeased. "How am I supposed to hate him now?"

I laughed, surprised that I still had the capacity to do so.

Khalid darted forward, keeping low to the ground. I relinquished Daniel to him. Someone had already belted Samantha into the helicopter, and the telekinetic was clearly unconscious. Christopher had Bee in his arms, halfway through the open door. Becca was wrapping some of her rune tape around Bee's neck—clearly a different variety than the explosive tape she'd used before.

Blood had thoroughly saturated the telepath's white body suit, spreading down to elbow and rib cage. At a guess, whatever fail-safe was in the patch the Chemist had forced on the telepath had been remotely triggered at the same time they hit our barrier, as an extra distraction. But if the plan had been to blow Bee's head off, it hadn't worked.

Not yet, at least. She was clearly dying, though. She'd lost a massive amount of blood in a matter of moments.

"We need to go on the offensive!" I snapped. "Everyone who's on their feet, to me. Everyone else, in the helicopter. Take off now!"

Christopher relinquished Bee to Becca. The demolitions expert pulled the telepath inside, then reached back to help Khalid with Daniel.

Aiden straightened, stepping up to my shoulder as the clairvoyant joined us. The sorcerer snapped out a mobile shield over just the three of us.

The others were too compromised. Or only functional enough to aid in their own retreat.

"Mission parameters?" Christopher asked. The white of his power limned his eyes, so much so that his gaze on me had actual weight. We were about to walk into some version of the future he'd started seeing for me in the depths of the fortress.

"Cover fire as we step through what's left of Samantha's barrier to assess." I glanced at Aiden. He nodded, removing two of his last five copper rings. I found myself hoping he hadn't lost the others, but had merely spent the magic contained within them and tucked them away. I glanced at Christopher next. "We take out anything that's designed to keep our transport from getting off the ground."

The clairvoyant nodded. "They're out of those quelling charges," he said, tilting his head. "And their ammo isn't tuned to any of the three of us."

"They had the chance to take me out—"

Aiden glanced at me so sharply that I amended my statement. "A chance to *try* to take me out, and they hesitated."

"You're going to go all Hallowed on them," Christopher whispered, speaking more to his magic than to me.

"Is it going to work?" I asked, trying for a light-hearted tone.

He grimaced, then said, "You walk away."

"And?" Aiden said, sounding dangerous.

Unfortunately, I didn't have time to luxuriate in that delectable tone.

"And… Emma saves us all. Like always."

We had no time for more chatter. Because there was only one reason an enemy combatant blew a major hole in your defenses and didn't immediately follow through. They were prepping.

I stepped through the destroyed barrier, Aiden's mobile shield around me. I assessed the scene ahead.

A single transport helicopter had set down as close to the far wall as possible—the source of at least some of the paratroops, I assumed. The area before us seemed oddly clear, until I remembered that Samantha had used everything she could reach to build the second barrier.

The merc troops had withdrawn to the far side of the courtyard. Nonmagical mercenaries, with a mixture of magical and nonmagical assault weapons. I'd never tested my Hallowed-amplified power on nonmagicals.

At least a half-dozen of them were clustered around what appeared to be a surface-to-air missile launcher.

Fuck.

"We disabled it," Christopher said, following my gaze.

"Well, they're clearly enabling it again," I muttered.

A woman was perched on the edge of the open side door of the black helicopter, which was larger than our own. She caught sight of the three of us, and a wide grin spread across her dark-skinned face. She wore her hair in a smooth bob and was dressed in a half-buttoned bright-red cardigan over pressed black wool pants.

Though the helicopter's rotor blades were still, the two remaining members of Gen 4 were already strapped in behind her.

Less than a dozen mercs?

I glanced toward the fortress. We hadn't been able to see the front door from behind Samantha's second barrier. If I were our opponent, I would have funneled troops inside in case we tried to escape the back way, or to create our own back exit. I flicked my gaze up to the ramparts, looking for magical shielding.

It took me a moment to pick up the telltale shimmer. More troops were stationed above.

The Chemist had brought a small army to collect me.

Which made sense. Because I had no doubt she'd studied my exit from another Collective compound—from the last Collective member who had tried to execute a kill order on the Five.

Taking out Samantha, Daniel, and Bee was a strong opening salvo. If I tried to initiate the Amplifier Protocol with just Christopher to anchor me, I'd probably kill us both.

And surrounding me with nonmagical mercs that I couldn't pull power from was a solid plan.

Except I wasn't just Amp5 now.

So I didn't just pull my blades.

I didn't start cutting through the Chemist's mercenaries, intent only on my target, intent only on finishing the mission as quickly as possible. Ignoring the body count that it would take to accomplish that.

No. Instead, I loosened my strict hold on my power. Everything I carried that had doubled, tripled in strength since my contact with the Hallowed. Everything I'd claimed and accepted from the time an immortal entity had invaded my body and tried to subsume my mind.

Everything that came with wings of energy, anchored to either side of the four active blood tattoos on my upper spine.

Christopher had joked that my starting a cult would be as easy as me walking down the street with those wings out. Wings that could be seen only by those who could see magic, but which I could nonetheless use to influence… well, quite possibly everyone.

I wasn't a fan of the idea of being able to weaponize my empathy, turn it outward. But I was done denying that ability.

Because I didn't have to kill anyone if I beguiled them. And not murdering people tore a little less from my already-shredded soul.

Aiden hummed in response to the appearance of my wings. My dark sorcerer might still have been livid with me, but he could appreciate pretty magic when he saw it.

Christopher chuckled. Darkly.

My power, layered with everything that made me Emma Johnson—the amplification, the empathy, and the ability to pull power to me—flooded the courtyard in an invisible wave.

Invisible to me, at any rate.

It crashed over the group of mercenaries scrambling around trying to get the missile launcher working. It lapped up the walls into the ramparts, where it slipped through shielding spells and curled tendrils of energy around every merc hidden from my sight.

Unfortunately, the Chemist was behind heavier shielding. My energy wave slammed into it, then slipped around until the helicopter and its occupants were surrounded.

Runes carved into the ground around the copter sparked in defense—not quelling my magic, but attempting to repel it.

"They fortified their landing pad," Aiden muttered.

The Chemist's eyes widened in utter glee as she nearly stumbled from her perch on the side of the helicopter. She pressed her hand to the inside of the domed ward protecting her from my weaponized empathy.

Then she had the gall to laugh.

Laugh!

As if I delighted her.

Snarling, I stepped forward.

"Wait," Christopher murmured, distracted. His own magic flitted over me, lingering on the blood tattoo that bound us.

"No more waiting," I snapped, taking another step.

The ground under my front foot depressed.

I looked down.

Fuck.

"No! Aiden!" Christopher shouted.

Aiden body checked me just as Christopher attempted to shove the sorcerer in the opposite direction.

The ground exploded underneath us, so violently that it shredded the remains of Aiden's shield and flung us back through the gap in the shattered barrier.

Ears ringing, every joint in my body aching, I rolled to my feet.

Smart.

I shook my head.

So, so smart to use mundane munitions against us.

I was out of practice.

I was facing one of my makers.

And no matter how much I wanted to insist I wasn't Amp5 anymore, the Collective still knew my weaknesses. They had tried to breed most of them out, after all. And what they couldn't lace into my DNA, they forced me to absorb from other Adepts.

Including accelerated healing.

By the time I'd oriented myself and keyed in on Christopher's white-blond hair, the dust from the explosion not yet settling, any wounds I'd sustained were already healing.

Except…

Except Christopher's hands were on Aiden's chest.

And he was… he was performing…

I stumbled the few steps between us, sliding to a stop on my knees.

Aiden was down.

Aiden was hurt.

Aiden wasn't breathing.

Then Khalid was at Christopher's side and tearing pages out of Aiden's notebook, plastering those pages over… over my dark sorcerer's bloody chest and… and…

I lashed out, amplifying anyone I could reach in the immediate area. Khalid gasped, shuddering.

I reached for Aiden's power specifically, trying to be gentle, trying to just tangle my power through his, but—

"Stop! Stop!" Khalid was shouting.

At me?

Christopher grabbed me, his hands on my face. I could feel the blood on his hands transferring to, then seeping into my skin. It sparked with power. Aiden's blood. Sorcerer power. "Gentle, Socks. Gentle, gentle. He's alive. He's breathing."

Relief shuddered through me. Inexplicably, it hurt. It woke me up to the situation.

The Chemist had gotten the better of us.

I watched Aiden's chest rise and fall, once, twice, three times.

Everyone was wounded or had been drained deeply enough that more amplification might cause more damage instead of helping.

Except Christopher.

I met the clairvoyant's gaze. He wasn't holding my face anymore, but he'd been watching me as Khalid and Becca took over bandaging Aiden, careful with his neck as they moved him onto a spinal board from the helicopter's cache of medical gear.

I stood up.

I stepped away. My gaze was on the opening in the shattered barrier, visualizing the Chemist waiting for me behind her shields.

How much did she want me under her control?

Enough to lay this elaborate trap.

Enough to sacrifice Bee and Daniel and Samantha just to secure me.

Would she kill everyone?

I wasn't certain I could get to her before she succeeded.

Unless…

Unless I walked right up to her.

Unless I broke all my own rules and made an idiotically ridiculous hero's play.

Amp5 would never have done so. She'd been trained better than that. She had always been made to understand that she was the Collective's most important asset.

"Please, Emma," Christopher whispered at my side. "I can't see that path clearly—"

I grasped Christopher's shoulders in my hands, my voice raw. "Tell me he lives, my Knox. Tell me Aiden lives."

Christopher's power flared, latching on to the blood tattoo on my T3 vertebra. Each of the other tattoos was dim. My tie to Bee was almost dormant again.

The clairvoyant inhaled shakily. "He lives."

I dropped my hands, turning toward the barrier.

"He's going to be seriously pissed at you," Christopher warned, trailing me. "Like, call-off-the-wedding, never-forgive-you pissed."

I glanced back once—checking the clairvoyant's expression, seeking to understand the solidity of his conviction, of what his magic was showing him. "Is there another path?"

Christopher opened his mouth.

"A viable path where I don't lose what I can't bear to lose?"

He grimaced.

That was a no.

If Aiden didn't get to the nearest healer—one of the many we currently had on call throughout Europe—then he wasn't going to make it. Even if I pulled my blades and Christopher and I carved through all resistance, through everyone ready to stop our helicopter from making it off the ground in one piece.

I turned my attention back to the courtyard. The Chemist was still standing beside the larger heli-copter, pressed up against the ward line that I could no longer see, because it wasn't coated in my magic anymore. Even across that distance, I could tell her gaze was trained on me.

I loosened the sheath across my back, handing it and my blades to Christopher. He slipped the loop over his shoulder. His own sword was in his other hand.

"But he lives?" I asked again.

"He lives."

"Good." I flashed the clairvoyant a smile. "I'm going to need pick up."

"Take me with you."

I laughed, my heart lying crushed on the ground, beating only for Aiden.

And why not? I was being a fool. Playing a fool's game.

"It's your turn to save everyone else this time, Knox."

He swallowed, then nodded.

"See you soon, my brother."

SIX

I RAISED MY HANDS, TAKING THREE LARGE STEPS INTO the courtyard. Christopher fell back toward our helicopter. I pinned my gaze to the Chemist and called, "I don't take another step until my people are out of your grasp."

"And what will I do with you without hostages with which to motivate you?" the Chemist yelled back, shaking her head and smiling broadly as if I might have been some errant toddler. Her accent was lilting, but I couldn't immediately place it. Not American, not Canadian, and not British. "I'll take your entire generation as guarantee of your good behavior."

"You take one more step in my direction, or have one of your mercs do so, and I'll initiate the Amplifier Protocol. My teammates would rather I drain them down to nothing than spend one more moment in your… care." Though not particularly good at banter, I could still sneer effectively. And I was trying to give Christopher time to get everyone on the helicopter.

The Chemist grimaced. It was brief, but I still caught it.

My own smile sharpened, and I purred, "You remember the Amplifier Protocol, don't you, Chemist?"

"It's Lindi," she snapped. "Lindiwe Fourie. Or overseer, if you must conform to your programming. And I seem to remember that you need skin-to-skin contact to—"

I flared my wings, putting on a show. "Care to test me? Just one more test for your creation… a brief glimpse of power before you succumb to your own death?"

Voices rose behind me, the words clipped and intense despite being hushed. Christopher was laying out the plan. No one else was liking it. But I could hear the magically muted thrum from the blades of the helicopter, so they were still readying for takeoff.

Predictably, Lindi's smile widened at my display. Her eyes gleamed with avarice—though it was entirely possible that was her magic I was picking up, even through the invisible wards that still ringed the landing pad and protected her helicopter. I had no idea what sort of Adept she was, but I knew that all of the main members of the Collective were far too powerful.

"Then what?" she asked, feigning that she was actually considering my proposal. "I let them go… and? Amp5 doesn't surrender."

"I think you'll soon discover that I'm nothing like Amp5."

She sneered, then scoffed. "The sorcerer. Really? I'd heard rumors of course, but please."

Instead of answering, I surveyed my immediate surroundings, as if I was readying an attack. Lindiwe Fourie would have seen all of us in action—and she had no idea how compromised the rest of the four were. For all she knew, I was currently in telepathic communication with them. That would have been protocol, after all.

"At least your blood, your DNA…" she finally said with an affected shrug. "It won't have been infected by the weakness degrading your mind."

"Well, you didn't breed me for my intellect," I said, unable to stop myself from grinning at a brief thought of all the things the Chemist had no idea I was now capable of doing.

"We are in agreement."

I waited.

Finally, Lindi beckoned over her shoulder without looking back. Shifting forward from the depths of the helicopter behind her, the Gen 4 telepath leaned in to listen to her orders, though his gaze remained locked to me. After a moment, the Gen 4 telekinetic also shifted forward to perch in the doorway of the helicopter, on the other side of Lindi now. His gaze flicked between the back of the overseer's head, me, and the helicopter preparing to take off behind me.

A look passed over and behind Lindi's head between the two remaining Gen 4 team members. I didn't have to be near to feel magic shifting between them. I had no doubt they were communicating tele-pathically. The telekinetic dipped his chin, just once. Then they both trained those blank stares back on me.

I also had no doubt that Lindi was controlling the last remaining members of Gen 4 with the same explosive patches she'd attached to Bee.

The team surrounding the missile launcher peeled away, running over to ring Lindi's helicopter. They stood just forward of the ward line encircling the landing area, guns trained solely on me.

I stalked forward, sending out tendrils of my power just in case someone with enough magic for me to grab happened to try to get by me. I had to trust that Christopher could handle any mundanes who managed to do so.

Lindi stepped back into the helicopter, still watching me. Its blades remained still, though I could see a pilot at the controls.

I paused just out of reach of the masked mercs. Standing with all their weapons trained on me, and the wind stirring my hair. I didn't bother raising my hands or making any idiotic show that I was surren-dering.

No member of the Collective was stupid enough to think that was what was really going on. And I wasn't going to try to playact anyway.

"Let her pass," Lindi said from inside the heli-copter. The Gen 4 telepath and telekinetic were still crouched just within the side door, their dull gazes trained on me. No weapons in hand. Because they didn't need weapons any more than I did.

The mercs tipped their guns down but kept them at the ready. One of them stepped back and pressed a hand to the ground, muttering under their breath. One of the runes etched into the dirt extinguished, then two more, creating a narrow passage. I probably could have walked through without the invitation, but I didn't need to show off any more than I already had.

And apparently, some of Lindi's mercs were of the magical persuasion. Bonus.

I glanced back.

The helicopter holding almost everyone I cared about in this world lifted from the ground, clearing Samantha's barrier wall, then briefly hovering over the far side of the courtyard.

Calhoun was at the controls. Through the still-open side door, I spotted two bodies stretched out in the interior cabin, Bee and Aiden. The others were strapped in, but aware enough to be looking in my direction. Samantha looked livid. Daniel was stone faced. Becca and Khalid had their hands pressed to the helicopter's interior, still actively fortifying its warding spells.

My Knox was perched in the open doorway, legs dangling in the air and his eyes blazing with the white of his magic.

He was tossing something in his hand.

Dark-blue magic flickered around a tiny circle of… copper?

One of Aiden's rings.

Grinning at him—understanding his plan—I tucked my wings away and crossed through the mercs without bothering to even look at any of them. I stepped through the opening in the wards, pausing before the side door to Lindi's helicopter.

Seated to the immediate right, the Chemist smirked at me. Then, thinking she was being sneaky quick about it, she abruptly leaned forward and touched something cold against my neck, an injector of some sort. "I thought you were better than this, Amp5."

I laughed.

The mercenaries ringing the helicopter swarmed forward. More mercs appeared on the ramparts surrounding the courtyard. I counted three rocket launchers without really bothering to scan the area as I twisted back to look at my team.

Whatever Lindi had injected me with curled coldly through my neck, over my shoulder and collarbone, feeling like it was heading for my heart. I assumed that was how it worked, needing to be pumped through my system once it hit my bloodstream.

From the helicopter still hovering overhead, Christopher flicked the copper ring forward. It spun outward for a moment, then was shoved sharply down by the wash of the helicopter blades. Flashing with the dark blue of Aiden's sorcerer magic, it hit the ground.

Magic exploded throughout the courtyard.

"Go!" Lindi screamed.

The Gen 4 telepath and telekinetic grabbed me, roughly hauling me into the helicopter. I didn't resist, even though they each still held enough magic that I could have stripped it away, leaving Lindi only husks to command.

The combat grade spell contained in Aiden's ring slammed into the ward protecting Lindi's transport. Even as my limbs started to numb, then tingle, and my magic drained away, I actually felt that boundary shudder.

Two more explosions followed—two more of Aiden's copper rings. Then those wards fell, slamming the entire helicopter back against the stone wall.

Lindi shrieked indignantly, issuing orders and generally sounding put out—and completely indifferent to the mercenaries who would have fallen in my team's final assault.

I shoved against the Gen 4s' hold, managing to get a sightline out of the helicopter. I watched as my team sped off, leaving Lindi's troops in disarray.

Lindi lunged forward, grabbing me by the hair and injecting me a second time. The Gen 4 telepath jerked me away from her, pressing me into a seat— and then shook his head at the telekinetic, as if calling him off.

Yeah, Lindi didn't have the Gen 4s as under control as she thought.

Everything went a bit mushy around the edges, including me. I was aware of being strapped in. I was aware of Lindi snarling orders, then doing more snarling into a phone. The helicopter apparently wasn't so badly damaged that it couldn't get off the ground.

The telekinetic shut the outer door, then strapped himself in beside me. The telepath did the same on my other side.

With Lindi fixated on issuing orders, the Gen 4 telepath curled his hand into mine, whispering through my mind.

Take us with you next time.

I met his crystal-blue eyes, not able to move any other part of my body. Unable to smile or squeeze his hand. But I whispered back through a telepathic connection that had been fortified in the brief moments I'd amplified him. *What's your name?*

I had no doubt that, just as Knox had named us all, the Gen 4s must have felt the same need to name themselves. To create identities beyond their designations, even if only ever shared between the five of them.

He hesitated for a moment. Then, as if revealing some dark truth that had never been spoken out loud, he murmured his name through my slowly fading consciousness.

Jason.

And him? I asked, meaning the telekinetic.

Kevin. Will you take us with you?

Yes.

The telepath offered the telekinetic a slight smile. The look that the telekinetic turned on Lindi in response was viciously pleased.

Gen 4 wasn't fully functional, Bee had warned me. They were violent sociopaths.

Just as I'd been bred and raised to be.

I forced myself to close my eyes, not wanting to wait until I couldn't do so of my own volition. I consciously let myself slip into sleep, knowing that my magic would eventually reassert itself. The Chemist who had mixed my DNA in a test tube thirty years ago or more would know about that ability. She'd know what the Collective had made me do—how many Adepts had died under my touch at their command—to reinforce that immunity.

But I already knew she'd miscalculate the strength of my resistance. Because I was too valuable to kill outright. And she would hesitate before running the risk of corrupting my magic accidentally.

I would wake up sooner, rather than later.

Then I'd make her regret drawing my attention.

A HARSH PINCH AND THEN SEARING PAIN BROUGHT me to full consciousness.

"There you are," someone said over my head. I couldn't place the accent. Hints of New Zealand, maybe? "I expected you to wake at least thirty minutes ago. How disappointing."

I squeezed my eyes shut at the next harsh pinch, and this time, I heard the pop that accompanied it. Agony streaked through my spine, radiating outward through every nerve ending.

"This is too high up the vertebrae for a safe collection," someone else murmured from behind me. Female. With an American twang. "And shouldn't we wait a little longer for the suppression serum to clear from her system?"

"Amp5 isn't so delicate."

As it came more fully into focus, I recognized that the first voice belonged to Lindi. Listening to her now, her previously unplaceable accent carried a South African tenor. Or maybe she'd just been raised in a variety of different places.

"And trust me," Lindi continued. "You don't want her more awake than she already is. I'm capable of separating out what I need from any lingering serum."

The second woman murmured her assent, though slightly doubtfully. Then the room fell silent.

I was strapped to a hard platform of some sort, with my limbs and head immobilized. It took me a moment to realize that I was facing a double door set into an otherwise plain-painted wall—because the medical bed I was on was cranked to the side to give whoever was behind me access to my spine. Machines and medical equipment were arrayed at the topmost edge of my vision, in what appeared to be the corner of the room.

A small space. Plenty of possible weapons within reach. And a badly secured door.

Unfortunately, I couldn't feel even a hint of my magic.

Another pinch at the back of my neck, and this time the needle scraped bone. My vision went black around the edges, and I struggled to not vocalize my pain. It was clear that I hadn't been given any kind of sedation or anesthetic. Or that if I had, the dosage hadn't been calculated correctly.

Or, even without feeling my magic within my reach, that I was immune or resistant to whatever they'd used as a numbing agent. As with most such things.

"Ouch," Lindi said, false sympathy laced through her tone. "Just two more extractions."

Yeah, she hadn't bothered with sedation beyond whatever she was using to keep me under in the first place.

And extractions? Bone marrow biopsies? Through the blood tattoos?

Was Lindi studying the blood tattoos? I had no doubt she'd put Samantha and Daniel through the same tests. So what would my marrow tell her…

DNA.

She was harvesting my DNA, and maybe its connection to the DNA that had been embedded under my skin—that she had embedded under my skin—to bind me to the other four.

Why did she need to know… ?

A flicker of movement drew my attention to the doors across from me. The upper windowed portion of each door was frosted, but for a brief moment I thought I saw someone trying to peek over the bottom edge.

Another harsh pinch and scrape, and this time, I didn't hold back the gasp of pain.

Behind me, Lindi clucked her tongue disapprovingly.

But as I'd anticipated, her assistant rounded the bed to check on me. Above her medical mask, her heavily lined blue eyes—witch eyes—were wide with a mixture of fear and concern. Not that I could feel her emotions with my empathy still effectively smothered.

Still, she met my own gaze in a way that indicated she'd had some proper training in compassionate care before the Collective had gotten hold of her. She gently pressed a cool cloth to my forehead.

"Sarah!" Lindi snapped, then jabbed me with the needle a fourth time. "Amp5 is a highly skilled, dangerous creature. You are not to touch her."

"I'm wearing gloves," Sarah said mildly. What I could see of her warm-brown skin was smooth and unlined, indicating she was young. Or at least that she appeared younger. She was wearing a lab coat, the sleeves rolled up. And the aforementioned latex gloves.

But just as I'd planned when I allowed myself to gasp, I didn't have to touch Sarah to take what I wanted from her. So when she turned away to wet the cloth a second time, I reached deep within and grasped hold of a faint shimmer of my power—power that would only grow in strength the longer they kept me conscious.

Sarah stepped back in front of me, pressing the cloth to my forehead again. I sent out a thread-thin tendril of that shimmer—all the power I could muster—and wound it through her, confirming that she was a healer, most likely with witch origins.

I stole the tiniest sips of that healing energy. It was a terrible irony that healers couldn't heal themselves, though they had robust immunities. But I could take that same power and use it to boost my own currently dampened healing abilities.

Sarah's head tipped to the side for a brief moment, as if she'd heard a whisper.

I didn't have much experience—okay, I didn't have any experience—with taking only tiny sips of power. If I hadn't been hampered by Lindi's toxin, I would have drained them both down without even needing the second touch.

But I didn't need to give Lindi any hints that I was more aware than I'd initially let on. The pain response had given me partially away. And even I couldn't easily fake out the monitors she presumably had attached to me.

Sarah stepped out of my field of vision again, and I carefully withdrew my tendril of power, allowing the energy I'd siphoned from her to settle into my system and spread as it willed.

Lindi stepped around the raised bed, crossing toward the equipment I could just see in the corner. Setting something under a microscope? My sight lines were seriously limited in my position.

Sarah wiped down the area at the base of my neck with something that stung at the injection sites. Then she started tearing open what I assumed were bandages.

Lindi didn't turn from the scope. "None of that is necessary, Sarah."

"Her magic is suppressed. She could bleed out without access to her healing abilities."

Lindi sighed and flicked her fingers offishly, not looking away from the microscope.

Sarah bandaged my upper back. Then the bed began revolving, turning me until I faced the ceiling. And again, for a brief moment, I saw that shift of movement behind the door. Though likely only because I was staring right at it.

Someone was watching us.

Someone smaller than either Jason or Kevin. Plus, it seemed unlikely that Lindi would allow the last two members of Gen 4 to wander around and eavesdrop.

The behavior of whoever was lurking outside reminded me of Opal...

My chest constricted, more pain flooding through me than I'd felt during any of Lindi's collections. I stared up at the ceiling, unblinking as I struggled to ignore, or at least absorb, that emotional onslaught. The dream walker had Aiden to get her through my... momentary absence. And Christopher.

Lindi sprang out of her chair and clapped her hands together. "Perfect!" She scooped up an injector of some sort and crossed to stand over me. "A little nap for you..." She pressed the injector to my neck. "And tomorrow, one more test before we begin."

A chill spread out from under the injection site, sliding almost lazily through my neck and upper chest.

And even as my eyes grew heavy, I could feel the sip of power I'd stolen from Sarah, that I'd used to boost my own immunity, rise up to counter Lindi's toxin. Just a tiny bit.

"I'm so pleased you joined us voluntarily, Emma," Lindi said. "This way, I didn't have to wait until you healed from any possible injury during your capture. And don't worry. I'll wean you off my magnificent serum just as soon as I can trust you enough to place a fail-safe."

Lindi hadn't needed to trust Bee to place the fail-safe she'd triggered when she attempted to kill the telepath as we'd made our exit from the fortress. But the Chemist, who had conceived us all in test tubes, presumably understood the difference between the telepath and me. Not psychologically, of course, but our physical attributes. Knowing what level of injury I could withstand, because she'd coded that resistance into my DNA.

The Chemist leaned over me, her eyes gleaming with an almost rabid intensity. "I've made so many breakthroughs, Amp5. Watching footage of your escape from the Peru compound, then analyzing everything I could find on all the magic you'd absorbed over the years. How your power grows, and how you trigger growth in all of the Five. I've had years to study you. Your DNA, specifically. And how it reacts when combined with other... not-so-stable strands. Did you think I wouldn't have other samples? I just needed a little bit more. Together, we will build a force that no other power can stand against. Not even you."

I'd underestimated Lindiwe Fourie.

I'd assumed that everything that made me Emma Johnson, not just Amp5, would be enough to let me walk away from the Chemist's grasp. Because she wasn't a black witch of Silver Pine's caliber. She wasn't a telepath of Chenda's power. And she wasn't remotely in Kader Azar's league either.

I slipped into sleep without a plan or a clear understanding of the situation, but knowing without a doubt that my magic was already recovering.

I was also aware that it might not be enough. I might not be powerful enough, or recover soon enough.

The Chemist might succeed.

And I wouldn't make it back to my dark sorcerer or my dream walker.

ALARM AND PANIC STREAKED THROUGH MY SYSTEM, electrifying every nerve ending and jolting me to consciousness. I couldn't see. I inhaled harshly, filling my lungs so much, so suddenly, that they hurt. I had so much energy abruptly racing through my system that it felt as though I were on the verge of exploding.

Completely untethered, power poured from me involuntarily, instantly connecting to and beginning to drain the five individuals nearest to me.

I heard startled shrieks.

I heard knees hitting the floor.

And I felt my body gobble up every lick of power it could grab, hold, and absorb. Just as my lungs had grabbed as much air as I could inhale.

As if I'd been drowning.

As if I'd been… deflated.

Shocked back into my… body.

"Clear the room!" someone shouted.

Footsteps… people scrambling, sobbing… doors sliding open, then shut.

My eyesight cleared, but the bright light overhead was almost as blinding.

I couldn't turn my head.

My chest hurt.

As if someone had beaten me, over and over again in the same spot…

I blinked rapidly, adjusting to the light.

Lindi was hovering over me, flapping her hand as if she wanted someone to give her something. Her other hand was braced against the side of the bed. She was panting.

She was one of the people I was currently draining of magic. Three of the others were in the process of trying to put distance between themselves and me. One other remained in the room.

Sarah appeared, her arm shaking as she passed Lindi something… whatever she was asking to be handed. Something other than whatever was currently wreaking havoc with my body and mind…

I managed another deep inhalation. I managed to settle back into my body. Partially.

I was fairly certain the Chemist had just given me an adrenaline shot.

And judging by the way my chest hurt, I could guess the reason.

I had flatlined.

Lindiwe Fourie had managed to actually kill me.

It wasn't my first near-death experience.

But I'd seen every other one coming. Or Christopher had.

I closed my eyes, forcing myself to focus on reining in my rampaging power.

Something cool hissed against my neck.

Perfect timing, my extremely alert brain informed me, momentarily sounding separate from myself. Due to the meds, I hoped.

I further stifled my magical reach, making it appear to have been suppressed by whatever Lindi had just injected me with. But the dose she'd given me was either too low, or I was gaining immunity to it. Because even as I slowly became numb, I didn't lose my grasp on my power—including all the additional energy I'd just stolen from the five Adepts who'd been in the room with me.

"Well, that was interesting," Lindi murmured, sounding oddly eager for someone I'd just tried to drain dry in a matter of seconds.

Someone replied—Sarah, maybe. I caught her tone and a hint of concern and fear, but not her words.

"I need her awake," Lindi snapped. "I shouldn't have to explain that to you. And I'm tired of being delayed."

I fought the instinct to tear myself free of whatever was restraining my head and body. I forced myself to relax into the bed, into the meds chasing the adrenaline through my system and attempting to dampen it.

"Amp5," Lindi said, louder. Commanding. "Amp5."

I blinked open my eyes as if barely awake—not feigning as much as I would have liked—and tried to keep my heart rate from giving me away. Not that I could hear a heart monitor anywhere around me.

"Lindi," I said, making a show of picking my words... slowly. "You aren't being terribly... careful with your new... toy."

The Chemist snorted. "We'll give you a moment to level out, Amp5. Then we'll continue the brain biopsy."

She stepped away. A door swished open... then closed.

I focused on all the power I'd inadvertently stolen. Most of it was healing magic. And for me, healing magic came with even more immunity. I let it spread instead of holding it, allowed myself to absorb it, even as my own magic continued to counter Lindi's toxins.

Sarah leaned into my view, not touching me. "It is better if you're awake, Emma. For the brain biopsy. You need to answer my questions, okay?" She blinked her blue eyes. Her unmasked face was a little fuzzy around the edges. I was more drugged than I thought. "And the quicker you answer my questions, the quicker this is all done."

I had to smile at that.

Sarah winced.

"It's never done, Sarah," I said quietly, not bothering to slur my words. "With the Collective. You have to end it to be done."

Sarah glanced back toward the door, clearly unaware that the room would have been rigged to constantly record audio and video. Or ignoring that fact. I had no doubt that Lindi, aka the Chemist, was a fiend for research and whatever else she justified through her version of science. She'd want everything she did to me recorded.

Sarah's brow furrowed. "I don't know this... Collective. I just know that—"

The door slid open.

A curt male out of my view said, "The boss needs you."

Sarah nodded, quickly walking away.

I stared up at the ceiling, slowly becoming aware that my head was bolted into some sort of cage apparatus. Nothing magical about it, as far as I could sense. But I could wiggle my fingers and toes.

So I did.

A quiet noise drew my attention to the left. To the workstation and all the equipment I'd seen during my first visit to the med bay. Well, my first conscious visit to the med bay. I thought I'd heard a cupboard door creak open. But I couldn't see low enough down to confirm whether there even was a cupboard under the workstation.

I stopped wiggling my toes and fingers, holding still while trying to see as much as possible around me. That disembodied inner voice I'd heard earlier had freaked me out more than I cared to admit. I didn't need my mind fracturing.

I also didn't need to be seeing things.

Magic tickled my senses...

Someone was moving toward me…

But they weren't invisible…

Crawling?

I caught a whisper of… clothing?

Then movement at the base of my bed. I tried to look past my nose, but couldn't. I stifled another impulse to tear myself free from the bindings across my arms and legs. From the metal cage encasing my head—which was no doubt bolted into my skull.

I could heal, would heal, from just about any wound, of course. But could I do so while flushing Lindi's suppression serum from my system? And taking on the Chemist's subordinates? And escaping?

Doubtful.

A fingertip brushed against my right ankle bone, barely touching. A soft flicker of healing magic slipped across my foot, radiating partially up my calf.

Potent healing power.

I didn't recognize the magic. Whoever was in the room with me, attempting to heal me clandestinely, wasn't one of the Adepts I'd just inadvertently tried to drain.

Voices filtered into the med bay, close enough to indicate that multiple people were just beyond the door.

The person, the healer, at the end of the bed flinched, then darted toward the workstation, still completely out of my line of sight. The cupboard snicked closed, almost silent under the quiet hum of the electronics and the lights.

The main door slid open before I could work through what had just happened.

Except… how large was that cupboard?

And though my own sense of magic wasn't acute even when I wasn't mostly incapacitated, shouldn't Lindi—who I was fairly certain had corrupted her innate healer abilities into something much, much darker—have been able to sense whoever was in the room with us?

The Chemist stepped into my line of sight, smiling broadly just as I put together a tiny bit of what was going on.

Lindiwe Fourie might have been powerful enough to have once been a main member of the Collective. But unlike most healers, who were often extremely sensitive to the power of others, her sense for magic was limited. Though presumably that wasn't the case when that magic was removed from her subjects—in blood, say. Or more specifically, in DNA.

Someone appeared to have free rein in Lindi's compound—assuming we were in another of the Collective's former enclaves. That someone had been spying through the door the last time I'd been conscious.

That someone held strong healing magic, but wielded it tentatively. And, I realized, without an emotional component. Except my own abilities were exceedingly suppressed, so my empathy might not have picked up anything from the brief skin-to-skin contact.

Also, the someone moving around undetected? They were small enough to fit in a cupboard.

"Shall we begin?" Lindi asked brightly, picking up a drill. Her attention was trained over my shoulder, presumably on the monitors showing my vital signs.

"Try not to kill me this time, Lindi," I said sneeringly. Then I threw her own insult back at her. "I thought you were better than that."

Anger flickered across the Chemist's face, but was quickly quelled. She didn't bother with the surgical mask that Sarah was slipping over her face as she stepped up to assist. "My staff overcompensated. I built you, molecule by molecule, Amp5. I know exactly how hard you are to kill."

"Keep telling yourself that, Lindi."

She sniffed as she crossed around behind me.

"Can you see the monitor above you, Emma?" Sarah asked quietly as she wheeled something into my line of sight.

A metal stand.

I looked up obligingly.

Sarah shifted the stand slightly closer, placing a monitor well within my line of sight. A series of images—shapes—flashed across the screen.

The metal stand, broken into pieces, would make an excellent weapon.

Once more, the urge to rip myself free from the restraints flashed through me so hotly that I had to clench my hands into fists to quell the instinct.

"Emma?" Sarah asked gently—an utterly hypocritical tone.

At least Lindi was completely aware of what she was. What lines she would and could cross for her science. What she was willing to destroy to bring her twisted vision to fruition.

"Yes," I snarled, reminding myself that brain damage would take far too long to heal. That cooperating at this stage was the strategic choice.

So I answered Sarah's questions while Lindi biopsied a piece of my brain—all the while, vaguely hoping they hadn't shaved my head.

Even when they finally removed the bolts from my skull, but before Lindi's suppression serum had taken hold of me again, I held on tightly to the whisper of healing magic the tiny spy had given me. I didn't even glance in the direction of the cupboard, or reach out with the tendrils of magic I now had back in my command. No, I kept myself still and shut down. Compliant.

What did Christopher always accuse me of? Other than being quick to decapitate and impossible to communicate with?

That my magic overwhelmed everyone's senses?

For once in my life, I hoped the clairvoyant's truth was actually founded in reality—not simply a way to lash out at me. Because maybe, just maybe, I was enough of a distraction that whoever was sneaking around Lindi's med bay wouldn't be discovered.

Because I had a sneaking suspicion I knew who it was. And that I'd seen him in Bee's mind.

I WAS NEXT AWOKEN BY A SHARP, HIGH-PITCHED, AGO-NY-filled scream. I regained consciousness so abruptly that it came with a wrenching pain through my head, neck, and spine, as well as complete disorientation. Blinking against far too much bright light, I tore free of the weak bindings at my wrists and across my legs, grabbing the people nearest to me while draining any and all magic I could sense nearby.

"No!" Lindi shouted from a few steps away. "I need her awake!"

Heedless of the Chemist's command, something stung my neck. Then all the people nearest me scrambled away and out of the room.

Lindi swore robustly in a lyrical language I didn't understand.

My vision came back to me, edged in black.

All the white light around me was reflecting off the walls and floors…

I was back in the med bay.

No. This room was larger.

I had knocked over the heavy, metal-frame bed they'd had me strapped to. One of those straps was still cinched to my wrist, the thick metal arm of the bed hanging off the other end of that strap. My other wrist was still bound to the bed. My legs were free, but unsteady.

I was bleeding from my inner elbow and both wrists. I must have ripped IVs free when I tried to lunge out of bed.

But I should have been healing quicker…

Lindi and Sarah, the latter masked once again, were the only people still with me. They were standing next to another bed on the other side of the room…

… hiding someone behind them.

I swayed on my feet. Whatever they'd shot me up with was starting to take hold.

"You gave her a full dose," Lindi snarled, not taking her eyes off me as she spoke to Sarah.

"How many of your techs did you want incapacitated?" Sarah sounded shaky. "She woke before she should have."

My blood stopped dripping on the white floor. I glanced between the healer, if that was truly what Sarah was, and the Chemist, trying to organize my hazy thoughts.

"Someone was screaming," I finally said.

"A dream, Amp5," Lindi said smoothly.

Motion drew my attention to a set of double doors to my left, both inset with glass to their full height, and not tinted. We were in an operating suite. Mercenaries in tactical gear crowded the hall beyond the door—presumably more of Lindi's nonmagical force.

I counted five mercs as my body shut down— telling me that today wasn't the day I was walking away.

I settled my black-edged gaze on Lindi.

And I smiled.

Sarah flinched.

My legs went out from underneath me without warning. I hit the floor with my knees.

As the full weight of Lindi's serum took hold of me, I keeled over in the pool of my own blood. And I saw... someone on the bed through the space between the Chemist's arm and chest.

I saw...

Red-edged... tear-filled... green eyes. Medium-brown skin... the smooth and slightly rounded face of someone... young...

Emerald... green... eyes...

I TOOK MY TIME RESURFACING TO CONSCIOUSNESS, fully aware it was happening—but keeping my breathing slow and steady to fool the monitors for as long as I could.

I felt a needle being inserted into the crook of my elbow. I reached for my magic, and it came to me—sluggish and thin, but far more present than it had been the previous times I'd woken.

I counted five magic users in the immediate area without opening my eyes. They included Lindi, Sarah, and the other tiny healer who'd been hiding in the cupboard.

Lindi and Sarah were engaged in a quiet conversation in a language I didn't understand. Terse requests from Lindi? And softer replies from Sarah... as if they were working on something together.

Still feigning sleep, I rolled my head in their direction and cracked open my eyes.

I was in the surgical suite still. My sight lines were restricted, but there was no black edge or haze to my vision. I was gaining an immunity to Lindi's suppression serum. And the longer she didn't know that, the longer it would take her to realize she needed to increase or tweak my dosage.

Lindi and Sarah were standing over the second bed. They were both wearing intricate headgear that I knew at a glance would completely hamper their ability to see me.

An IV line, currently attached to my arm and filled with my blood, ran directly across to a person lying facedown in the next bed.

A quiet whimper floated across the room to me.

Then Lindi, not looking away from whatever she was doing, made soothing noises.

Soothing noises? From the Chemist of the Collective?

Another pained gasp rose from the person in the other bed. Or rather, the test subject.

I opened my eyes wider, shifting my head so I could see better.

No… not a person…

A child.

Their face was turned in my direction but blocked by their arms, which were spread upward and cuffed to the bed.

Anger rushed through me, shoving the effects of the serum still lingering in my system back in a gigantic wave.

I sat up.

Someone came at me from the other side of the bed. I didn't even bother glancing at them. Instead, I latched onto and grabbed their magic. Then I yanked.

They fell on my bed, across my legs, gasping and panting.

Someone else came at me from behind. They hit the floor writhing as I did the same to them.

The doors burst open. Mercs poured in, with machine guns trained on me.

I wrenched at the cuffs binding me to the bed, which had been doubled after my last inadvertent awakening.

"Stop!" Lindi shouted. "Unless you want me to damage his spinal cord."

I paused to assess the situation.

"Get out!" Sarah pushed back her headgear, commanding the mercs. "This is open surgery."

"Germs are not the issue," Lindi murmured. She hadn't taken her gaze off whatever procedure she was performing on the fully aware child.

The child healer who had hidden in the cupboard.

The mercs backed off, hovering in the still-open doorway.

"You're hurting the child," I snarled.

"A necessary evil," Lindi said without looking at me. "You were awake for your procedure as well. That was also necessary. I'll grant him the same short-term memory loss that I granted the Five."

My heart rate picked up, but not out of fear. Not for myself, anyway. I couldn't see what Lindi was doing exactly, but I could clearly see where she was working—at the top of the boy's spine—as well as the white of bone beneath her fingers.

She had him flayed open.

While awake.

With his hands gripping the top edge of the bed tightly, the boy was looking at me now. His hair was shaved, just as my hair had been shaved when I was his age. My own hair still fell around my shoulders.

"Give him something for the pain," I snarled.

"The… how do I put this so you understand…" Lindi mused. "The spine is like an electrical system. The reason the blood tattoos are so effective, so ingenious—"

I snorted.

Lindi ignored me, continuing. "It's because magic is also energy, energy that moves through our bodies, conducted through our nervous systems. I tried sedating Hel6 for the first procedure. Then dampening his pain for the second. Neither took."

A chill ran through me, and I glanced down at the IV that still connected me, connected my blood, to the boy. This was Lindi's third attempt at trying to force a blood tattoo on him?

"Why bind him to me?" I hadn't meant to vocalize the question, but Lindi answered readily.

"My attempts to bind remaining members of Gen 4 all failed. Even with my previous success with Gen 5."

"Because you killed their amplifier."

"Perhaps…" Lindi couldn't outwardly shrug while performing surgery on the boy's spine, but it was implied. "Whether or not that was the case, I had no way to test it. But now I believe it is the unique DNA I mixed for you that is the key."

Under other circumstances, some part of me would have respected her for not fobbing the murder of the Gen 4 amplifier off on the Collective as a whole.

Except I knew it simply meant that we weren't people to Lindi. She'd dreamed us up. She'd programmed our DNA, then grown us in test tubes, presumably implanting multiple viable fetuses into our surrogate mothers.

The two other Adepts I'd drained—techs or healers, I really didn't care—finally stumbled to their feet behind and beside me. One of them grabbed an injector from a nearby rolling tray.

"No," Sarah said, her gaze fixed on me. "We need her awake." Then she glanced over at Lindi and added, "For the boy's sake."

Lindi huffed, but didn't correct her assistant.

Sarah met my gaze again. Then she nodded— just the tiniest dip of her chin—as if to confirm whatever she hoped I was piecing together from the conversation.

The boy was just another experiment to Lindi. Who was trying to correct some… flaw in her experiment with a blood tattoo and… my blood?

I met the boy's pained gaze and spoke coolly. "Tie him to me and he'll belong to me. Just as the other four belong to me."

Lindi laughed quietly, confidently. "And you belong to me, Amp5."

I settled back on the bed, stretching out on my side with my arm dangling off the edge, so I could keep an eye on the boy but not impede the blood flowing from me to him.

The more time I was awake without the suppression serum in my system, the more my magic would recover.

Sarah swallowed harshly. Then she put her headgear back on and stepped up tightly next to Lindi, hands held up and ready to assist.

The boy whimpered involuntarily again.

Lindi made the same idiotic soothing noises again.

But I knew as I locked my gaze to his that he'd done it to draw my attention.

So emerald-green eyes filled with pain met emerald-green eyes filled with all sorts of promises.

I'd be taking the boy with me when I left.

Bee hadn't been trying to manipulate me in her mindscape after all.

The boy was real.

And he was one of us.

A sixth-generation healer. So where were the other five of his generation?

And why wasn't Lindi using the Gen 6 amplifier to bind the healer instead of me?

SEVEN

SURFACING AGAIN CAME IN WHISPERS THROUGH MY nerves. Small-scale flushing. The shimmer of my own power stirring within the blood tattoos on my spine, as if responding to outside stimulus. A light breeze across my face that smelled… clean and clear, but somehow canned as well?

My shoulder blades and the back of my head were cushioned… by smooth, but thick fabric under my hands…

Then I could wiggle my toes… and fingers.

I swallowed, my mouth and throat uncomfortably dry.

I reached out with all of my other senses… feeling nothing.

I was either alone or surrounded by nonmagicals.

I opened my eyes.

And instantly knew where I was—in one of the Collective's stasis chambers. A dome of what looked like glass—actually a thick, transparent composite—

arched over me. Not enough space to sit up within. Not enough space to fully bend my knees or stretch out my arms.

No matter.

I wasn't going to be sticking around.

Keeping my movements minimal as the rest of my body regained awareness in a flood of painful prickling, I carefully removed two IV lines and a number of sensors attached to me. All the while, I systematically engaged and released muscle group after muscle group.

The needle marks on my arms instantly clotted, then healed over with only a trace of pink. The older bruises beneath—from repeated jabbings, most likely—had almost faded.

If my healing abilities were reasserting themselves, then I had gained immunity to Lindi's magical suppression, which I assumed had been steadily fed to me through one of the IVs.

I ran my fingers around the edges of the stasis chamber, looking for an internal latch for the lid, and using my toes where I couldn't easily reach with my hands. I could have twisted around, but then I wouldn't have been as primed to deal with someone coming in and checking on whatever monitors I'd just deactivated. Or whatever alarms I'd triggered.

No latch.

I was going to have to exert some brute force.

Something clicked within the four corners of the chamber. Then the lid lifted upward with an expulsion of air, seemingly of its own accord and on no discernible hinges. An upgrade to the version of the chamber in the fortress compound that Daniel had been stuffed into.

Interesting…

Had I triggered a fail-safe?

Or had someone hacked the internal systems?

I waited a moment, expecting someone in the room beyond that I still couldn't see or sense to notice that the lid had opened.

Nothing else happened.

The light breeze I'd felt before—the air being filtered into the chamber—had dissipated. Meaning… someone hadn't deliberately opened the lid? Rather, had they simply shut down the unit, allowing a fail-safe to force it open so I wouldn't asphyxiate?

I curled my fingers around the edges of the lid, exerting just enough pressure to realize that it opened on one side, sliding to the right on supports I couldn't see.

I pushed upward. The lid moved sluggishly on dormant hydraulics, opening up a narrow space before getting stuck. Once again, I considered just busting my way out. But the noise of doing so might draw too much attention.

So I wedged my head, neck, and shoulders through the opening instead, scanning what I could see of the area around me. I appeared to be in a cross between a med bay and a storage room. Gray metal with riveted seams sheeted the walls. Minimal medical and computer equipment, all of it set along the wall near the head of the chamber. No windows. A single round-edged steel door, with what appeared to be a pressure lever set in the center like a steering wheel.

Now that was odd.

A mechanically sealed door? Why tuck me away in a space with a handle on the inside?

Apparently, I wasn't supposed to wake up ahead of schedule. Specifically not per Lindi's schedule, at least.

Twisting, I wedged my back against the bottom lip of the lid, my head still hanging out. The ceiling was clad in more of the same riveted metal. Elbows bent at my sides for leverage, I pressed upward with both hands. I was weaker than I would have liked— weak enough that I might have been held 'in storage' for a lot longer than I hoped.

Christopher was right about how pissed Aiden was going to be.

But I would worry about that later.

The lid slid slowly back, about halfway. Enough for me to twist around again, then to sit, perched in an awkward crouch, and dangle my legs. The lid didn't seem inclined to slide back all the way.

I was dressed in a gray tank top and panties, the fabric of both flimsy enough that they were likely single-wear disposables. My skin was more impervious than the stupid outfit. But then again, I wasn't supposed to be breaking out.

All things considered, though, the clothing was a bonus. I usually found myself naked in these sorts of situations.

I slid forward, balancing on the edge of the stasis chamber with both hands, testing my legs to make sure they were holding me. They were, but I still felt as though I hadn't properly moved in days. Possibly weeks.

I tamped down on whatever emotion wanted to clog up my throat at that thought. Of how long I'd been parted from my Opal and my dark sorcerer. Of the completely inert tattoos on my spine.

My power reserves were currently only a gentle simmer. I had no doubt that my immunities and abilities were reasserting themselves throughout my system. I just didn't know how deep a well of magic I had to draw upon.

That problem, however, was easily solved.

I would take what magic and energy I needed to get back to my life. To be done with the Collective. One last time.

Something clicked and then started humming, drawing my attention to the equipment lined up along the wall at the head of the chamber. The computers appeared to be rebooting.

There had definitely been a glitch in the system.

One of the two IV lines that should have connected to the stasis chamber from the outside was lying on the floor. It appeared to have been yanked out, because the other line and the sensor cables that fed into the chamber were still connected.

Yanked out… why would anyone… ?

My brain caught up to the reality of what I was seeing, and my heart beat a little wildly, off-kilter. An inappropriate and ill-timed reaction.

A teammate who'd managed to infiltrate the compound—or even just a staff member with a grudge against Lindi—would have hidden their sabotage. But... a three- or four-year-old genetically constructed child who had emerald eyes and glints of red threaded through his medium-brown hair... a child who should have been... playing... learning... not...

A child who shouldn't have been the one to help rescue me.

He would have just ripped the IV line free. Maybe it had been the only thing he'd had time to do in between security sweeps.

Though that didn't explain the computer system currently rebooting.

What would Lindi do to the boy if—

I moaned, then struggled through a burst of irrational, useless anger. I shut my eyes, bowing my head and clenching my hands into fists until my too-long nails bit into my own skin. My hair fell forward, long and dark red. They still hadn't shaved it.

All emotions were liabilities. In this moment, in this reality, at least.

So I swallowed it all down.

I shut it all down, all the rage, all the frustration.

I wiped it all from my thoughts, from my system.

Then I scoured the small room for weapons. Nothing. Not even any of those preloaded injectors.

Because Lindiwe Fourie wasn't an idiot.

As far as I'd been able to figure out so far, the Chemist had two glaringly large blind spots. Three if I counted utter arrogance, which I didn't—since it was a trait that most powerful people wielded with generally good results, for themselves at least. Myself included.

The first blind spot was that Lindi couldn't sense the presence of the magically inclined. At least not acutely.

The second was the boy. The boy was somehow consistently circumventing whatever restrictions the Chemist had placed on him. Through magical means, perhaps. But more likely just through the skill set that had been programmed into his DNA.

And I could work both of those flaws to my advantage.

Unarmed and barely better than naked, I crossed to the door, took a moment to figure out how to unlock it, and started spinning the locking wheel. It opened with a whisper of air that told me that the room had been mildly pressurized. Again, I had no idea why.

I stepped over a high threshold constructed out of more of the same gray metal, rounded at all four corners.

Where the hell was I being held?

I WALKED THROUGH THE TIGHT CONFINES OF THE metal-clad hallway—or perhaps the walls, floor, and ceiling were actually constructed out of metal plates riveted together?—without bothering to sneak around. Not that there was anything to hide within or behind. All the doors on this level were flush mounted into the walls, each equipped with the same wheeled handle that I was fairly certain indicated a vacuum seal.

When I figured out where the hell I was, I already knew I wasn't going to like it. Metal didn't usually dampen my power or my reach, but being surrounded by it on all sides was making me irrationally itchy. Mostly between my shoulder blades, around my dormant blood tattoos.

I loathed being irrational.

I could have crossed all the way to the clearly marked stairwell—a bright-green sign with a picture of a stick figure walking up stairs glowed above a doorway at the far end of the hall. The sign added to the already-too-many levels of weirdness of the space.

What sort of nefarious lair had clearly marked exits?

I should have just busted my way out. I had no doubt I was going to come up against Lindi's mercenaries eventually, if not the Chemist herself. Just like I should have, had I followed my training, had I allowed the Collective to continue to control my actions, my choices, left the other four to die while I destroyed the last member of the Collective who'd tried to hold me, to execute me. Silver Pine.

But I hadn't then.

And I wasn't going to do so now.

Eight years ago, I hadn't killed Silver Pine when she was all that had stood between me and freedom. I'd thought I had. Then she'd surfaced and come after me again.

But I didn't need to kill Lindi to vanquish her.

I just needed to destroy her life's work.

Or, more specifically—to rescue that life's work. The boy.

So I paused at the next door, then the next, and the next, finding the rooms beyond either empty or filled with boxes and equipment.

A stasis chamber identical to the one I'd just awoken within occupied the fourth room. Somewhat ironically—since he'd technically helped Lindi shove me into a similar chamber—it was holding the Gen 4 telepath. Not that I usually dealt in irony.

The power hadn't gone out in the room as far as I could tell. Before entering, I spent some time trying to figure out how to disable the door so I couldn't be locked inside, but didn't come up with anything viable quickly enough. So I pushed it all the way open until it was flush with the exterior wall, then used the latch that was already built into the design to keep it from swinging shut. If I kept an eye on it, no one should be fast enough to unlatch it, slam the heavy door closed, and spin the locking mechanism before I could get back into the corridor.

All the IV lines and monitoring cables were still attached to the stasis chamber, which meant that the Gen 4 telepath who called himself Jason was going to be just as doped as Daniel had been when he'd woken.

I didn't know how to operate the chamber, or how to properly hide my tampering. So I just ripped all the lines free, then pulled the power cords on the chamber and the monitoring equipment, hoping to trigger the same safety feature response that had shut down my own chamber.

The hum of that equipment faded into silence. Jason's eyes remained closed, but he appeared to still be breathing, not distressed. Yet. But I might have to break the—

The stasis chamber popped open before I could finish the thought, confirming that whatever mode Lindi was using to keep us on ice, she needed us to continue breathing. When the power was cut and the oxygen cut off, the lid eventually opened.

The Chemist's operation felt more than a bit sloppy around the edges. Even haphazard. It was entirely possible that she didn't even know about the safety protocols on her own equipment.

But someone did. Because that someone had rebooted my chamber, perhaps remotely, to give me a window to escape. And I was fairly certain that specific someone wasn't the same person who'd ripped out the IV line that had been feeding the toxin into my system.

All the monitors had gone dead in Jason's room when I pulled their power cords. No backup power source had reawakened them, but I assumed that alerts were currently flashing on some other screen—in the main medical chamber, if not the compound's security hub.

I grabbed the lid and shoved it fully open on its dormant hydraulics, casting a quick glance over the still-sedated telepath within. His light-brown hair was shorter than it had been when I'd seen him at the fortress—not shaved, but clipped close to his skull—not giving me any sense of how much time might have passed. He was clad in a tank top and boxers. The gray color and flimsiness matched my own. No visible wounds marred his tanned skin.

I didn't have time to waste babysitting, so I left him to wake on his own. I stepped back through into the hall, finding the Gen 4 telekinetic, Kevin, confined in another stasis chamber one room over. His darker-brown hair had also been clipped short. His light-brown skin likewise showed no apparent wounds.

As I'd done in the other room, I carefully latched the main door open, tore out every line and cable I could see, then fully opened the stasis chamber after its automated safety feature unlocked the lid.

Keeping an eye on the exits—I assumed the far end of the corridor had another exit—I searched the rest of the rooms between me and the nearest set of stairs. The sort of signage on the stairs was part of some mundane building-safety code, wasn't it? But why would a member of the Collective bother with such things? Or with sealed doors that could just be latched open to prevent accidents?

I was worrying about things that didn't actually need answers, because I didn't know where I was yet. Because I didn't know how long Lindi had managed to confine me. But also—more logically—because I couldn't implement an escape plan until I knew the layout of the compound.

I was practically blind.

But no longer powerless.

And yes, apparently I was so on edge that I had to remind myself of that fact, while attempting to shut down my verging-on-obsessive observations.

Making it to the end of the hall without coming across anyone else—including the person I was actually searching for—I considered trying to disable the door to the stairwell before heading back the other way. But it didn't appear to lock from either side. Safety first!

This was verging on ridiculous.

I didn't have a terribly firm grasp of physics or mechanics, but I was also fairly certain that shoving something through the door's round handle would do nothing to disable the matching mechanism on the other side.

No one was sneaking up on me in a hall this narrow anyway. Or getting past me. So I left it for the moment. Once the Gen 4 telekinetic was functional again, I wouldn't need to worry about how to secure our exit.

I paused on my way back down the hall, checking on Kevin, the telekinetic. He was perched on the edge of his stasis chamber and dropped his hand from rubbing his face as he met my gaze. He had torn the IVs and monitor lines free from his body, not knowing I'd already disconnected them from the chamber. A trickle of blood ran down each of his arms, staining the white fabric of the bed. But I didn't need evidence of his slow healing to let me know his magic was drained—or, more accurately, that his power was suppressed by Lindi's toxin. Standing just within the doorway with only a couple of meters between us, I might have known he was an Adept of some sort, but I wouldn't have picked up that he was telekinetic.

"The stairwell isn't secured," I said, my tone brusque to curtail any conversation. Just in case he was going to chatter on about me releasing him. I gestured in the direction I'd just come.

He nodded curtly, pushing off the bed to test his strength. I stepped back into the hall so he wasn't forced to display any weakness in front of me.

If Lindi occasionally woke the remaining members of Gen 4 to do her bidding, she likely didn't keep them as doped as she'd kept Daniel and Samantha. I would have expected my presence to have triggered some tightening of the Chemist's security procedures—but hadn't seen any evidence of that yet.

Jason, the telepath, was even more awake, bent over the keyboard of one of his room's computers, fingers tapping away. He'd powered up and restarted the system, with what appeared to be multiple security feeds now occupying one of the screens. He was searching for something, generating lots of scrolling text. Just as Samantha was the most technically inclined of the Five, I guessed that Jason was Gen 4's tech.

Three injectors had been tossed to the side of a wheeled metal cart in the corner of the room. A top drawer on the cart was hanging open, clearly rifled through. There hadn't been any meds in my room.

Adrenaline injectors.

And three shots…

I sighed internally.

It explained how Jason had gotten up and running so quickly, but three shots was too much.

Way too much—even for one of the Five. Impulse control and self-preservation were most definitely one of the major flaws in the Gen 4s' programming. Kader had once suggested that the generation before my own hadn't been able to think for themselves—and had hinted of how that 'flaw' had made them both superior and inferior to the Five.

Jason could obviously think for himself.

"Your mind is very active," the telepath said without turning around.

"Stay out of it," I warned, though I hadn't felt any intrusion.

He glanced at me over his shoulder. His eyes were a clear crystal blue, no sign of magic within them. "I can only feel you in general. Due to the pathway you opened."

When I'd amplified him on Bear Island, he meant.

"You will stay out of my mind," I said quietly.

"And if we need to communicate?"

"I will initiate. And you'll go no further than I invite."

He nodded stiffly, then turned back to the computer. "Security won't attempt to take this level."

I glanced briefly at the camera feeds he'd accessed. Not knowing the layout of the compound yet, the images only added to the itch that had taken up permanent residence between my shoulder blades. But I didn't need to know the general layout or have full access to the feeds to understand why security wasn't going to come down a narrow hall to confront me directly—or the two other uber-powered Adepts I'd just awoken.

"Do you know where we are?"

"Not where."

"You haven't been here before?"

"On site, yes."

Okay, he was even more terrible at communicating than I was. Probably because I was forcing him to speak out loud. "Explain yourself," I snarled.

His shoulders stiffened. "The overseer maintains a mobile base."

Everything clicked together at once—including the metal walls. Dread filled me, becoming a sickening weight in my stomach. I ignored it.

"A freighter?" I asked.

"Yacht."

"It's rather large for a fucking yacht," I snarled, betraying far too much anxiety. But… just the thought…

The threat of death by drowning wasn't something I'd ever confronted before…

He blinked at me, then frowned. Not concerned or angry… just thinking. "A mega yacht," he finally said.

That made far more sense, though it wasn't any less daunting. "Are we in port?"

He shrugged. "Not if the overseer can avoid it."

"International waters?"

"Usually."

We could have been anywhere.

Anywhere in the world.

I inhaled, and accepted the parameters of the mission on the exhale. Keeping a yacht filled with highly valuable assets mobile required a multitude of things only found on land. Which meant that not only could the yacht itself be commandeered, but there had to be at least one helicopter perpetually on board.

If Lindi was on site, she would never leave herself without an escape vehicle. Which also meant that, international waters or not, we'd have to be close enough to land for a helicopter or a smaller boat to be a feasible choice.

Pushing myself into action, I stepped forward, looking closer at the security feed the telepath had accessed. The top right corner of the monitor on the right was rotating through exterior shots of... a large pool. Deck chairs. What looked like endless water through white metal railings, gleaming under faint starlight. It was dark, either late night or early morning. So we were well south of Norway now.

"Shortsighted," I said, my tone steady once again. "Easy exploit."

Jason nodded.

"Are Gen 6 usually on site?"

Jason paused his scrolling and typing to look at me questioningly.

"The overseer's yacht is set up as its own self-contained settlement," Kevin said, picking up the thread of our conversation as he filled the doorway behind me. "It's unusual for her to bring us here."

Like Jason, his tone was flat, almost to the point of being devoid of inflection.

Had I ever sounded so... empty?

"We're on the move," Jason added, pulling up a map. "I've got current coordinates but not the projected destination."

"Might not be one," Kevin muttered, pushing off the door frame. "Yet." His gaze settled on me. His eyes were bloodshot. And not from lack of sleep or crying.

"How long can you function on that much adrenaline?" I asked. Not because I was concerned, but because I actually needed to know for the mission.

He shrugged belligerently. "With you to amplify us? Couple of days."

"If you don't stroke out," I snapped. But before he could offer up a retort, assuming he was actually capable of questioning a commanding officer, I turned back to Jason. "Can you get access to external comms? Even just to send our current coordinates?"

"No text or email from this station. I might be able to get you—"

The monitors started winking out—one, then two, then all three.

The telepath raised his hands from the keyboard. "That's us locked out. Get me to another terminal, and I'll get you a satellite uplink."

Nodding, I turned toward the hall. But both Gen 4s, standing shoulder to shoulder, stepped into my path and offered me their hands.

They stood utterly still. Their expressions were blank. Submissive, even with multiple shots of adrenaline crashing through their systems.

"That adrenaline hasn't had time to settle," I said dismissively.

The telepath blinked, just once. "You need us operational."

"For now, functional works."

My gaze fell to the patch on Jason's neck, then to the one on Kevin's. Both so close to the color of their skin that they were practically invisible. Lifting my hand to my own neck, I already knew what I would find. A slightly raised area that tingled with magic at my touch.

Not my magic. Lindi's. I shouldn't have been able to determine that by touch. My senses weren't usually tuned to magical spells or items.

But the magic the Chemist wielded was annoyingly powerful.

Jason's and Kevin's eyes had followed my fingers. Lingering on the patch adhered above my carotid artery.

I let my hand drop without comment. I would deal with the patches later—if necessary, by taking Lindi's magic and forcing her to feed me the disarming spell.

I stepped around the telepath and the telekinetic, but not before I caught the glance they exchanged. A thread of power shifted between them, indicating they were communicating telepathically.

"We will not harm you," Kevin said to my back.

"And as long as you don't threaten someone I love," I tossed back over my shoulder, "then I won't harm you."

They glanced at each other again, following me out into the corridor.

"Can you give us a list?" the telepath asked. "Of who you love?"

I laughed, completely involuntarily. Then I realized Jason wasn't joking. It was very possible that the Gen 4s didn't actually know how to joke. Or even what a joke was.

But then, neither did I really.

"Yes. I'll make you a do-not-harm list."

They each nodded once, then took up positions behind me as I headed for the exit I assumed was at the other end of the main hall. I hadn't needed to see much of the security feed to understand that the footprint of the mega yacht was massive, even on the lower levels.

That was to our benefit.

At my silent prompting, after we'd passed the rooms I'd already searched, the telepath started checking the rooms on the left. The telekinetic started on the right.

"Tell me about the sixth generation," I said.

"There is no Gen 6," Jason said.

"What about the boy?"

"The boy?" he echoed.

"With the… he's about three or four, light-brown skin, green eyes."

They each shook their heads.

Damn it. That meant that if he wasn't in another stasis chamber on this level with us, I was going to have to hunt down the boy instead of just heading straight for the bridge and taking the ship. Either that or have a very pointed conversation with Lindi— assuming she was even on site.

Or maybe that was supposed to be 'at sea'?

The skin between my shoulder blades, where my wings rooted on either side of my still-achingly-empty blood tattoos, was crawling now, not simply itching.

Not only were my escape options severely limited if we were in international waters, but I had the two Gen 4s and a child to rescue. Children, even genetically constructed children, were fragile. And I already knew that the Gen 4s had no sense of self-preservation and no impulse control. Losing team members in Moscow and on Bear Island would likely have exacerbated both of those flaws.

I was also aware that I'd severely underestimated Lindi.

The Chemist had held me for longer than I would have thought possible. Even with me walking right into her waiting arms.

I reached up and over my shoulder, feeling for tender skin or a spark of magic from the blood tattoos. Finding neither.

"How many tattoos can you see here?" I asked Jason.

He tugged down the back of my tank top, not touching my skin. "Four."

"She didn't manage to tie the boy to me," I murmured. But maybe that hadn't actually been Lindi's goal. Maybe she'd wanted to tie my magic to the boy, but not have him bonded too tightly in reverse?

THE TWO REMAINING MEMBERS OF THE COLLECTIVE'S fourth generation of super soldiers understood the layout of Lindi's mobile-base mega yacht far better than I did. Granted, I'd never actually been on a yacht. Or many boats of any kind, for that matter.

Jason and Kevin rode their adrenaline shots with a focused determination through the time it took for us to swiftly traverse the next two levels, both of which appeared to be dedicated to utility and storage, with no sign of medical or security personnel, the boy—or Lindi. Apparently, we three had been 'stored' in the lowest level of the ship. I tried to not let the idea of being surrounded by thick metal walls while submerged suffocate me, psychologically speaking. But when the first porthole window had appeared, the tightness in my chest eased enough that I felt a little more in control of my reactions, as well as my ability to make assessments and decisions in the moment.

Which was good, because the Gen 4s felt as though they were posed to either implode or explode—to the detriment of any living creature on board, including myself.

I couldn't force them into freedom. I wasn't even sure that 'freedom' as a pure concept was even an option for them. Even Bee, for all her grandiose intentions and declarations, had felt compelled to pilot them. But given the opportunity, I would have liked to help them make the choice. A choice dictated solely by themselves, for themselves.

We made it all the way up to the employee- and crew-quarters level while avoiding confrontation. Yes, according to the Gen 4s, Lindi referred to her mercenaries as "employees," and they were housed alongside her techs, her corrupted healers, and other staff.

At every point, it became even more clear that the yacht's security was seriously lacking. It hadn't been built with any doors or stairwells that needed an ID or a handprint to open or access—presumably for safety reasons. And because the telepath could sense the nonmagically inclined just as well as the magically inclined, we were able to simply choose the best routes to avoid confrontation once we got up to the occupied decks.

The unyielding darkness beyond the portholes confirmed that it was still the middle of the night. But the fact that no alarms were blaring or flashing, despite Jason having been locked out of the security system, supported the idea that we were still benefitting from unknown help.

How far that help would extend or last, I had no idea. I did, however, have an idea of who was helping us—and it wasn't an unusually skilled four-year-old child. Best guess? The healer. Sarah. And I seriously doubted that she was aiding us simply out of the goodness of her heart.

I didn't mention my suspicions to the other two. I didn't give them any information that might add to any possible confusion on their part. Or, rather, any possible disjointed loyalties. Because I clearly remembered them aligning with the Chemist when I'd given myself up.

But then, in giving myself up, hadn't I done the same thing?

My neck was itching around the edges of Lindi's fail-safe patch. I knew the sensation was most likely psychological, though, so I ignored it.

Jason's movements began to turn jerky as we passed a number of tiny cabins—all currently empty but obviously inhabited—along a darkened corridor. The walls were still constructed out of metal, but were painted an off-white and featured added touches of decor. The floor was a fake-wood laminate, mimicking oak, by its color.

"Three people up ahead," the telepath murmured. He'd vocalized all his observations to me so far, but I could feel the shift in energy between him and Kevin every time they spoke telepathically.

I remembered when having Bee in my head, connecting me to the others, was a comfort. Not that I would have admitted that at the time. Because I also remembered when it was an annoyance. When it felt like I had no choice but to accept the continual mental contact. No chance of any privacy, even in my own mind.

"Is there a comms station on this level?" I asked quietly.

"In the shared common area," Kevin murmured. He checked the name on the next door to our right, wrapping his hand around the handle, then looking at Jason questioningly.

Jason nodded. Kevin entered the cabin, leaving the door open. Dim starlight filtered in through the porthole window. When we'd entered this level, Jason had indicated there were three more levels above us, including the medical bays and laboratories, the upper deck suite and security, plus the main bridge. We could have hit the engines first before ascending from the lower decks, but commandeering a still-functioning boat was the quickest way to escape—at least before confirming whether there was a convenient helicopter to steal on the main deck.

And yes, I was aware that the idea of 'escaping' in a mega yacht was highly ironic. So it was a good thing I didn't much bother with ironies.

As we waited on Kevin, Jason pressed a hand against the wall. If that hand, and the arm attached to it, hadn't been shaking, I wouldn't have thought much of the gesture. Bee occasionally touched walls and doors when she was trying to scan through them. It helped her focus her power.

But Jason was just trying to stay on his feet.

The telepath lifted his head, meeting my gaze. And I realized that what I'd taken to be burnout from too much adrenaline… wasn't.

In the cabin behind me, Kevin had found and was pulling on tactical gear. Yes, I was still in the tank top and underwear. Presumably, the telekinetic knew the merc who occupied the cabin, and therefore knew the gear would fit his lanky frame. I usually didn't much care about what I was wearing. But a telekinetic preferred to have pockets. Lots and lots of pockets, filled with lots and lots of objects their magic could manipulate.

"Are you about to break?" I asked Jason, not specifying what exactly I meant and not dropping the telepath's red-rimmed, crystalline-blue gaze.

"I'm functional," he said, pushing away from the wall with effort. "I feel… more stable with you than I did with Amanda in my head."

I nodded, not surprised. "The amplification forms a bond. Don't worry, it dissipates."

"And what if I told you that neither of us wants that? That neither of us wants to be… what they made us?"

Kevin stepped back out into the hall, now clad in black tactical gear and carrying a short, sharp-looking knife with a black hilt. His feet were still bare, suggesting the boots in the cabin hadn't fit. Ill-fitting shoes could be a liability in a close-proximity fight, even more so than bare feet. And any fight on a yacht, no matter how large that yacht was overall, was going to be in close proximity.

"No other useful weapons." The telekinetic flipped the knife in his hand, offering it to me. When I shook my head, he offered it to Jason.

The telepath also declined. He hadn't taken his gaze off me while he waited for me to address his last statement. I continued to say nothing.

Jason shook his head a second time—answering a different telepathic communication from the telekinetic.

"We'd rather die," Kevin said, no inflection in his tone as he slid the knife into one of several built-in thigh sheaths on the pants he wore. "If you can't take us with you."

"We don't want to be puppets," Jason said.

"Killers," Kevin added, watching me with an intense, fixed gaze.

They both stood close enough to touch me, but held themselves stiffly.

"They made us…" The telekinetic shook his head, glanced both ways along the corridor, then continued, "They made us kill our amplifier."

My stomach soured. "Why not do it themselves?"

Kevin shook his head again, swallowing harshly. So some emotions were intense enough for the Gen 4s to feel. They weren't automatons.

"Everything was a lesson," Jason said quietly. "She tried to… go against her programming."

"She wasn't an empath?"

Jason blinked, surprised. "Are you?"

"Unfortunately."

The two Gen 4s exchanged looks as more telepathic conversation passed between them.

Then Kevin grunted and said out loud, "That's why."

Ignoring whatever they had going on in their internal conversation in favor of more pertinent information, I asked, "Did your amplifier try to help you escape?"

Jason shook his head. "She tried to… negotiate."

"With the Collective?" I couldn't help the note of disbelief and the layer of sarcasm that came with the statement, but regretted it instantly when Kevin and Jason stiffened and turned away from me.

They might have been the sociopaths that the Collective had tried to make all of us. But they clearly weren't beyond… caring for each other.

Kevin stepped away, scanning the names on the next two doors, then tapping one and glancing back at Jason. This time, it was the telepath who went inside the tiny cabin to forage for clothing.

I briefly thought about trying to continue the conversation with the telekinetic, but it wasn't relevant to our current situation. "Are you still fully functional?" I asked instead.

He nodded stiffly, back to dutifully following orders and responding to a commanding officer. "Limited access to my power. But more than capable of handling Lindi's mercenaries."

As long as they weren't armed with more of that magically imbued ammo.

"Will your people come for you?" Kevin asked. Again, the question was flatly delivered, yet somehow searingly intense.

I realized that I was picking up random emotions again, even without physical contact. Which meant my magic was continuing to reassert itself. Good.

"If we need them," I said curtly.

Jason stepped out from the open cabin, tugging on a thin sweater over jeans. He'd also found sneakers that apparently fit. "Delane must be on shift," he said, explaining why he hadn't outfitted himself in tactical gear.

We continued down the corridor, moving quietly but quickly toward the communal area and the three mental signatures that Jason had identified. Kevin tapped another door as he passed, looking at me and presumably indicating that he thought the clothing within would fit.

I shrugged and kept going. My skin was still a weapon, after all. So having easy access to it while my longer reach reasserted itself was the strategic tactical choice.

I was a step from the next door—this one was open—when a figure exploded from its depths and crashed into me. He locked his arms around me, grappling as we slammed against the far wall, and I hit my head hard enough against its metal surface that my vision went momentarily black around the edges.

The completely nonmagical merc who'd caught me off guard suddenly began convulsing. His grip across my neck, pinning me to the wall, intensified as his arm locked into place. Then, foaming at the mouth as he tried unsuccessfully to scream, he slumped to the side and hit the floor without trying to break his fall.

Most definitely dead. His brain turned into mush.

Jason stumbled, quickly righting himself. He was bleeding into his right eye—more than simply a few broken blood vessels.

"I had it under control," I said tersely.

Two more people barreled into the hall ahead of us from the common area. Then behind us, metal met metal as the stairwell door we'd entered the current level through banged against the wall.

We were about to be caught between attacking forces.

The telekinetic hit the two nearest figures with a wild blast of magic. Both were Adepts, one in workout gear and one in what might have been pajamas. They flew backward, slamming against the stairwell door ahead of us. One of them managed to throw up a flickering shield of some sort right before they hit the door—possibly witch magic, but my senses were still dulled from Lindi's suppression serum. Still, they went down and didn't get back up.

"These are employees," I snarled.

The clothing of the two Kevin had hit confirmed even more clearly that our breakout hadn't been made general knowledge yet. Again, someone was covering for us in security—or else someone who'd screwed up by letting me escape was trying to cover their ass by containing the situation before it made them look bad.

"Don't kill them," I added bluntly, forcefully.

The telekinetic nodded, turning back the way we'd come.

I wasn't sure he or Jason understood… well, nuances. Or fine lines. I grabbed his shoulder. He jerked, reflexively grabbing my wrist.

I allowed him the moment, allowed him the attempt to brush me off, break my hold.

He pitted his strength against mine, his hold and his push backed by his still-slumbering telekinetic magic.

He lost the power play.

When he finally met my gaze, his dark eyes were a bit wild. Not with a clear emotion, but something more… feral? Primal?

"Don't kill anyone," I said again, slowly and definitively. "You'd rather be dead, remember?" A little chunk of my own soul—apparently it wasn't ripped entirely to shreds yet—tore as I used his own words against him. His own deeply internalized despair, of being controlled, of being a puppet. Of being uncontrollable.

"Yes, amplifier," he said tonelessly.

"Neutralize. Conserve your magic." I flashed Jason a look. "If you burn out, I can't carry you both. I'm not going to waste my own energy amplifying what can't be amplified."

Harsh, brutal pronouncements. And part of me already knew I was lying. At least in part.

Because I couldn't actually sacrifice myself, not any more than I'd already done. Aiden would never forgive me. And Opal...

My little witch had already lost one mother. She wasn't going to lose me as well.

My orders seemed to galvanize Kevin and Jason, though.

I released the telekinetic's shoulder so he could head back along the corridor to face whatever was coming up from behind us. Since they hadn't attacked already, I presumed they'd paused to assess the situation, aka facing off with the three of us in a narrow hall.

I moved for the common area, slightly surprised that Jason stuck with me. Though I could feel the brush of magic that indicated he was still connected to Kevin mind-to-mind.

Beyond the open door, a large room opened up, subdivided for different activities. A huge flatscreen TV was set on the far-left wall, facing a large sectional couch pieced together in different configurations. Smaller screens attached to gaming units were situated in the corners of the room, along with clusters of chairs. Cluttered bookshelves lined the wall facing the windows. A pool table and another table for some game I didn't recognize sat in the center of the area. And a kitchen with a few smaller round tables was set next to the windows on the far right.

I still couldn't tell if it was approaching dawn or past nightfall. All I could see through the deep-silled, round-cornered windows was an endless dark ocean under starlight.

Though eating something wouldn't have been a bad idea, the three computer workstations tucked against the wall immediately to our right were more relevant to our current needs.

Before entering, though, I stepped past the doorway, checking the vitals of the two people Kevin had left crumpled in front of the stairwell access. Technically, they were blocking one of our escape routes, but that wasn't why I dragged them back inside the common area and set them gently on the couches.

Jason was sitting before one of the computers, tapping the trackpad and scrolling through apps.

The unconscious woman in workout gear was a witch. The male in sushi-print pajama bottoms was a sorcerer, but his power didn't feel like combat magic. A tech, probably.

The sound of doors banging and metal crunching filtered up the corridor. Kevin.

"He's locking people in the rooms?" I asked Jason. And not conserving his telekinesis by doing so—though that was arguably better than slitting everyone's throats.

The telepath nodded, not looking away from the computer screen. "Looks like the satellite link is still working. I need a phone number."

I straightened. And then I just stood there with my mouth open, ready to speak, while my mind went suddenly and awfully blank.

"An emergency contact number?" the telepath asked, sensing my conundrum without having to read my mind. "Where you leave a coded message…"

The Collective had always used such things. Numbers to call for pickup, or if you got separated from the team or needed access to the nearest safe house. And I'd never used them. I always got my team through our missions.

I didn't know the phone number of anyone I would actually call, though. I'd really only ever called or texted Christopher, and he'd programmed his info into my phone. I didn't know anyone's email either. I just didn't—

Opal.

I knew Opal's school email, because it was one of the things the Academy made a parent or guardian confirm. It was dream_walker_chick at the Academy server… but was that .com or .org or something else?

"I need… a video app… thingy." I knew I sounded utterly idiotic as the words tumbled out of my mouth, but I couldn't remember the name of the app that we'd used every day for months. "You click a green box…"

"Like… for a video chat?"

"It works with an email address."

Jason fiddled with the keyboard, then finally opened an app that looked similar, if not identical to the one on Aiden's iPad—and, more importantly, on Opal's phone. He reached up and adjusted the camera that was mounted to the monitor.

Though I had no doubt that Lindi had her employees' conversations monitored, apparently even she understood that she couldn't guarantee loyalty without also allowing people to contact their family and friends.

I slipped into the desk chair as Jason vacated it. It took me a moment to figure out where to type in a new email address. Other contacts were listed on the left side of the screen. The center, where the video should stream, was blank.

"I need our exact coordinates," I said to Jason.

He settled at the computer next to me. "I'm not sure I can get an update here. We might have to break into the security hub. Or make it to the bridge."

"Do your best."

I pressed the green call button… and waited.

I STARED AT THE BLANK SCREEN, WILLING THE VIDEO call to connect. Quiet had descended in the corridor, so Kevin had the mercs on this level under control. Jason took over the computer station to my right, staring at the screen intently as he tried to access the security systems he'd already been locked out of once.

The telepath was bleeding from his ear. Some of the blood had crusted, but some of it was still fresh. From using his telepathy while his system was functioning on little more than administered adrenaline.

It was going to take serious luck for me to get him and Kevin to the deck—to the bridge or the yacht's helipad—without carrying at least one of them.

Some sort of digital glitching appeared on the screen. Still no picture. Then… something… moving… the background?

"What's happening?" I hissed to Jason. "Is it connected?"

He leaned in to peer over my shoulder, pointing at something at the bottom of the screen as if it was an answer to my question. But before I could snarl at him further, the screen brightened.

With blue witch light.

My chest squeezed, and I leaned closer to the screen and camera. "Opal? Opal?"

The image froze again.

Jason was shoving something at me—a headset with a built-in microphone. But before I could put it on, Opal's voice came through the computer's speakers.

"Mom? Emma?"

A wave of emotion washed through me. Relief, I thought—except it left me cold and a little shaken, as if it had been followed by a spike of pure anxiety.

The screen started moving again. On a slight delay, perhaps? I caught glimpses of bedsheets and a side table. Then another light flared, and suddenly Opal's eyes were all I could see.

"Mom?" she cried, tapping on her screen.

Maybe she couldn't see me?

"You called... your daughter?" the telepath murmured, reaching over my shoulder and using the mouse to click icons on my computer screen. The video camera? And the microphone?

Ignoring him, I kept my focus on Opal's sleepy visage and uttered three words I never thought I'd say.

"I need Kader."

She blinked at me, tears filling her eyes. And I desperately wanted to talk to her, to soothe her, but I wasn't certain how long the connection would hold.

"You're okay," she breathed. Then she shook her head. "Okay, okay. Kader." The picture jostled, as if she was running with her phone. It dipped, and I caught a glimpse of glowing red eyes—Paisley. Then the walls of the upper hall and the stairs.

The house surrounding Opal was darkened, but not pitch black. But the sun set late during summers in the Pacific Northwest.

"Is there a message function?" I asked the telepath, not taking my gaze from the screen. "For the coordinates?"

"I don't have our current position," he said. "The only data I have is a half-hour old."

"Just type in what you have."

He leaned around me. His reserves were so low that I had to stifle the urge to amplify him as he brushed against my shoulder and arm. He started typing numbers into a chat window.

"It's Emma!" Opal cried. "Grandfather!"

The video feed went almost black for a moment. Then Kader Azar's face filled the screen. He looked haggard, like he hadn't slept for days. He stared at me, his eyes flicking around the screen as if he was taking in every part of me that he could see. Only then did he glance at Jason hanging over my shoulder.

The telepath looked at me sharply. I actually felt a brush of his magic against my mind.

"Coordinates," I snapped, understanding that he recognized Kader Azar but not having time to mollify him.

"Sent," the telepath said dully, sounding almost wounded. Even betrayed.

Kader sat down on something, still holding the phone aloft. Then Opal climbed onto what I realized was the couch in the front sitting room. The dream walker leaned into view of the screen. Paisley did the same over Kader's other shoulder.

The elder sorcerer huffed, holding the phone farther away so I could see the three of them.

"We're on Lindi's mega yacht," I said, barely holding on to the confusing mixture of emotions, all of which combined seemed likely to undo me. So I ignored it all and remembered the now, the mission. "Jason sent a message with our coordinates. At least our coordinates as of about thirty minutes ago."

Kader tilted the phone toward Opal. "A message?"

She shook her head, biting her lip. But just as Kader was pulling the phone away, her eyes widened. "There!" She grabbed for the phone.

"Send that to your father," Kader said. His tone was rough, demanding.

But I didn't mind one bit. Because now I knew Aiden was alive. Christopher had promised as much, but…

"Done," Opal said.

Then Kader was holding the phone again, and he no longer looked at all composed. "Giving yourself up?" he snarled. "Ridiculous."

"How is the rest of the team?" I asked.

His jaw clenched, and for a moment, I thought he might not answer me. "Those I'm in contact with are fine." His gaze flicked toward Opal, and that was enough to let me know that they were keeping things from the little witch.

She leaned her head on Kader's shoulder, then said sweetly, "Aiden harvested your DNA from the others' blood tattoos and tried a teleportation spell. To get to you."

Kader momentarily closed his eyes—but couldn't completely hide his pride at the little witch's intelligence-gathering abilities.

My stomach completely soured. Teleportation was extremely risky. But I tried to keep my tone even. "It didn't work?"

Kader opened his mouth, but Opal answered first. "Christopher was pissed," she said. "Because

Aiden hadn't healed yet, and then he wiped himself out magically."

"Blood magic," Kader sniffed offishly. "Unreliable."

Opal flashed me a grin. "But it took them to somewhere in South Africa."

"What?!" I cried. "How... how many of... them?"

"All of them," Kader said tightly. "The rest of Gen 5, my son, and the damn cat."

Mercury Dunkirk's goblin cat? Why would—?

But Kader continued, not giving me time to question him. "A spell like that could have... should have killed Aiden."

Opal's eyes widened in panic. "What?"

The sorcerer grimaced, then scrubbed his hand over his face. He'd managed to hide that bit of information from the dream walker.

"Teleportation is... complicated," I said. Then I narrowed my eyes at Kader. "The cat?"

He waved his hand, dismissive. "Ask the clairvoyant."

Chenda spoke up from somewhere in the background. "Is that Emma?"

"Yes!" Opal cried.

"Oh, thank goodness. Did you mention the warding?"

"Not yet," Kader snapped.

"Well?" the self-styled Mystic of the Golden Peninsula said offishly, still off-screen. "What are you waiting for?"

"The amplifier is not an idiot! There were more pertinent things to discuss. She understands that Lindi has her well warded."

Opal snatched the phone from Kader and did what appeared to be a somersault off the back of the couch. She crouched down, and her face filled the screen.

My heart felt heavy and warm in my chest. "Hello, my dream walker."

Her eyes filled with tears. "I've been looking for you. Three weeks… Emma…" Tears spiked at the edges of her bright-blue eyes.

I'd been out of contact for three weeks? That was a shock. I struggled to absorb it without letting it show on my face. "I'm almost home."

She nodded, sorrow etched across her face.

I firmed my tone. "Nothing is more important than getting home to you. Nothing."

Her eyes flicked up to the top of her screen, reading something there. Presumably a text message. Then a wide smile swamped her face. "Aiden's coming for you. He's near. He's nearby, Emma."

I grinned back at her, despite being aware that even with thirty-minute-old coordinates, a mega yacht in the middle of international waters wasn't going to be simple to track down. Nor was getting on or off that yacht going to be easy.

"I love you, Opal mine."

She opened her mouth—

Then the computer died, along with all the lights and other electronics in the room.

I sat there in the dark, looking at the black screen and feeling utterly hollow inside. Then Kevin stepped in at the doorway, joining Jason in staring at me. The weight of their expectations pulled me back from the bleak edge.

"My team is on the way," I said, sounding just as hollow as I felt. "No ETA. But apparently, they were already nearby." So perhaps Aiden's teleportation spell had been partly successful?

I struggled through another moment—all my emotions conspiring to overwhelm me, with terror the most prevalent—at the thought of Aiden using such a spell…

I stood up abruptly. The desk chair spun back into the darkened room, hitting the far wall with a thump. "We have another member of the team to collect."

Jason regarded me with deeply shadowed eyes, barely highlighted by the starlight filtering in through the windows. If Aiden's teleportation spell was to be trusted and the yacht was in the ocean somewhere near South Africa—so ahead of BC, time zone-wise— that would put us in the dark hours before dawn.

And yeah, I wasn't going to read into that at all.

"You have a daughter," the telepath finally said. It wasn't a question.

"A chosen child, yes," I said stiffly, stepping around them as if I expected them to simply follow. Though I got the distinct impression they were reassessing their situation—via the telepathic communication I could feel passing between them.

Jason closed the distance to me and touched my shoulder lightly, instantly letting go when I paused. "But... you know... love?"

I met his gaze, then glanced at Kevin. Then I nodded and simply said, "We are capable of loving. Yes."

The two of them fell into step behind me without another question. No interrogation about Opal being with Kader—one of the architects of the Collective. No demands that I lead them straight off the yacht instead of continuing to search floor by floor for the boy.

And when their energy waned enough that they faltered, I started amplifying Jason and Kevin, going against all the warnings my own system seemed to scream as I did so. Not for fear of harming myself. But from a concern that I was adding more fuel to a fire that was already burning out of control within each of the remaining members of Gen 4.

But because that was a completely illogical observation, based on nothing more than feelings and the thread-thin, glitchy magical connection between us, I ignored it.

If Jason and Kevin trusted me, then I should—I would—trust their own assessments of their capacities.

EIGHT

BY THE TIME WE CLEARED THE EMPLOYEE AND medical levels of the mega yacht, Jason was stumbling so badly that I had him slung over my shoulder. Kevin was bleeding into both eyes. Everyone who tried to stand against us as we passed had been either knocked out by the telepath or the telekinetic—in the latter case, not as gently as I would have preferred. All the rest of Lindi's crew, we'd locked into their cabins and med bays.

I still hadn't found the boy. Or even felt a hint of his magic.

I still had no idea where Lindi was.

Frustratingly, the nonmagicals in Lindi's crew outnumbered the magically inclined. So short of randomly punching people and carefully amplifying the telepath and telekinetic, I was oddly useless. That made me even more itchy—especially around Lindi's fail-safe patch on my neck. I'd had to stop myself from scratching at it more than once.

I was exceedingly aware—even as Jason and Kevin became more driven, more reckless with their own personal safety as I amplified them—of how many of my hard edges had been blunted somewhere between escaping the Collective the first time and falling in love with Aiden and Opal.

Looking for the boy was part of that softening. Amp5 would have simply commandeered the yacht, then overseen the fallout. But Emma Johnson didn't want the boy to be a casualty in her war against the Chemist. Her war against her own creation.

Even that observation—that hint of philosophy regarding my so-called creation—only emphasized the cracks in my training. Cracks that could be used against me…

"Three mercs," Jason murmured. "Just beyond the door."

Kevin stepped in front of Jason and me. The door in question led to a stairwell beyond, which led to the upper deck. Finally.

As before, Jason was the only one of us who could sense the mundanes. As before, that was seriously irksome.

The telepath abruptly pulled my hand away from my neck, frowning at me. I'd been scratching at the damn fail-safe patch. Unaware that I was doing so.

Kevin snapped up a shield—which he could indeed make out of thin air. A technique that Samantha would undoubtably salivate over—as a barrage of magically charged bullets sped our way. Again, I couldn't feel that magic, but I could see its dark-blue flicker. Lindi had some powerful weapon makers on her payroll.

Kevin's shield shuddered. Then it died.

Shoving Jason, who really couldn't stand on his own, through an open doorway to our right, I crouched and twisted past Kevin's legs. Then I leaped toward the three mercenaries approaching at a run, taking two of them out at the knees. We went down in a tangle of limbs, kicking and hitting. The third merc spun, still standing as he trained his gun on me.

Taking a knee from another merc to the chest for my inattention, I managed to get a leg free, kicking upward at the standing merc's elbow. They shifted at the last moment, and I braced myself in anticipation of being shot even as I continued to quell the first two mercs I'd taken down.

The standing mercenary lurched. Gripping his gun even tighter in both hands, he started convulsing and foaming at the mouth.

Jason had gotten to him.

Unfortunately, even while getting his brains scrambled by a telepath, the merc didn't let go of his gun—or the trigger. One of the three shots he got off before falling skimmed the side of my temple.

Even I had a bad reaction when I got shot in the head with a magically fueled bullet.

Everything went black.

I lost control of my limbs, my body.

Then pure pain exploded through my skull, wiping out all my other senses.

I WAS AWARE OF BEING PICKED UP—PRESUMABLY BY one of the two still-functional mercs, because I couldn't feel any magic from whoever was carrying me.

I was aware of being moved… somewhere.

Then set down.

Then… time… passed… punctuated by the hum of electronics and the quiet murmur of… voices.

I blinked, coming fully aware in an instant.

And then I was off the bed with my hand around someone's throat and power pouring from me, flooding the too-bright room.

"Stop!" a voice shouted.

I couldn't stop. So much energy was coursing through my system that I couldn't even focus my eyes.

The person I was choking gave up fighting me, going limp.

Someone else—the person who had shouted, maybe—was keening in pain.

The room blinked, blinked, blinked into view.

A med bay.

But we'd cleared this level…

Sarah, Lindi's assistant, was dangling from my hand. Not dead, but I had definitely strangled her near to it.

Kevin was stretched out on the other med bed. Unconscious. Blood was everywhere—his blood, presumably. His chest was bandaged in multiple places.

Jason was on the ground between me and the telekinetic, curled up under the assault of my untethered power. That same power was flowing around two mercenaries stationed on either side of the door—the two I'd taken down before… getting… shot?

I'd been shot.

In the head.

I touched my temple with my free hand. My bandaged temple. Then I rubbed my chest where it also ached.

"Adrenaline shot," Sarah croaked against my hold. Her barely open eyes were viciously bloodshot.

"Well, that's better than a death curse," I said.

The mercs were looking around, dazed. As if they'd been under compulsion and were just now coming out of it. Their gazes settled on me, and they reached for guns they no longer had. Their eyes then flicked behind me to where a plethora of weapons were piled on a nearby steel cart.

I released Sarah. She dropped straight to the floor as I launched myself back over the bed.

I got to the weapons before the mercs.

Palming what I thought looked like a modified Glock, I flicked off the safety by pure muscle memory and pointed the gun at the mercs. My arms were shaking from too much adrenaline. But even more so than the gun, it was the smile that spread across my face—or perhaps more a maniacal baring of teeth— that got the mercs' hands up and them taking a step back.

Jason moaned again.

I reined in my magic.

Sarah clawed herself up the side of the bed, slumping across it and gasping for air. The telepath was panting similarly from his prone position on the floor.

The telekinetic hadn't moved a muscle. Apparently, my power hadn't perceived him as a threat.

"Knock these two out," I snarled, gesturing to the mercs, and not quite back in my own body yet. Not quite fitting my mind into that body, or in control of the energy coursing through my limbs.

Jason tried to push himself off the ground but didn't make it. Sarah did. Stumbling around the bed, she grabbed two injectors from a drawer just behind me, then turned to the mercs.

They eyed her distrustfully.

I stepped up behind her, alternating my gaze between the mercs. "Either she knocks you out," I said softly, "or I shoot you in the head. The person I was eight years ago wouldn't have hesitated in the hallway, even before being shot. But I'm a mother now, and I'm trying to not be… so much of a killer."

Exchanging a glance, the mercs nodded, then allowed Sarah to inject each of them in the neck. They succumbed quickly, dropping at the healer's feet. I didn't bother to catch either of them, crossing to check on Jason instead. Sarah didn't move any further, swaying on her feet.

The telepath was propped up against the base of Kevin's bed. I crouched before him, offering him my hand. My arm was still shaking.

"The adrenaline was a bad idea," I said mildly.

He closed his eyes, tilting his head back as he grabbed my hand. I gently amplified him. His reserves had already been low, but I had inadvertently drained him while abruptly awakening, and he barely had a whisper of power left. Which was fine. I could work with only a whisper.

"I told him," Sarah croaked, slowly rounding the bed. "About your extreme reaction to adrenaline, but…"

She hadn't gone for any of the weapons while my back was turned, confirming that she'd patched me and Kevin up voluntarily.

"It was you who shut down my stasis chamber," I said without looking at Lindi's assistant.

"Rebooted," she said quietly. "And no… I had a friend do it."

"A friend in security?"

"He was."

I looked at her then. She just swallowed. Painfully. "Is he dead? Or…"

"I'm not sure," she said, closing her eyes for a moment. "Dead, I think."

"Lindi killed him?"

"Yes."

"Does she know you were working with him?"

She bit her lip. "I don't think so."

"Is this about the boy? Is the boy why you're helping us escape?"

She flicked a gaze to the Gen 4 telepath and telekinetic, then cleared her bruised throat. "Yes?"

That was more a question than a solid confirmation. Sarah hadn't known I would wake the other two. They scared her.

As they should have.

"Who is he to you?"

"Just a boy. Just a child. I didn't… I didn't sign on for this." She waved a hand at me, then Jason.

"Where is he?"

She shook her head. "I… he was with me, but…"

Something hit the side of the mega yacht, hard enough to knock Sarah back a few steps. She grabbed hold of the bed.

With the adrenaline still flooding my limbs, I easily kept my footing. Hell, I was practically floating anyway.

That first hit was quickly followed by two more.

Then all the blood tattoos on my back flared with power.

Backup had arrived. And they'd broken through the yacht's shields, judging by the suddenness of that power surge.

I laughed darkly. "Time to go."

"We're pinned in here," Sarah said shakily. "In medical."

"Not for long," I said, helping Jason to his feet, then releasing him as I crossed to Kevin.

"You can't move him," Sarah protested.

I wrapped my hand around the telekinetic's wrist, gently seeking out his power and tangling mine through it.

"He'd rather be on his feet," Jason said in his strange monotone. "Die on his feet."

"But…" Sarah cut off her own protest. "I don't understand any of this… any of it at all!"

"I need to know where the boy is," I said, pinning my gaze on the healer before she could dissolve into hysterics.

She stiffened, then jutted her chin out. "He's better off with me."

"But you don't understand any of this," I said mockingly. And yeah, I was aware I was being an asshole, but at least I had the adrenaline still coursing through my system to blame. This time.

I quelled my rage—my almost-desperate need to simply snatch the boy and get to my team by any means, to reunite with my dark sorcerer. I made an effort to communicate. It didn't help that my neck was itching around and under Lindi's fail-safe patch so badly now that it actually hurt.

"My team is here. They just took down whatever wards Lindi had in place." The blood tattoos had settled into a steady hum at the top of my spine. "They'll be coming for me. There will be fewer casualties if we meet them on deck."

Sarah's bloodshot eyes widened. Then her gaze flicked between me, Jason, and Kevin.

"Yes," I purred, rather darkly. "More of us. Except these other four haven't been poisoned by Lindi for the last three fucking weeks."

I might have yelled that last little bit, because Sarah blanched and stumbled back, putting the second bed between us.

Kevin moaned quietly, his eyes flickering open and settling on Jason. Then he smiled, almost gently. "Not dead yet?"

"No," Jason replied, not smiling back, but with emotion actually warming his tone. "Not yet."

I released Kevin's wrist. "We're pinned. But we're also only steps away from getting off this boat."

The telekinetic nodded, understanding my unvoiced orders. He slowly got off the bed. Jason didn't help him, and neither did I.

Sarah was watching us, mouth open in disbelief.

"Does the boy have a tracking device?" I asked her.

"What?! Of course not."

"Where does he room?"

"Normally... with Lindi. There's a suite on the upper deck. But I checked there. I... know where he likes to... play."

"He doesn't play," I snapped. "He survives."

She inhaled sharply, then grabbed for her throat. Yes, breathing deeply after almost having the life choked out of her was going to hurt until she could find another healer.

"I swear... I didn't... understand. I thought he was Lindi's son... she said he..."

"Shared DNA means nothing, Sarah," I said, still unable to soften my tone.

Kevin stepped back to the cache of weapons they'd stripped from the mercs, thoroughly checking each before holstering or sheathing them. Jason stripped an extra holster from one of the sedated mercs, then did the same.

"Those tattoos..." Sarah murmured, forgetting to be afraid of me for a moment. "Lindi said that..."

Her gaze flicked to Jason and Kevin. Then, rather wisely, she clamped her mouth shut.

"Lindi said that the blood bindings stabilized my team." I completed the thought for her. "But why does the boy need to be stabilized? He's a healer."

Sarah still said nothing, her thinned lips beginning to whiten.

Yeah, that was what I thought.

There was a reason that whatever combination of DNA the Collective had tried to breed into the sixth member of each generation of super soldiers hadn't resulted in a viable fetus, let alone a fully realized person.

"Is he dying?"

Sarah shook her head. "No, he's… healthy. Top percentile."

I had no idea what rating system she'd be using for a child, but I ignored that thought. It was well past time to be moving. Samantha was probably already on deck and blowing things up. Even a mega yacht couldn't withstand the telekinetic—my telekinetic—on a rampage for long.

"You head for the deck," I said to Jason and Kevin. "I'll find the boy."

"No," Kevin said. "We stick together."

"I'll be more efficient alone."

"And we won't make it without you," Jason said quietly.

"Then stop jumping in front of bullets," I hissed. Yeah, I had put together why I'd woken to find Kevin riddled with gunshot wounds. "You might have a better chance."

My neck was suddenly insanely itchy—so much so that it was clouding my judgement, all my senses still strangely off-kilter from the adrenaline.

I reached up and viciously scratched at it.

"No!" Jason shouted, lunging for me.

The fail-safe patch tore off under my too-long fingernails.

Everyone froze. Sarah had thrown her arms up in front of her face—instinctively worried about getting hit because my inadvertent and abrupt removal of Lindi's fail-safe was going to trigger said fail-safe and blow off my head.

The tiny tingle of magic that still resided in the skin-colored patch fizzled, then died. I flicked the patch off my fingers.

Sarah started hyperventilating. "That… that… should… impossible… that's… impossible."

Jason reached up, fingers clawed, for his own neck, his own patch.

I grabbed his wrist. "It's how my magic works. I build immunity." Apparently, all the itching hadn't been just psychological. Good to know.

He grunted, not completely believing me.

"She… she's…" Sarah was trying to get her breathing evened out. "Even Lindi can't remove them that easily."

I released Jason's wrist, narrowing my eyes at the stuttering healer. "Does she have one on the boy?"

"No!" she cried, aghast.

"Oh? That's one step too far for you?" Apparently, I wasn't done with the mocking.

She flushed. "I wasn't a fan of the conscious spinal surgery either."

I turned away. Jason and Kevin instantly crossed by me, stepping through the sliding door to secure the corridor. My amplification had them on their feet again, but I had no doubt they'd burn through it rapidly.

"Wait!" Sarah cried. Then she softened her tone. "I… I'll find the boy… I… no one knows I helped you…" She glanced down at the unconscious mercs. If they woke anytime soon, they'd likely tattle. "I'm… I can walk out of here, get the boy, and bring him to you without anyone stopping me. Or questioning me."

"Lindi isn't going to hand him off to you," I snapped, tired of talking when I could have already been heading home.

"He trusts me," Sarah said, not addressing how she was planning to get the boy away from Lindi. "He'll come with me."

I shook my head at her, stepping into the corridor. It was empty except for Jason and Kevin waiting on me.

The healer called after me. "You just said… you're a mother, right?"

"I'm immune to that sort of manipulation."

She jutted out her chin. "It's not manipulation." She glanced between the three of us, deliberately. "Just… I'm starting to understand."

I followed her gaze, just for a moment. Kevin and Jason stared steadily back at me. They were running on fumes, magically and otherwise. The sooner I got them on deck, the better.

"If you take too long," I said to Sarah, "you might end up facing my team, not just me. And they won't hesitate to take you out."

The healer nodded. Then without another word, she stepped past us, turned right, and headed down the corridor.

I looked at the Gen 4s. "I'll get you on deck. Then I'll come back for the boy."

Kevin stiffened as if responding to an attack. "We'll stay with you."

"You'll only slow me down. I'll take my own telekinetic, and telepath, if needed."

Kevin nodded stiffly.

A remote look settled over Jason's face, informing me that he was reaching out with his magic. Then he whispered, "Amanda is here," like maybe he hadn't believed me.

"Yes." Assessing the way he was standing so close to the wall, presumably so he'd have something to grab for if he went down, I slung Kevin's free arm over my shoulder. "I don't bluff."

AS I'D SUSPECTED, EVEN THOUGH SARAH HAD INSISTED that we were pinned down in medical, we didn't meet much resistance on our way out and up to the upper deck.

Samantha had a way of drawing attention.

Plus, we'd already made our way through a good number of Lindi's mercs. Or more specifically, the

Gen 4 telepath and telekinetic definitely had a score to settle with the Chemist and her people.

The luxury yacht had transformed into a battle-field by the time we made it up to the main deck. A crumpled helicopter was partially submerged in the pool, the tile surround was severely cracked, and the deck chairs and umbrellas were splintered and scattered. Scorch marks tinged with dark-blue sorcerer magic marred the white metal railings and the polished wood of the deck. Mercenaries—not a mark on them, but still breathing—were piled up around the exit, as if they'd been in the process of fleeing.

I knew without a doubt that the helicopter was Samantha's work, the magic was Aiden's, and that Bee had shut down the mercenaries' minds.

Jason and Kevin continued to flank me as we skirted what I assumed were the upper-deck cabins. And possibly the main security hub since we hadn't come across it yet. But, having never been on a mega yacht before, I still really had no idea what was supposed to be where.

I did, however, hear the whirling blades of another helicopter—this one still airborne. And I could feel more magical explosions coming from the other end of the yacht. Plus the draw of the blood tattoos. All four of them were thrumming in earnest now.

After being below deck for so long, and with my system still fighting off the last lingering effects of Lindi's suppression serum, I was forced to continually squint under the barrage of sunlight glinting off the crystal-clear blue water. Dawn had apparently come and gone while I was recovering from a bullet to the head. But even in full daylight, I couldn't discern any hint of land within the expanse of blue.

The three of us rounded the upper cabins, and the area at the stern of the ship widened to reveal a helicopter landing pad.

And the helicopter currently landing.

But I only had eyes for the dark-haired sorcerer in a black suit practically hanging out of the side door of the copter. He pinned me with a blazing-blue, murderously intent gaze in return.

I had never seen Aiden completely outfitted in a black suit before, including his dress shirt. His face was as gaunt as it had been the first time I'd laid eyes on him, and he definitely hadn't shaved.

But none of that mattered. All that mattered was me running, leaving the Gen 4s behind to cover my back, moving as fast as possible to close the distance between Aiden and me.

Bee, and my Knox, and Samantha were crowded behind Aiden in the copter. Fish was flying it. But I didn't break my gaze from my dark sorcerer.

He didn't smile.

His expression didn't soften as he leaped from the copter, still a meter above the deck.

I grabbed him with my magic, amplifying him even before I got my arms around him. He stumbled under the assault, but then I was there to hold him up.

He wrapped his arms around me, crushing me to his chest with my face buried in the warmth of his neck.

I didn't have any words. I knew I owed him some, but all I had was my power. And that I gave him freely, filling his severely depleted reserves swiftly and without restraint.

The helicopter set down, its rotor wash having its way with our hair and clothing as it did. Aiden pressed his face to mine. His cheek was wet with tears, his jaw rough with his short beard. His grip was tight, possessive.

Leaping from the copter, Samantha dashed past us. Aggressively placing herself between us and the two remaining Gen 4s, even as Bee shouted, "I told you they're with Fox in Socks, Zans!"

The telepath sounded tired. Her power was still dim. And what I could see of her neck was heavily bandaged. She didn't get out of the helicopter, which confirmed just how hurt she still was.

I tipped my chin up to whisper in Aiden's ear, "Christopher told me you'd never forgive me."

"He's right," Aiden snarled viciously, not easing his grip on me one bit.

I tried to pull back slightly to see his face, and he granted me only that tiny sliver of freedom. "Does that mean the wedding is off?" I'd been trying to be playful, but I sounded… not playful, not in the least.

"It means you will spend the rest of our lives together making it up to me."

"I can do that."

I lifted up on my toes, just enough to brush a tender kiss across his lips. He sighed harshly, as if I'd wounded him all over again. And didn't kiss me back.

Christopher appeared on my left, his power simmering around his light-gray irises but not yet fully blazing. Without getting between me and Aiden, he wrapped his arm around my shoulders and rested his forehead against my temple. "I really don't like to be the one doing the rescuing, my Socks."

"I know, my Knox."

He huffed, pissed and pleased at the same time. "And… I have one more thing to ask—"

"No," Aiden snarled, loosening his hold on me just enough to practically bite the clairvoyant's face off. "One of you can go!"

Christopher backed off a step—an unusual retreat that spoke volumes about just how on edge my dark sorcerer was, and must have been for the past three weeks. "We talked about this. Emma is the only—"

"I forbid it," Aiden said. His magic churned around his hands, sparking against me where we still touched.

"The boy?" I asked, interjecting myself into their stare-off.

Christopher nodded. "Yes." And then the goblin cat was suddenly perched on his shoulder, blinking its bulbous eyes at me.

It took me a moment to realize that Christopher was wearing a backpack, and that the cat must have been in its depths a moment before. "The cat?" I asked idiotically.

"Yes," Christopher said. "You're going to need Sweetness, and this…" He held a new phone out to me.

"I'm going to… need the cat and to make a call?"

"You're going to need pictures—"

"Absolutely fucking not!" Aiden shouted.

The little goblin—who had apparently been named Sweetness sometime in the last three weeks—hissed at the enraged sorcerer.

"You fucking go," Aiden said, trying to get himself back under control. "Or Daniel. Emma has done fucking enough. For all of you."

I pieced the conversation together, interjecting again, "I'm the only one who can get the boy?"

Christopher nodded, though the bulk of his attention and magical sight was still trained on Aiden. Aiden, who I'd just pumped full of power. Aiden, who was definitely on the verge of becoming unhinged.

Speaking of power, Samantha was unleashing a barrage of it—followed by the sound of a lot of metal crumpling—behind me. Daniel, leaving the copter primed to depart, stepped out to press a hand on its hull, reinforcing the wards protecting it.

The shielding the sorcerer and the nullifier must have erected over and around the landing pad before setting down the copter was being sporadically peppered with munitions fire that was then quickly quelled by the telekinetic. Bee had moved into the mouth of the copter's side door, her feet dangling and head tilted as if she was having a conversation—presumably with Jason and Kevin, who had followed me and were now hovering a few steps away. The entire side of Bee's face was darkly bruised and puffy.

Lindi had made a solid attempt at murdering the telepath.

"We'll go back," Jason said, stepping closer to me, though his gaze was locked on Bee.

"No," Christopher said, sweeping his gaze over the Gen 4 telepath and telekinetic. "Everyone else dies."

The goblin cat jumped off the clairvoyant's shoulder, then sauntered over to sit beside Samantha's right ankle. It then proceeded to lean against her leg as it hunched over and cleaned its butt.

"That's a… cat, right?" Kevin asked.

No one answered him—because Aiden chose that moment to round on Christopher, actually making an attempt to shove me behind him. "You can't even guarantee that Emma makes it back in one piece."

"She'll be alive," Christopher snapped. "Her alive is better than the rest of us dying painful deaths."

"If whatever is in this fucking yacht is capable of killing all of you, then it's capable of killing Emma. The future is changeable, clairvoyant!"

"Yes," Christopher said, keeping inexplicably calm as he met my gaze over Aiden's shoulder. "Emma is that change."

Aiden half-growled, half-howled, as he turned back to me. "Emma. Opal needs you."

"I'm not leaving a child behind, Aiden." I pressed my palm against his cheek. His skin was hot, as if he was fighting off an infection. My sorcerer was still hurt, barely healed.

He shut his eyes. A terrible, mournful sob tore from him, sounding as if it had cracked open his chest even as he tried to suppress it. Then he was pulling me to him, hands buried deeply in my hair, and his mouth covering mine in a harsh, painful kiss.

Not claiming. Not possessive. Just pouring pure terror through our empathic connection.

His emotions rampaged through my entire system until I trembled under his wholly intentional assault—using my own empathy, and my inability to block it, against me.

It was underhanded. Devious, even. And far more effective than any of his words or demands could ever be against my own stubborn nature.

Aiden broke the kiss almost as quickly as he'd started it, tearing off a piece of my soul as he did so. Then he took a deliberate step back from me and looked over to Fish. "Daniel?" The sorcerer's expression was completely blank, shoulders so stiff that he looked like he was in pain.

That same pain I could still feel echoing through me.

Fish stepped closer on Aiden's prompting. He paused to grasp my shoulders, just staring down at me.

"We're going back," Jason abruptly announced. "We want Lindi."

"Please," Bee said. "Please… just stay. Let Emma get the boy and let all of us walk away. Please trust Knox, our clairvoyant."

Everyone ignored her, including the aforementioned clairvoyant. A deliberate snub on Christopher's part.

Daniel dropped his hands from my shoulders, then looked at Aiden.

My dark sorcerer grabbed my hand and threaded three copper rings onto my fingers. Aiden met and held my gaze as his power sparked under his palm, triggering something within the rings.

Then Daniel laid his hand over Aiden's and added his power to the mix. A wash of cold ran over my hand and wrist, then up my arm and across my shoulders and chest.

A dual shielding spell.

Under other circumstances, I would probably have questioned Aiden and Daniel's ability—and inclination—to work together cooperatively.

"Can someone neutralize the patches?" Jason asked. He and Kevin were watching Aiden and Fish casting closely enough that they had to be sensing the magic slowly encasing me.

Right. The two Gen 4s still had Lindi's explosive devices adhered to their own necks. The Chemist could have taken Jason and Kevin out at any time during our breakout. She still could. Except she was the sort to only cut her losses at the last moment, or in trade. Like trading my team for me.

The Chemist wouldn't so easily destroy her assets. But now that she was effectively trapped on the yacht with all of us? That was a far different scenario. Unless she thought she could still turn the Gen 4s against us?

But I didn't have to know them any better than I already did to understand that Jason and Kevin would rather die than be used. Used again.

Daniel crossed to the Gen 4s with Christopher and Samantha. All three of them leaned in to examine the fail-safes embedded into their necks.

"I said no!" Bee cried, trying to make it to her feet but still pressing a hand to the side of the helicopter for support. "It doesn't have to be—"

"We don't leave teammates behind," Jason said, his tone as harsh as I'd ever heard from him. "And we don't sacrifice one of our team for another." His gaze fell on me for a moment, then he looked away.

Kevin nodded in stiff agreement.

Bee settled her fierce glare on me, one fist clenched, the other hand still propping her up. "You command them now. Tell them—"

"They're their own people, Bee. If they want to defy a clairvoyant..." I glanced at Christopher, prompting him.

Feeling my regard, Knox stepped slightly away from us all, presumably to help clear his sight from all the influence we must have been inflicting on him. The white of his magic flickered over his eyes.

Bee's gaze settled on him, hope radiating from her.

Christopher nodded to whatever his magic was telling him, then turned his attention to Kevin and Jason. "I can't see you clear of what is going to kill the rest of us if we try to go with Emma. I also can't see you succumb. Yet."

Jason and Kevin looked at each other, magic shifting between them to indicate a telepathic conversation.

Then Kevin said, "For our team, Lindiwe Fourie dies."

Amanda moaned.

"I'm not going to try to stop you," I said. "But we can deal with Lindi another way. I presume Samantha has plans to sink the boat."

The telekinetic flashed me a wicked grin. "Oh yeah! And there are just so many fun ways to do it!"

As if called forth by that pronouncement, a second barrage of magic peppered Daniel's shield. Or maybe a third? It wasn't even leaving residual in its wake.

"Emma," Aiden whispered.

I turned toward him, instantly stepping within my dark sorcerer's embrace. "I'll be right back."

"I'll be here, making certain there's something to come back to."

"I know."

"Aiden," Daniel barked. "Some help?"

Ignoring the nullifier for just a moment longer, my deadly sorcerer brushed a kiss over my lips. A kiss that was annoyingly dampened by the shield that had completely encased me, anchored in Aiden's copper rings. A shield that wasn't going to last long against my own power.

If I was going back for the boy—and facing the future that Christopher currently saw killing everyone but me to do so—I needed to go now.

Aiden stepped away, leaving me hanging in the echo of the almost-kiss for a moment longer. He crossed to Daniel, conferring with him about neutralizing the fail-safes.

I met Bee's gaze. Her light-brown eyes were weary and reddened, and drained of the hope I'd seen in them just a moment before. "Do you want me to amplify you?"

She nodded, reaching for me, but I didn't step forward to touch her. I simply homed in on the blood tattoo etched into her skin and bone—the binding constructed out of my blood and DNA and magic—and began to feed power into it.

She gasped. I held her gaze for a moment longer, until she dropped her hand, then her chin. Unable to look me in the eye.

Behind me, Samantha used a lazy swipe of her hand and a push of her telekinesis to counter another round of munitions fire before it could even hit the shield around the landing pad. "They're not even trying now," she muttered crossly.

"They're fortifying," Daniel said. "While wondering why we haven't left yet."

Samantha shrugged, playing at belligerent and bored. "We'll show them soon enough."

Crossing to them, I amplified Fish, the telekinetic, and Christopher, then topped off Aiden as he pulled a black marker out of his pocket and started drawing a complicated rune on Jason's neck. I couldn't discern the patch that held the fail-safe from Jason's own skin.

The rune must have been similar to the ones etched into the copper rings I currently wore, because as soon as Aiden finished drawing and moved to Kevin, Daniel added his own power to the spell.

The creepy goblin cat wound around my ankles as Christopher took his backpack off and handed it to me. Then he tugged the phone partly out of one of the backpack's outer pockets, showing its location to me.

"Pictures?" I asked, slipping the otherwise empty backpack on and tightening the straps.

He shook his head, just once. "I loaded everything I had on my phone. Of Opal, of Paisley, and us at the farm."

"For?"

He shook his head another time.

Okay, then.

"Point me in the right direction, Knox," I ordered.

He leaned in, brushing a kiss against my cheek, then whispering in my ear, "I still see you, Emma. With black roses in your hair, gazing up at Aiden."

My chest tightened. "And I'm going to need to know that?" I asked, not really wanting the answer.

He grimaced. "You're going to need to know that."

Well, that was disconcerting.

The clairvoyant pressed an earpiece into my right ear. "I'll guide you for as long as I can." He pivoted slightly and pointed back the way Kevin, Jason, and I had come, toward the mostly glassed-in entrance to what I'd assumed was the upper cabin deck.

Aiden had finished with Kevin. Making certain the earpiece was secure, I closed the space between him and me, twining my fingers through his.

"I love you." I squeezed his hand, though not as gently as I probably should have.

My dark sorcerer nodded stiffly, keeping his lips pressed tightly together and jaw rigid. I nodded, my heart aching, thinking he wasn't going to speak as I stepped away.

But the moment after our fingers parted—our arms still stretched out between us—he called, "My father and the mystic have taken over the wedding planning."

I blinked at him over my shoulder, utterly aghast.

Aiden grinned at me. A wide, vicious, wickedly pleased baring of his teeth.

I huffed. "Is that my penance?"

He shrugged.

Christopher threw his head back and laughed. Samantha joined in.

I shook my head at them all, gesturing to the goblin cat. "Come, Sweetness." Then I stepped beyond the edge of the helicopter landing pad and Daniel's shield.

I dashed for the door Christopher had indicated, dodging as the intermittent magical assault turned my way. The two remaining members of Gen 4 swiftly followed, tucking as close to me as they could while we ran.

Ahead of us, three mercs spilled out of the glassed-in entranceway, guns raised and homing in on me. They fell under a telepathic assault from Jason before they had any chance to get their first shots off.

The entrance featured a security pad of some sort, so I leaped over the downed mercs and grabbed the door before it swung shut. I deliberately didn't look Jason's way as he stumbled while following.

The adrenaline he'd taken had long worn off. And my amplification wasn't going to be enough with him already so depleted by Lindi's toxins, plus the forced long sleep. In taking down the mercs, he'd spent too much power, too quickly.

I didn't need more anger to keep me moving forward. But the spike of it as Kevin kept Jason on his feet to follow me inside the upper deck suite helped cut through the trepidation that had taken up residence in my chest. Concern, even fear, of the future that the clairvoyant had shoved me into. A future that Aiden knew enough about that his own anger, barely relieved by having me returned to him whole, had blown through the carefully crafted facade he'd spent his entire life perfecting.

Metal crunched behind and to my left. I glanced back. A large section of the railing tore free from the side of the yacht, then swept across the deck.

Mercenaries had gathered between us and the helicopter pad, their weapons trained on the three of us who weren't shielded. Well, as far as they knew. Under the touch of Samantha's telekinesis, the metal railing crashed into, then sent those mercs flying off the other side of the yacht, limbs flailing as they tumbled into the sea.

With one hand on her cocked hip and a smirk on her face, Samantha picked up a series of life rings with a casual flick of her other hand and threw them overboard as well.

I raised my voice. "Try to keep the ship afloat until I get back!"

The telekinetic grinned, manically pleased. "No promises."

I snorted. With the goblin cat twining around my ankles and two unstable teammates at my back, I let all my power loose to undulate around me.

Then I stepped through into the future that Christopher had seen ending the lives of everyone I was leaving behind on the deck.

NINE

THE FIRST CORPSE I'D SEEN ON ANY PART OF THE UPPER deck not wearing tactical gear was sprawled out in front of what I assumed was the main security station. We had already crossed through some sort of front room, replete with mahogany wood flooring, marble accents, and plush fabrics. It must have been an entertainment space of some sort, given the full bar and the stainless steel kitchen beyond. It looked clean but untouched.

The goblin cat simply wandered off between rooms. Literally walking through the wall.

Jason huffed in surprise, but I just kept going. Unintentionally bonded to me or not, sent with me by a clairvoyant vision or not, the cat and its wanderings didn't interest me.

The second room of the upper deck suite—originally a stateroom, perhaps?—had been converted into the central hub of the rather lame security Lindi had monitoring her mobile compound. Jason and

Kevin pressed into the monitor-filled space ahead of me, shoving a second corpse aside in his wheeled office chair without a second look. Then they systematically checked every monitor.

Looking for Lindi.

I took a moment to examine the corpse who'd fallen just beyond the door, as if fleeing, and then the other security officer hanging off his chair. They were both dressed in blue collared shirts and dark-blue pants, walkie-talkies and key cards clipped to their belts.

At one point while dying, the first corpse had started foaming at the mouth. His fingers were clawed and stiffened, indicating a painful death.

The corpse in the chair had blue, bruised lips. The rest of him was seemingly untouched. Until I turned over his wrist and spotted marks—also blue, the size of three fingerprints.

I'd seen those kinds of marks before, left by healers who had twisted their power into something much, much darker.

"Blank spots," Jason said quietly, calling my attention to one of the monitors. He appeared to have paused some of the footage he'd found.

"In the video? Or the coverage?"

"Coverage."

I stepped closer, and Jason hit play.

Sarah appeared on-screen, stepping out into a white-walled corridor. Followed moments later by me, Jason, and Kevin. Sarah turned right, and the camera footage Jason had accessed followed the healer. When she stepped out of frame, a new camera and angle picked up her movements, over and over again.

I glanced at the corpse, understanding now that he had been Sarah's… friend. The friend who'd rebooted the systems in my cell, forcing the stasis chamber to open. "He was tracking her," I murmured. "Watching her back."

Jason nodded. Then he sped up the footage. I looked away as it glitched and jumped forward, hating the visual stimulation. He hit play again.

On the monitor, Sarah was now talking to Lindi.

And Lindi was holding the boy. Not by the hand. By the forearm.

"Where are they now?" I asked, my gaze riveted to the boy. His head was bowed, fist clenched at his side.

In the footage, Sarah glanced at the boy. Twice, as if she was trying not to but couldn't help herself. I leaned closer to the monitor. The back of the boy's neck was exposed, but the camera wasn't close enough…

Jason sped up the footage again. When I looked back, he had paused at a moment when Lindi's attention was distracted by something off-screen. Sarah reached for the boy, settling her hand on the back of his neck.

Trying to… heal him?

The boy flinched away from Sarah, and she pressed her lips together, then straightened and spoke to Lindi.

"No audio?" I asked as I leaned closer, still trying to see the back of the boy's neck.

"No." Jason hit fast-forward again, just a bit of a bump. I didn't look away this time.

Lindi practically shoved the boy at Sarah, then stomped off. Jason's fingers flew over the keyboard, and the footage split, the same screen showing Sarah walking away with the boy—not touching him, but he was following. A second monitor showed Lindi crossing toward and speaking to an older security officer. Not either of the corpses I'd just examined. Then she snarled something and started up the hall at a brisk clip.

Simultaneously on both monitors, the boat shifted enough to jostle everyone.

"Samantha," I murmured. Lindi had been distracted by one of Samantha's volleys—after my team had breached the wards, but before the Gen 4s and I had made it to the deck.

Kevin grunted in agreement.

On the second monitor, Lindi took off with the older security guy. On the first monitor, Sarah grabbed the boy and ran in the other direction. The feed jumped, Sarah's security-officer friend continuing to switch cameras to follow her movements, and the healer darted through a set of wooden double doors, disappearing with the boy. The feed didn't shift cameras or angles again. It just continued to hold the same static shot.

"Sarah or the boy don't come back out?"

"No," Jason said. He fast-forwarded again until Lindi reappeared and passed through the same double doors. Then the same static shot was held for a moment. "That's the live feed now."

"No cameras beyond that door? That's the blank spot in security?"

The Gen 4 telepath nodded, his fingers flying over the keyboard again. Camera feeds flashed up on all the other screens. He was cycling through them, looking for Lindi.

"She came in here first," I said, glancing down at the corpse still sprawled in his chair. "She killed Sarah's accomplice."

"How do you know?" Kevin asked with a frown. The telekinetic was leaning against the back wall with his arms folded—guarding the exit while conserving energy.

Not needing to linger, I crossed toward the corridor. "None of the rest of us are poisoners. Not by touch, at least."

"We haven't confirmed Lindi's location," Jason said.

"I don't need cameras to tell me where to go, telepath," I said mildly. "I have a bossy clairvoyant to do that."

I paused for a moment in the doorway, reaching out for my Knox—more with my mind than my magic, because we were tied that tightly now. My wings unfurled, sprouting between my shoulder blades, then settling down my back. Closed, at rest. For the moment.

Kevin grunted disconcertedly behind me.

And he hadn't even seen my full power unleashed yet.

As if on cue, Christopher's voice came through the earpiece in my ear. "Left, Fox in Socks."

I stepped out into the corridor, over the second corpse—presumably also killed by Lindi. Then I turned left, trusting the clairvoyant more than I'd trusted him in a long time.

For the boy.

THOUGH THE YACHT ROLLED FROM TIME TO TIME IN what felt like a very unnatural way—presumably due to Samantha—we made it safely to the set of double wooden doors we'd seen the boy, Sarah, and Lindi all step through. We hadn't spotted any other mercs, but raised voices—Lindi shouting orders at someone, and then quieter tones—greeted us from beyond the doors. However, the main living space was empty when we slipped inside the suite.

More luxury furnishings filled the area, which featured an open kitchen beyond it. But this part of the upper deck suite actually looked lived in. Various books and notebooks were strewn on the couches and coffee tables. A white lab coat had been tossed over the back of a chair. A small pile of shoes tucked to the side of the main doors nearly tripped Jason as I gently closed those doors behind us.

"How difficult is it to keep track of one boy?" Lindi snarled from somewhere deeper into the suite to our left.

Sarah's murmured response was too quiet for me to pick up, but Kevin immediately veered in their direction, Jason on his heels. Both of the Gen 4s were flagging. I kept pace with them for a moment, feeling somehow—perhaps through my stronger connection with Knox—that I was heading in the wrong direction. But keeping my hands on their shoulders to amplify them… right up until I couldn't anymore.

A double set of glass doors led to a large breakfast nook off the side of the kitchen. The sparkling ocean view through floor-to-ceiling windows was spectacular, but Lindi had converted the nook to an office, replete with white boards covered in numbers and symbols that I had no idea how to interpret. Gene sequencing, at best guess.

As well, given the older security officer seated with his back to us in front of a bank of computers, the room also operated as a secondary security hub.

Half of the camera feeds rotating through on one of the screens were glitching in and out of focus, or filled with fuzz. As I peered over Kevin's shoulder, more fuzzed out, one after another.

Fish was screwing with the security feeds.

I couldn't feel the nullifier's magic, but I'd seen the results of him interfering with tech signals before. A nonmagical tech would have just shut the system down.

The older male, presumably the head of Lindi's security, snarled in frustration, slamming his hand on the desk. "We need to evacuate! We should have been gone the second your monsters got out of containment!" As far as I could pick up, he was nonmagical.

With her back also to us, Lindi was leaning over his shoulder. She was dressed in casual clothes but had a silk scarf knotted around her neck, her gaze riveted to the monitors. "Not without the boy!"

Standing at the back of the room, behind the other two, Sarah risked a glance toward the door. She looked ill—reddened, puffy eyes and sickly pale, as if she was fighting off some sort of infection.

Lindi had hit her with something.

And even though the Chemist couldn't sense all the power we three carried, though the other two were probably dampened under my onslaught, apparently Sarah could.

Had Sarah lost the boy? Or hidden him somewhere?

The healer's gaze flicked deliberately back the way we'd come.

I squeezed Jason's shoulder, projecting my thoughts toward him. *I'm going to the boy.*

The telepath's back stiffened, and I could feel the question he was forming before he actually voiced it in my mind.

The Collective means nothing to me, I whispered down that thin telepathic connection, stepping back as silently as possible.

Now Kevin stiffened, glancing at me questioningly.

Lindi will pay for our teammates, Jason murmured in my mind.

That's your choice.

I already knew Lindiwe Fourie wasn't getting off the yacht alive. The other four who made us the Five, all of us cooked up in a test tube by the Chemist herself, wouldn't let her walk away.

But I needed no such vengeance. I had a family to get home to.

We're right behind you.

I nodded, though I wasn't so certain of that. Whatever Christopher had seen, whatever only I was capable of walking away from, had yet to occur.

THE LAST REMAINING MEMBERS OF GEN 4 WAITED TO launch an assault on their creator until I was all the way down the other end of the suite, having passed multiple unused bedrooms and bathrooms.

Feeling magic come up against magic, I glanced back up the hall just as Sarah stumbled out of the nook, fell to her knees, and vomited all over the marble floor of the kitchen.

The door at the very end of the hall had three aftermarket locks adhered to the wall just above the handle. It was closed—the only closed door along the corridor—but the locks were unclasped. I opened it, already knowing what I would find beyond.

The small room was decorated in a riot of blues. The low, pinewood-framed bed was neatly made. Dozens of brand-new-looking toys were neatly set on shelves. And covered in a fine layer of dust.

I opened the top drawer of the bureau—a drawer too high for a child of three or four to reach. Some of the clothing within was still in its plastic packaging.

Following a whisper of power—Knox's power riding and directing my own in a way I'd never felt before—I crossed to the closet, opened the doors, then kneeled and pulled out a pile of neatly folded blankets and pillows.

I ran my hands over the paneling I'd exposed, then found a latch. Lower down than I would have guessed.

And easily reachable by a four-year-old.

I knew that he couldn't have piled the pillows so neatly after him if he'd gone through it alone. But Sarah could have covered it up behind him.

I opened the panel, finding a narrow opening rather than the cubbyhole I'd expected. Beyond it, a metal-rung ladder was welded into a metal-clad tube-like passage. An emergency escape route?

I shoved my head through the opening, gazing up and then down. There was slight wear on the lower rungs. Plus, given that I finally had a sense of the layout of the yacht, the only level above the upper deck suite was the bridge.

This was how the boy was getting around the ship undetected. Well, undetected by Lindi, at least.

I wasn't certain what was worse. The fake child's room, indicating that Lindi had made some attempt to offer the boy a bit of space and comfort. Or the fact that she obviously had no idea he was wandering the ship rather than sleeping in his bed or playing with the toys.

Wandering the ship and seeing everything she did in her labs. And in between those excursions, being tortured himself for the advancement of her goals.

I went in feet first, taking a moment to drag the blankets and pillows back into position as much as I could before closing and latching the door.

Apparently, the yacht did have emergency systems and egresses built into it. That made sense, though Lindi's blindness to the boy's movements was still sloppy.

And now she'd trapped herself in international waters with me. So I qualified as another of her blind spots.

"One level down," Knox murmured through the comms in my ear.

Medical. And Lindi's labs, unless I'd gotten completely turned around. But why would the boy retreat to medical? Maybe because that was where he usually found Sarah?

Or where he'd now seen me multiple times?

I WASN'T REMOTELY SURPRISED TO FIND THE GOBLIN cat sitting with its back to me, cleaning a paw as I exited through a hidden panel into an empty med bay. I had found the emergency egress door already hanging open as I made my way down. I was, however, a little thrown as I crawled onto the cool white flooring and watched the creature Christopher had dubbed Sweetness dip that same paw into a congealing pool of blood.

That blood had seemingly erupted from the nose of the mercenary sprawled across the floor, partway through the doorway. I hadn't realized the doors on the medical level were automated. Or at least some of them were. The mechanical door to this particular med bay was trying, over and over again, to close against the merc's thigh.

There were more corpses in the corridor beyond.

And something in the air.

Something that tickled across all my exposed skin, something that prickled as I inhaled, scraping the insides of my nostrils and throat.

"Stop that!" I snapped at the cat as I straightened, not bothering to close the egress behind me.

The cat tossed me a huffy look over its shoulder, but it stopped licking the blood still coating the gray skin of its paws.

I raised my hand to the nearest air vent, noting that the runes on one of the three copper rings Aiden had slipped onto my fingers had already dimmed. The shielding spell was being eroded by my magic.

No air stirred against my palm. Nothing was coming through the vent. But I couldn't deny the taste in my mouth or the burning sensation coating my throat now. Someone had gassed this level, or was in the process of doing so. And the mercenaries most definitely weren't just unconscious.

Someone was trying to bring me down? Or the boy?

But, in either case, why hadn't the mercs been masked against it?

I stepped through the door as it opened automatically, glancing down at two more corpses as I passed. The goblin cat minced around my ankles, mewing in protest as if dead bodies leaking blood were suddenly distasteful.

I had a feeling Sweetness was mocking me.

I ignored that feeling.

I glanced right—no bodies, and a clearly marked exit just a few steps away. I glanced left—at least a dozen corpses littered the white-painted, metal-clad corridor. Jason, Kevin, and I had crossed through this level on our way to the upper decks, locking mercenaries and employees in the med bays as we'd moved. However, open doors along the corridor made it clear that those we'd locked up had been released— which in turn made it likely that at least some of those mercs and employees were the bodies now sprawled out around me. But I didn't take the time to examine them in detail. Dwelling on all the death that Lindi had wrought wasn't my mission.

I stepped left, noting the burst pustules around the mouth of the next downed merc. The corpse beyond that was a woman in a lab coat. She was lying in a pile of bright, green-tinged vomit.

An unnatural color.

Something shivered up my arms and across my collarbone. Instinctively, I flared my wings, and the feeling receded.

It wasn't gas in the air that I was sensing.

It was magic.

A sickly layer of magic.

It had settled around my ankles, but as I slowly traversed the hall—stepping around corpse after corpse with weeping sores and bleeding orifices—I stirred that magic up. Along with the first inklings of true fear.

Terror skittered down my spine as I scooped the cat up and set its yowling, shivering mass on my shoulder.

The second anchor of the shield that Aiden and Daniel had coated me with—the runes etched into the second copper ring Aiden had given me—sputtered and died on my finger.

What had Lindi unleashed in medical?

And why? Why kill her own crew?

I could understand her killing Sarah's friend in security—or perhaps both the corpses there had been working with the healer. I could understand Lindi lashing out at Sarah, though she obviously didn't know that her assistant was actively working against her. Simply that she'd lost track of the boy.

My chest started aching. And not because the poison—the plague?—that I was currently walking through was creeping up my bare calves, trying to grab hold of me.

Because I already knew the answer to my question.

Maybe it was another unheard whisper from Christopher. Though the clairvoyant remained quiet over comms, the power embedded into his blood and DNA etched under my skin maintained a strong hum that informed me his sight was trained on me.

It became difficult to breathe.

The skin of my arms began to itch in earnest, reddening. I could feel my power, all my magic and the immunity that backed it, expanding within me, rising to the surface to counter whatever plague was in the air, infiltrating me on every level, through every pore, every breath I took.

And faltering.

The third rune-scribed ring died.

Everyone else dies, Christopher had said. Even Daniel's nullifying power would have eroded under the continual assault unfolding around me, no matter if I'd been continually amplifying him. Just as the shield rings hadn't held.

My eyes were leaking, and I wasn't certain it was actual tears or blood wetting my cheeks.

I kept walking.

I kept following the trail of corpses, until I reached the final med bay at the end of the hall.

"I'm sorry, Socks," Christopher murmured in my ear as the automated door whooshed opened for me. "Black roses in your hair… smiling up at Aiden with your magic bright in your eyes."

I stepped into the med bay I'd awoken in multiple times. Or another space just like it.

Pain… pain… radiated through my limbs. My immunity was still struggling to counter the magic I'd breathed in, was continuing to breathe in, that magic still burrowing into my skin. Pustules formed on my arms and legs, then burst.

I fell to my knees, too far from the bed to catch myself.

I could feel the boy now, through the choking miasma of power, of poison.

The boy.

Not just a healer.

I knew—I already knew.

I started crawling.

A healer, even one as powerful as Lindi could create, shouldn't have been so difficult for the Collective to breed. Lindi wouldn't have needed my DNA, presumably mixed with her own, to create a sixth-generation healer.

My wings were dragging on the floor now. Despite them being made of pure power, I couldn't hold them up any longer. They shredded with every forward movement I made to reach the boy. The bits of magic and manifested energy I left behind disintegrated in my slow, painful wake.

I fell forward, managing to turn my face at the last moment so I didn't smash my nose on the white tile floor.

The goblin cat jumped off my shoulder as I fell, mincing forward with its tail in the air and asshole on full display.

I got my hands under me, but not my knees. My legs were no longer responding to my mental commands.

I pressed my palms to the floor. I pulled myself forward.

I was so close.

The asshole cat started purring, madly, loudly. Sidling up along the cupboards underneath the monitor cabinets, crossing back and forth.

The cupboards in which the boy had hidden.

Hidden from Lindi.

To watch as she took samples from me, nearly killing me in the process.

The cat was immune, I realized. The goblin cat was immune to the boy… to the plague bringer that Lindi had finally managed to create. With my DNA.

I turned my head just in time to vomit to the side, rather than in front of me.

Blackened blood spewed forth from me, spackling the floor. Not the green sludge I'd seen in the corridor. Shredded bits of my lungs, maybe? The others had died more quickly than I was dying, perhaps.

And then, I was finally close enough… close enough to reach a shaking hand to the latch on the cupboard. My arm was streaked with blood, my wings just the barest wisps of magic across my back.

I blinked and blinked, only to realize that the sheen of red that overlaid everything was… a lens of blood coating my eyes.

I got the cupboard door unlatched and open a crack, but then couldn't work my fingers… couldn't hold up my arm… or my chest any longer…

I was… dying.

I had trusted the clairvoyant, and he'd sent me to my death.

Again.

The cupboard slammed all the way open, barely missing my forehead. The magic propelling it crashed over me, crackling through my chest and shredding the remainder of my wings.

I fell the rest of the way, my face smacking against the cold floor.

And I didn't get back up.

I couldn't even… close my eyes.

I caught a glimpse of green… emerald green.

Then an absolutely terrified shriek.

All the pain just… faded away.

Because the pain always faded right before I died.

The great and powerful Amp5, taken down by a four-year-old boy. A plague bringer who wielded magic my amped-up system had never encountered before.

TEN

AWARENESS CAME WITH PAIN, SO MUCH PAIN. I COULDN'T breathe against it. Couldn't move or even react.

A sliver of energy slowly bloomed, a sliver of warmth pressing against that pain... emanating from my... right... rib cage?

That didn't make any...

A bony... spine... was pressed against me. A tiny... warm body that radiated a trickle of power. The person sniffled, then burrowed back against me more.

I still couldn't move.

I still couldn't open my eyes or speak.

The pain was too much for all my senses.

I accepted it.

I stopped fighting it. Instead, I tried to relax the body I couldn't yet command, relax into the pain.

Pain meant I was still alive.

Or... that I'd actually died. And then my immunity—or rather, my genetically imposed sense of self-preservation—had kicked in.

So I accepted it was going to hurt, going to continue to incapacitate me.

I lost some time in that haze...

Then slowly... ever so slowly, I became more aware of my surroundings. The cold tile under my bare arms and legs, hard under the back of my skull... I'd fallen face forward... had I rolled over instead of drowning in my own vomit? Or...?

The boy.

The boy was the warm, almost insubstantial presence at my side.

And was that... purring?

The damn goblin cat was on my belly. Clawing at me.

No... kneading?

"Asshole," I croaked through cracked lips and ragged throat.

The purring and kneading increased.

And if I could feel the cat's claws, then the other pain was receding.

Socks?

Bee's voice whispered through in my mind.

"Still here," I said out loud.

We need you to come to us.

I opened my eyes, blinking up at the dark ceiling. The power had gone out.

And... the tile was cool and wet with pink-tinged water, not just my blood and vomit.

I managed to move my arm, settling my hand on the goblin cat across my belly. It half snarled, half... huffed? Sounding pissed and utterly dismissive at the same time. I curled my other arm in, realizing the boy was resting his head on my bicep. I hugged him tighter against my chest, gently. His skin was burning.

He was… hurt.

I sat up, knocking the cat off me—yowling indignantly—as I somehow found the strength to haul the boy into my lap.

He came to awareness with a shriek, tearing out of my arms and scrambling back in the shallow water. He pressed his back against the cabinet, his feverish gaze not seeming to see anything at all. He tried to crawl into the cabinet, but didn't make it all the way before collapsing.

Drained.

Physically, mentally, and magically.

"Hey," I croaked, realizing I sounded absolutely destroyed, and would likely come off as ridiculously creepy to a young child. "My name is Emma."

The goblin cat crossed to the boy and shoved itself into his lap awkwardly.

The boy's gaze fell to the cat, then rose to meet mine. He managed to settle back into the cabinet. He was so tiny that the water now coating the floor was high enough to cover his bare feet up to his ankles. He was wearing a gray T-shirt over elastic-waisted jeans, both soaked in bloody water.

"What's your name?"

He didn't answer.

It was possible he couldn't speak, having grown up alone. We Five had had each other, as well as tutors and trainers.

"Apparently, my sister Samantha got a little carried away." I whispered in an attempt to soften my voice. Then I splashed lightly at the water surrounding us. The yacht had definitely sprung a leak.

The boy blinked those emerald eyes at me—eyes that were almost exact replicas of my own—trying to focus. His skin was still flushed. But I could feel his magic already trying to reassert itself.

The plague-bringer power, not the healing.

Because he couldn't defend himself by healing people. And his genetic code would have had just as much self-preservation woven into it as my own did.

"Sister?" he asked. His eyes were wide and distrustful. His voice carried a hint of Lindi's accent, confirming that she had been playing caregiver, at least at some point.

"Yes. Not by blood, nor do we share the same parentage. I don't think." Every word I forced out of my mouth hurt. I could taste blood. My arms and legs were still covered in large weeping pustules.

The boy opened his mouth to speak again—but then flinched at the sound of belabored footsteps in the water beyond the doors. Then the sound of someone falling with a groan.

Not one of mine, I hoped.

The boy's long eyelashes were spiky with unshed tears. Or maybe his fever was so high, that was just sweat. Maybe he didn't know how to cry.

"We should go," I said.

He flinched again as if I'd reached for him, and a tiny pulse of power fizzed out before it hit me.

Bee wasn't talking to me anymore. I had a feeling that Lindi and her mercs were keeping everyone busy. Or something else had drawn the telepath's attention.

Had one of them been hurt? The four blood tattoos were all still simmering on my upper back, but that told me nothing of Aiden. Or Jason or Kevin.

"I can't," the boy practically shouted, literally folding in on himself. "I'm danger."

The goblin cat upped the amperage of its purring. Seemingly unconsciously, the boy ran his hand down the cat's back in a rough pet. The creepy goblin cat was likely the first animal he'd ever had contact with.

"That's Sweetness," I said. "Either my brother Christopher or my daughter Opal named it… him, I think. While I've been here on the boat with you."

The boy tried out a few more heavy-handed pets on the goblin. At least as heavy-handed as a four-year-old could be when mostly drained of power. He dropped his gaze, staring at the water-covered floor.

I knew the moment my empathy reasserted itself, because I could feel a hint of the fear rolling off him.

No. Not fear. Self-loathing.

"I'm danger…" he murmured again, rocking slightly.

"No," I said firmly, not caring about how destroyed my voice sounded. "I'm dangerous." And then to prove my point, I stood up. I needed the edge of the bed to support myself once on my feet, but I remained upright.

He blinked up at me. "How?"

I leaned toward him, smiling. "I can take magic. Anyone's magic. I can take your magic. Also…" I feigned a shrug when he remained warily silent. "I'm strong and fast."

He didn't look at all convinced. "Lindi hurt you."

Nodding, I removed the backpack that had somehow remained on my back—slowly and painfully. I found the phone Christopher had put in the outer pocket. It looked intact, the facial recognition identifying me even with the slowly healing pustules that cracked and seeped when I spoke.

"I let Lindi take me," I said.

"Why?"

"Because I was protecting a bunch of people I love."

He scrunched his forehead.

Not understanding the word love.

One of those emotion-borne pains I had no defense against skewered my heart. I ignored it.

I opened the photo app on the phone, finding a recent picture of Opal with her arms wrapped around Paisley's neck. The demon dog was in her large blue-nosed pit bull form. The little dream walker was grinning widely enough to reveal her crooked eyeteeth.

The boy made it to his feet, dumping the cat on the floor as he crossed the few steps to my side. I lowered the phone so he could see what I was looking at.

He stared at the photo long enough that the cat jumped up on the bed, hissing and shaking water off his paws.

Finally, the boy looked up at me. I wondered if he'd noticed that Opal's skin was almost the same shade as his own.

"I have something else that makes me even more powerful," I said, my tone strong, even if ragged. "More powerful than whatever Lindi can do to me." I looked down at my arm, drawing the boy's attention to my healing skin. "More powerful than you."

"Dangerous," he whispered.

"Yes. Because I have people who belong to me, people to love, to protect."

He reached up for the phone, and I gave it to him. He cradled it in both hands.

"That's Opal. My daughter. And Paisley," I said. "They're waiting for me at home."

"Home," he whispered.

It wasn't a question, but I answered anyway. "Yes. Would you like to come meet them?"

"I hurt… you. I hurt… Opal?"

I knelt in the water next to him. His gaze remained riveted to the phone. "I can stop you from hurting anyone, ever again."

He trembled a little, meeting my gaze. "Lindi… tried… to stop me." He tugged at the neck of his gray T-shirt with one hand, turning slightly toward me.

The wound on his upper back, where Lindi had tried to adhere the blood tattoo, was healed over but bruised. The skin was completely darkened there, almost black. As if whatever magic Lindi had bound to him was dead.

I had no idea why it hadn't worked—since the Chemist was the architect of the original tattoos, as well as of our DNA. I presumed it had to do with the boy's power. The reason that there'd never been a sixth member of the Collective's super soldiers before him.

"I can keep the power that makes people sick at bay without hurting you," I said, hoping I wasn't lying. "We… my family and I… can help you learn to wield it."

A wave of panic rushed through him, and he dropped the phone.

I grabbed it before it hit the water, which was definitely higher than it had been before. The level was creeping up the boy's lower calves now.

More power pulsed out of him.

I was drained myself, barely on my feet, but I somehow managed to catch that involuntary casting.

And absorb it.

The boy's eyes widened, then dropped down to my exposed collarbone and arms. I followed his gaze, watching as more of the pustules healed on my arms.

"You?" he whispered. "Take?"

"Yes."

He rushed toward me in a stumble, reaching for me with both hands, and I swept him up in my arms. Crushing him to me as I straightened.

I tucked his head into my neck, under my chin. Then, as gently as possible, I sought out the plague-bringer power trying to reassert itself in him and pulled it to me, absorbing it for myself. Not to cast, but to build up my immunity further. Hopefully.

He gasped, but then pressed his head against me hard, as if trying to burrow under my skin.

I took all the plague-bringer power I could feel within him, slightly concerned that I was also stealing his healing abilities, but knowing I had to prove myself to him.

Prove I was more dangerous.

Footsteps in water approached, far down the hall. But I easily picked up the magic of the person approaching. My own power was slowly simmering back to awareness.

Lindi had gotten by Jason and Kevin, then.

She'd come for the boy herself.

I tried to settle him on the bed, but he fought against letting go of me. So when I swiveled to the door to confront the Chemist one last time, I did so with a four-year-old clutched to my chest.

No matter.

I didn't need hands to bring down Lindiwe Fourie.

I was already reaching out for her power before the doors had fully opened. She kept walking, her hand stretching out to touch me. She was disheveled with bloodstains on her clothing. From the fight with the Gen 4s, no doubt. The silk scarf was askew on her neck. She splashed through the calf-deep water a few steps before she stifled a groan. Before she realized what I was doing.

The boy lifted his head, watching his creator's arrival impassively.

My hold on her was weaker than I would have liked, so I reached for the hand that Lindi was attempting to grab me with.

"Oh, good," I said, making skin-to-skin contact—and absorbing the quelling spell she'd been trying to cast against me. "I'm going to need your magic."

The Chemist tried to rip her hand free from mine, struggling as I pulled more and more of her energy—her magic—from her.

The boy pressed the palm of his hand to the side of my neck, his arm still wrapped around me. Then he lifted the other hand toward Lindi, as if he was trying to feel what I was doing to her.

"The Collective are powerful," I said, speaking to the boy while I drained the Chemist. My voice was no longer ragged. "They'd have to be to try to control the likes of us."

"Stop... stop!" Lindi fell to her knees in the water, begging. Her arm twisted in my grasp, most likely painfully, when I didn't let go.

I leaned over a little so I could look her dead in the eyes. So the boy could look her in the eyes. "No."

"You need me..." she croaked. "Hel6... needs... you belong to me. Both of you."

"Give me a healing spell," I said, my tone flat and demanding. "For the boy. He's drained and hurt."

She tried to shake her head, to deny me, but I yanked harshly on the dregs of her power.

"A healing spell," I demanded again. "And I won't be the one to kill you."

I wouldn't have killed her in front of the boy anyway, but she didn't have to know that.

Lindi rallied, gathering the last of her power and feeding it to me with intention. She didn't take the opportunity to try to kill me. I could feel the gentle, calming energy of her magic rising under my hand. It wasn't malicious.

I released Lindi's hand. It fell limply as she listed to the side, barely catching herself on her other hand. Her entire body was trembling with the effort of holding herself partially up.

The water was well up my calves now.

The yacht had definitely sprung a major leak.

I pressed my hand to the boy's chest. He didn't try to stop me as I fed Lindi's healing power into him. His skin cooled, his eyes clearing.

Turning away from Lindi even as my system continued to absorb every last drop of the power I'd pulled from her, I set the boy on the bed. He let go of me this time, not making a sound. My arms and legs continued to heal as I stepped over to the cupboard and scooped up the small backpack that had been tucked in with the boy. It was heavier than it looked. I felt the hard edges of books within it as I slung it over the boy's back and helped him draw his arms through the loops.

He was distracted by my phone again, having scooped it up from where I'd placed it on the bed, but he couldn't figure out how to turn it on. Instead of taking it from him, I angled it to trigger the face recognition. It opened on the picture of Opal and Paisley. I showed the boy how to swipe right, then left, revealing photos of the house and Aiden in the garden.

The boy swiped the screen again, blinking down at a picture—a selfie—of Christopher and Opal.

"Family," the boy muttered.

"Yes."

He wrapped his hand around my wrist and tried to push his power into me. It didn't work, but I responded to the need, the concern behind the action. "I can take the power, every little bit of it. You won't hurt anyone else."

He looked down at the phone again.

I tugged on my own backpack, then scooped up the goblin cat and put him on my shoulder.

Lindi was sobbing quietly to herself, the water lapping at her waist now.

"I belong to you?" he asked quietly, not looking up from the picture of Opal. "Not Lindi."

"No," I said. "But you can belong with me, if you want."

He looked up at me, then down at the phone.

Ignoring the need to move, to snatch him up and run back to Aiden and the others, I forced myself to remain with him, to allow him this one moment. To allow him to make his own choices. But I couldn't wait much longer—and I wasn't sure I had the words that would convince him if that's what it came down to. Definitely not words a four-year-old plague bringer would understand.

He tapped the photo screen, then he tapped his chest. "Picture?"

I took the phone from him, opened the camera app, and held the phone toward him to take his picture. He grunted, letting me know I hadn't quite understood the need he couldn't articulate himself. He reached up, tapping the hand I was holding the phone with. "You. Me. Picture."

Understanding, I leaned against the bed and angled my face in front of the phone. The boy snuggled up next to me, staring up at the screen. My face was red and slightly pockmarked, but mostly healed. The damn cat, still perched on my shoulder, reared up on his hind legs and plopped his two front feet on the boy's head so that all three of us were now framed within the camera screen on the phone.

Surprise flitted over the boy's face.

And he smiled, laughing so quietly that it might have just been an expulsion of air.

I smiled, completely involuntarily.

Then I took our picture.

Straightening, I reopened the photos app on the phone and showed the boy the picture we'd just taken. "My first ever selfie," I said.

He gazed at the picture again, murmuring to himself quietly.

Because we needed to go, I took that exchange as assent, dumping the cat off my shoulder and stepping over to Lindi. "I'm going to need just one more thing from you, my maker," I purred.

She flinched, actually attempting to scramble back from me.

But I simply grabbed the end of her silk scarf, tugged it from around her neck, and turned my back on her for the last time.

One end of the scarf was wet, but it would do what I needed it to do.

The boy didn't protest when I took the phone, then carefully tucked it into his own backpack.

"What's your name?" I asked him gently, showing him the scarf.

"Hel6," he said.

"That's your designation. Mine used to be Amp5. But my name is Emma."

He nodded, but then pinched his eyebrows together.

"How about I call you Six?" I asked, tightening his shoulder straps. "Then you can decide later what you want your name to be."

He smiled tentatively. More copying my expression than a true emotional response, I suspected. But then he said, "Six. Okay." He touched the back of my hand. "Emma." He looked at the goblin cat and said, "Asshole."

I laughed, completely and utterly involuntarily.

Another of Six's quiet sounds—of joy?—threaded through my own amusement.

I scooped the seriously pissed-off cat up from the bed. His ears were pinned back, and he looked as though he was a moment away from taking a swipe at me as I dumped him on my shoulder. He dug in with his claws. "I think the cat prefers to be called Sweetness. Asshole is actually a... swear word."

"Bad word?"

"Some people think so." I held out the scarf, level with his eyes. "I'm going to put this on you."

He nodded, suddenly resigned as he grabbed the straps of his backpack and hunched forward protectively.

"Next time, you can blindfold me," I said.

"Yes?"

"Yes."

He nodded, more focused now.

"Do you…" I glanced over to Lindi, who was still pressed up against the wall and panting in pain. The fact that she hadn't passed out after being so thoroughly drained by me was a testament to the power of the Chemist. I hadn't expected anything less. It was just fortunate—for me—that my arrogance outweighed hers.

The water was near my knees now, and up to Lindi's ribcage. I cleared my throat, entirely certain I was doing everything wrong.

"Do you want to say goodbye to Lindi?" I asked.

Six stood up on the bed, beckoning me toward him. I stepped closer, and he leaned into me, his gaze shifting from one of my eyes to the other.

I was even less certain, completely uncertain, about what he was doing.

On my shoulder, the cat ducked and bobbed his head as if trying to get the boy's attention. But Six's focus remained fixed to me.

"Green…" he said quietly.

Emerald-green eyes.

"We have the same eyes," I said, tamping down on all my concerns—that Six was too young to make his own choices with any true understanding of consequences. That it might just be the binding of the botched blood tattoo drawing him to me. That he might have simply imprinted on me because he'd seen enough reflections of his own eyes to recognize our shared DNA. "Yes."

I could make him all sorts of promises—of a home, a family, of being taken care of, being loved—but he didn't have any context to understand those either.

I deliberately turned to look at the Chemist—my maker. Then, not understanding my own impulse to force the issue, I said, "Goodbye, Lindi."

Six cocked his head, following my gaze. He blinked down at Lindi as if he didn't really recognize her. Then he echoed, "Goodbye, Lindi," and looked back at me expectantly.

Ignoring the sour feeling in my chest that had nothing to do with magic and everything to do with not wanting to ruin a child's life any more than the circumstance of his creation had already done, I wrapped the scarf over Six's eyes, doubling it.

He didn't need to see what lay beyond the doors. He never needed to know how many people he'd hurt, he'd killed. In his panic.

Then I picked him up, cradling him against my chest. He wrapped his arms around my neck and laid his head on my shoulder.

My heart felt swollen and hot in my chest, pressing against, then overwhelming the sour concern I'd been fighting only a moment before.

A completely different sort of love, I decided. Yet another pain for me to weather, to endure, to embrace, and to celebrate.

"Let's go home," I whispered, turning my back on Lindi without another thought.

"Okay," Six whispered back, pressing his face into my neck as if once again trying to burrow under my skin.

ELEVEN

THE WATER WAS HIGH ENOUGH AS I STRODE TOWARD the medical-level exit, heading for the stairs, that the corpses strewn through the corridor had begun to float. The air-sealed doors on the lower levels were starting to make much more sense now.

But… how much water could a mega yacht take on before it actually sank?

I ended up just pushing forward, shoving my way through the floating dead—only to discover that Six's body count stretched up the stairwell. So I backtracked to the emergency egress. Despite the rising water level, the corpse in the room was still somehow blocking the doors from automatically closing. I simply yanked it out of the way and headed for the open panel.

Struggling to keep Six's head above water and the cat on my shoulder, I somehow managed to squeeze all three of us into the narrow confines of the chute. Then I started climbing the ladder, one-handed, all the way up to Lindi's suite.

As I crawled out into Six's closet, all of us soaking wet, the cat finally retracted his claws from my shoulder and back, then took off through the bedroom. Six pulled off his blindfold, looked around his room without any reaction, then wiggled in my arms until I set him down.

He offered me one end of the scarf. Not quite certain what was expected of me, I took it. Then he started to try to tie the other end around his neck.

"You are not a dog," I snapped before I could stop myself, grabbing his hands.

Six looked up at me, wide-eyed.

Scared to be separated from me? But wanting to walk on his own?

Understanding what he needed, I kneeled and tied the scarf around his wrist, then helped him do the same to my wrist.

I let him walk at my side, though I desperately wanted to scoop him back into my arms. We followed the goblin cat out into the hall, then into the grand room beyond.

Six's fingertips brushed mine when the kitchen and the eating nook came into view. But I assumed it was the sight of the large pool of blood and the two bodies that had disconcerted him. He was slightly too short to reach up and fully grasp my hand without me bending to the side, so I did so.

One of those bodies was Sarah.

Six didn't try to dart forward, though. His expression remained neutral. Watchful, even.

The goblin cat slipped through the partly open wooden doors, disappearing into the corridor beyond.

Kevin, the Gen 4 telekinetic, was sprawled across Sarah's lap. Sitting with her back against the wall, she had her hands wrapped around his neck. The blood wasn't all his. As I approached, I noted that the older security guy was down in the converted nook. The fact that his head was twisted the wrong way around instantly informed me that he'd died by telekinesis. Given the pool of blood, I wasn't sure whether he'd taken some other mortal wound as well before his heart stopped beating.

Lindi must have triggered Kevin's fail-safe after he'd killed her head of security, resulting in the massive neck wound that Sarah was still valiantly trying to heal, even though she appeared practically dead herself.

I crouched by Sarah. Six was a quiet, steady presence at my side. The healer's hands, wrists, and forearms were slicked in Kevin's blood. Unable to sense her magic, I reached out to touch the side of her neck.

She inhaled shallowly before I made contact.

"Not dead," I said, for Six's benefit. Kevin wasn't so lucky.

The plague bringer just grunted in acknowledgement.

It was possible I should have insisted he keep the blindfold on. Except I already knew, given my own so-called childhood, that Six was no stranger to death. To what he could do.

I reached for Sarah's magic with my senses again, still not able to feel even a hint of it. Healers occasionally killed themselves, gave too much of themselves. Sarah had put everything she had into trying to heal Kevin. Unsuccessfully. Since Bee had survived Lindi's fail-safe, it should have been possible for others to do so. But the Gen 4 telekinetic had been all but spent, even with my careful applications of amplification. Bee had had Aiden, as well as Khalid and Becca, to keep her stable enough to get her to a healer.

I gently removed Sarah's hands from Kevin's neck, then pushed him off her. She slumped to the side.

I hefted her over my shoulder, my other arm still tethered to Six, and straightened. I couldn't carry Kevin as well, and he wouldn't have wanted me to choose his corpse over the healer who'd drained herself trying to save him.

I'd barely known him, but I knew that much.

Six pressed his hand against my leg as I turned toward the heavy wooden doors at the main entrance.

"Not dead," he said.

"Yes, not dead."

THE OUTSIDE DECK LOOKED LIKE A WAR ZONE NOW. TO be expected, since Samantha was involved. But I was surprised and most definitely pleased that she hadn't managed to sink the yacht. Yet. Though the crack that completely bisected the deck, running down one side of the hull and groaning with every swell, made it clear what had caused the leak in the lower decks. A leak that was only going to get worse.

With Sarah limp and heavy over my shoulder, I hovered just beyond the door, not wanting to drag Six and the unconscious healer any farther without shielding. The helicopter and my team were still under fire, but the attacks were erratic, targeted to what appeared to be weak spots in the shielding. Indicating that only a few mercs were still fighting back, or they had limited ammo.

I pinned my gaze beyond the battle-scarred deck and met Aiden's blazing blue eyes. He was already running to me, Christopher tucked at his shoulder and a flickering blue mobile shield around them both. My deadly dark sorcerer was drained, after having not been wholly healed to begin with.

Tightening the circumference of his own waning shield, presumably in response to Aiden going mobile, Fish jumped into the helicopter, sliding in behind the controls.

Bee was slumped off to one side, bent over a body. Not Samantha.

Six's magic welled, then stuttered. An involuntary reaction, I thought. His power triggering to protect him from a new onslaught of the unknown— the new people and the discordant environment.

"That's Aiden," I said to him, touching his head gently. "And Christopher. You saw pictures of them on the phone. They're with us."

"Us," he murmured. He pressed his shoulder into my leg, but his attention was riveted to Aiden and Knox.

Aiden stumbled to a halt a few steps from me, his gaze settling on the boy and suddenly wary of approaching. Christopher didn't pause, already reaching for Sarah and pulling her off my shoulder and onto his.

An alarm sounded, loud enough to hurt my ears. Six slapped his hands over his own ears and shrieked. I picked him up, pressing one side of his head against my chest while covering his other ear with my hand.

"Time to abandon ship," Christopher shouted over the din, grinning maniacally. Then, completely unshielded, he jogged back to the helicopter with Sarah over his shoulder.

Even if he couldn't see his own future, the clairvoyant had always relied too much on his sight of others to parse his own mortality. It was always disconcerting to watch him doing so.

Samantha literally dropped out of the sky to my right, the deck cracking even more under her feet. "Whoops," she said, laughing madly. "Now it's really time to go." She dashed off toward the helicopter, shouting over her shoulder, "Don't worry, Socks. I left them the lifeboats... well, some of the lifeboats."

I realized the gunfire had stopped.

Aiden reached for me, touching me lightly on the shoulder and enveloping us in his shield. His gaze was on Six. I was already amplifying my dark sorcerer.

As I filled his reserves, the shield around us strengthened, and the blare of the emergency siren faded.

I released Six's head, and he looked at Aiden with a dispassionate gaze. "This is Aiden," I said. "Aiden, this is Six."

"You belong Emma?" the boy asked.

Even in the whispered question, Six's accent held too much of Lindi. Too much, because I wanted the boy to be mine. And only mine.

But none of us were a family because we were biologically related. So I shoved away the pain that I knew would only grow as I allowed myself to love the boy with emerald eyes like mine, and I looked to my dark sorcerer. Looked for him to anchor me, to make this transition smooth for Six.

"Yes. I am Emma's." Aiden leaned closer, sandwiching the boy between us to brush a tender kiss across my lips. "And she is mine."

Six nodded. "Family."

"Yes…" Aiden croaked through the emotion that was apparently clogging his throat as much as it was mine. "Let's get back home." He met my gaze. "Amanda needs you."

All the softness brought forth by the moment hardened in my chest. "And I told her not to need me," I said coldly.

Aiden flashed me a brilliant smile, and for a moment, all I could do was blink at him idiotically. Then he chuckled and reached for Six, waiting until the boy reached back. The sorcerer took Six from my arms, untying the scarf from around my wrist with a quick tug, then turned toward the waiting helicopter.

Six peered at me over Aiden's shoulder, and I forced myself to follow, forced myself to soften my face and smile—nicely. Not, you know, my supposedly toothy death glare.

"I'm right behind you," I said as we neared the helicopter, close enough for the whirling blades to play havoc with my hair. I stepped away from the comfort of Aiden's shield, crossing to Amanda, who was still slumped over the body I'd seen her with when I arrived on deck.

Leaning against a section of the railing that was miraculously still intact, Bee's yellow hair had fallen around her face. Her expression was vacant in a way that made me think she was reaching out with her mind, straining to talk to someone far away.

Except Jason, the Gen 4 telepath stretched across her lap, was beyond her reach. Beyond anyone's reach.

Excepting a necromancer, of course.

He was lying with limbs sprawled, as if Amanda had hauled him into her lap.

"Just leave me," she whispered, not bothering to acknowledge my presence any other way.

I ignored her, noting the gun still held in Jason's hand...

The back of his head was blown open. I frowned.

"Emma!" Samantha yelled over the sound of the helicopter fully powered up. "We need to go. Now!"

I glanced over to see her hanging half out of the copter's open side door. Aiden was there as well, holding Six so the boy could see me.

The yacht groaned.

The crack across the deck opened up a little more, at least a meter wide now.

"Emma!" Samantha snarled, frustrated and a little pained.

While it had been rather obvious that she had caused the slowly widening crack in the first place, it now became clear that the telekinetic was also holding the yacht together. A remarkable display of power and control. Not that I would ever say that out loud within her hearing.

"I told them to leave me," Amanda said tonelessly. "Lashed out… hurt them."

"Aiden?" I growled.

"No," she said.

I pulled Jason out of her lap without warning.

She screamed and hit me with the dregs of her power. I took everything she had to throw at me in one sharp yank, without even laying a finger on her.

She screamed a second time, then broke into sobs.

"It was me!" she shrieked in despair. "I… I felt the telekinetic die, and—"

"Kevin," I interrupted her. "His name was Kevin."

She blinked at me, so pale that she looked to be near death herself. The bandages on her neck were infused with fresh blood. The wound that should have already been healed was bleeding again.

"He… he told you his name…" Her gaze fell on the telepath. She shook her head, then clenched her fists. "Of course he told you! You weren't trying to... you weren't—"

"Forcing myself into his head."

"Yes!" Bee snarled. "I felt Kevin die, and I called to you, but I couldn't... you didn't come..."

"I was a little busy."

"Well, you always are, aren't you?"

"Yes. Including right now." I glanced over at Aiden and Six. They were both steadily watching me.

I would be judged by more than one person by how I handled this... situation. There hadn't been any pictures of Bee on the phone, but I had no doubt that Six could feel the connection between us—the blood binding of the tattoos etched into our spines—no matter how thin that tie currently was.

"We're going," I said, trying to keep my tone steady.

"He shot himself." Bee started to sob again. "Because I called him to me, because I invaded his mind... if only for that moment."

"Jason wasn't ever going to survive the death of his last remaining teammate."

"How do you know?" Bee snarled.

I crouched down, meeting her eye to eye. "Because neither would I."

"He... they... they aren't tied like we are..."

"No." I held out my hand to her. "Just accept that this was his final choice, for himself. And it was his choice, wasn't it? Because you could have stopped him. You could have forced him to obey you."

"But... he... I called him."

"And maybe he came to you because he wanted to see that you were okay. Or… he wanted to see the blue of the sky, feel the wind, just one last time. You remember, Bee. You remember what it felt like…" My voice cracked. "When we…"

She met my gaze steadily. And then…

I saw the moment she decided to believe. To believe my version of whatever the hell had gone on between them that had resulted in Jason putting a gun in his mouth and pulling the trigger.

"When we…" she whispered. "Made the choice. Our first choice."

"To die free."

She nodded.

"Are you with me?" I asked, echoing the vow we'd extracted from each other, however inadvertently, when we'd first escaped the Collective.

"To the end."

She settled her hand in mine. But when I helped her to her feet, she couldn't stand on her own. So I scooped her up, already amplifying her as I carried her back to the helicopter.

Christopher pulled Bee from my arms, passing her to Samantha. Then the clairvoyant pulled Six from Aiden's grasp as we all climbed aboard and tried to get belted in. The boy—the plague bringer—remained warily stiff in Christopher's arms, his emerald eyes fixed on me right up to the moment the clairvoyant deposited him back into my lap, and Aiden stretched the seatbelt to accommodate us both.

The yacht bucked underneath the copter. With a shouted warning, Fish got us up off the landing pad.

Aiden and Christopher scrambled, checking that everyone else was belted in. The goblin cat appeared out of nowhere—though he might actually have just been under the seats—to yowl indignantly at being tossed about. Christopher unceremoniously stuffed him in an empty backpack and thrust him at Samantha. Sarah was awake and strapped in beside the telekinetic, her tired gaze resting on Six in my arms. Across from me, Bee's head settled on Knox's shoulder the moment he sat next to her.

I saw the clairvoyant struggle to accept the contact from the telepath. His magic-free gaze fell on Six, who was quietly watching us all, before he nodded to himself and visibly made the choice not to push Amanda away.

I might have gotten the telepath who made the four of us the Five onto the helicopter. However, the other three were a long way from accepting her back into our lives.

I didn't blame them.

But as Fish flew us away from the now rapidly sinking yacht—with at least a dozen lifeboats scattered around it like specks among other debris—Aiden settled his hand on my knee, and I couldn't bring myself to feel anything but relief.

I WAS WRONG, AS IT TURNED OUT, ABOUT MY CAPACITY to feel. An occurrence that I wouldn't have minded repeating under the right circumstances.

Around the time that Fish sighted land, Six settled his hand on the back of mine where it was resting over Aiden's—my dark sorcerer still gripping my thigh.

The boy was playing with a runed copper ring. Aiden must have given it to him, along with a calming spell no doubt. Eyeing the three spent rings still on my fingers, then the single copper ring that still adorned Aiden's hand, Six tried slipping his ring onto each of his fingers. It was too big though, even for his thumb. His concentrated focus was so fierce that I could actually feel it through our near-constant empathic connection.

And that, I understood.

I understood mimicking behavior until figuring out how to be... well, not normal... but not a pure sociopath. Not just a killer.

I pressed a kiss to Six's head. He left the ring on his thumb, curling all his fingers in so it wouldn't fall off his hand. Then he burrowed into my arms. Huddled together, we two fell asleep with Aiden and my blood-bound siblings to watch over us.

Safe.

And on our way home.

TWELVE

A whisper of malignantly tainted magic drew me out from under Aiden's arm, which was heavy with sleep. I pulled on my silk robe, padding silently into the hall. The house was quiet and dark enough that I knew we were still sheltered in the deep of the night.

Aiden and I had only set foot on the property a few hours before, staying awake just long enough to wrap our arms around Opal and for the dream walker to meet the healer—the plague bringer—we'd brought home with us. Christopher, Samantha, Daniel, and the sullen Bee had managed not to outright murder Kader or Chenda at first sight, and I was thankful that Aiden's half-sister Ocean wasn't home to get caught in any crossfire. The young witch was doing her summer internship with Olive, the herbologist of the Godfrey coven.

I crossed the hall to my sitting room, finding Daniel sprawled out on his back across my small couch. The nullifier was clad only in blue plaid boxers and snoring quietly. The tattoo that bound me to him for life was a quiet simmer on my T1 vertebra. The couch was too narrow for Fish's bulky frame, and his head was canted at an awkward angle.

Bee was curled up in a tight ball on a blow-up mattress tucked under the curtained windows. Despite the warm night, she was practically cocooned in a striped wool blanket. Aiden had grabbed the mattress and blanket, still in their original packaging, from the attic, making me suspect he had an entire survival kit stored up there that I had no idea about.

The telepath's blood tattoo on my T2 vertebra was still a bare simmer. She had needed another intensive round of healing during our stopover in Johannesburg, which had been the primary delay in our return.

Aiden had called in one of the Azar cabal's private planes and kept the crew on continual standby. While we waited on Bee being stable enough to travel, I learned that Becca and Calhoun were on the mend, with Daniel contacting them to let them know I was safe. Until the nullifier told me, I hadn't even known that Mark had gotten wounded getting everyone strapped into the helicopter, then back to Norway. Aiden checked in with Khalid, safely back in France, to update him as well.

In between her rounds of healing, Bee had tried to reach out to Samantha, Daniel, and Christopher multiple times. Even while making sure she had everything she needed to heal properly, they barely acknowledged her presence.

I, of course, could still viscerally recall the moment she'd attacked Aiden. When she'd tried to murder my dark sorcerer, or at least severely incapacitate him. And I could forgive a lot. Hell, I'd forgiven Christopher for throwing me in front of a death curse.

But not that.

Daniel was also still so livid with the telepath that he wouldn't have been sleeping in the same room as Amanda, except it had become rather obvious that the other three had placed her under a rotating guard.

I wasn't getting involved in any of their games.

Still... I pressed the door open just enough to slip into the room, crossing to Daniel. Far more gently than I'd probably ever touched him before, I shifted his head back to center.

His eyes opened in slits, blazing with the bright white of his power, then closing the briefest of moments later. As if it was his magic that was assuring his safety under my hands while the nullifier continued to sleep deeply.

As we'd all made our way to bed after our arrival, and in a moment of uncharacteristic softness, Samantha had admitted that she'd never slept so soundly as she did just a door down from me. The same might have been true for Daniel.

Ignoring the door that led to Samantha's room, in which Chenda was currently residing—it was sealed with robust magic I could feel but not see—I crossed to the end of the hall and peered into Christopher's room. The clairvoyant was sprawled on his front, completely naked, his golden skin bathed in moonlight streaming in the open window. I took a few steps into the room, listening for that whisper of power that had drawn me from bed.

Nothing.

I tugged up the sheet that Christopher had kicked into a crumpled pile at the corner of the bed, pulling it over his lower half. I didn't have any issue with nudity, but we did have two children in the house. Plus I assumed that Chenda, who was leaning heavily into her self-appointed mother/grandmother role, might not want to accidentally stumble upon such a view.

"Socks…" Christopher whispered in his sleep.

When he didn't wake further, I backtracked down the hall, finding Paisley waiting for me at the door to Opal's room. I touched the demon dog lightly on the head, then gently ran a hand down her newly healed neck and shoulders. She raised her chin, stretching back against my touch and smiling at me with red-hued eyes.

I could practically taste the night air and the warm summer scent it carried emanating from her. She'd just returned from checking the perimeter of the property.

"All secure?" I asked teasingly. Even with all of us ensconced deeply in desperately needed sleep, no one would manage to come within steps of the outer boundary wards without us knowing.

Much to Aiden's chagrin, Kader had apparently spent the bulk of his babysitting time fortifying my dark sorcerer's wards. So much so that we'd had to enter the property one at a time when we'd returned. Samantha had been ready to murder both Kader and Chenda on sight simply for that perceived slight.

Paisley flashed a doubled row of teeth in my direction. Then she shoved past me and trundled into Opal's room. My little dream walker was curled up on the far side of the bed, facing the windows. Samantha hadn't bothered removing more than her boots, socks, and belt before apparently collapsing on the side nearer the door.

Paisley glared at the telekinetic, then looked at me and huffed.

"Have you been banished from the bed?" I asked quietly.

The demon dog snuffled offishly.

"Maybe if you didn't kick in your sleep…"

She pinned slitted red eyes on me, unamused. I rested my hand on the top of her head, reaching for any unusual power signatures in the bedroom. The tattoo that bound me to the telekinetic pulsed powerfully, underpinned with a seemingly boundless energy.

"Fuck off, Socks," Samantha muttered into her pillow, not otherwise moving a muscle.

The dream walker didn't stir.

And the impressive pillow fort Opal had built in the corner of the room—for Six—was empty.

As I'd already suspected. As I'd known. Because even without a blood tattoo to bind us, the plague bringer's power was slowly becoming embedded under my skin.

I swiftly crossed back into the hall and headed down the stairs, Paisley at my heels. I had drained Six so thoroughly on the yacht, after he'd already expended most of his magic himself, that not even a glimmer of that magic had reasserted itself. Yet.

The rest of the house was warm, dark, and empty.

The goblin cat was perched in the middle of the kitchen island. He swiveled his head, glancing over his shoulder and blinking his bulbous eyes—just once— at me before giving me his back again.

The cat had a spectacular attitude. Annoying enough that I might have banished the beast to the barn. Except Six had figured out that the little goblin, or perhaps all felines in general, was immune to his touch. And the four-year-old healer needed to volun- tarily touch someone other than me.

He needed to learn to trust himself before he could truly trust me.

Even though Aiden had held him in those last moments on the yacht, Six had refused to be held by anyone else in the aftermath. Not even Daniel, who wouldn't have been able to withstand the plague bringer when he'd unleashed the full extent of his power on the yacht, but who could certainly nullify it at the source while in contact with Six.

I really hadn't known what the hell I was doing with Opal, who despite her relatively young age, hadn't been a child when she'd found me. So I understood that Six needed all of us. All of the Five, plus Aiden, Opal, and Paisley. He was young enough that all of us, working together, might have some chance to help him live a full life. Without fear.

Paisley trundled toward the French-paned doors that led out to the back porch. The demon dog and goblin cat were in the refusing-to-acknowledge-each-other's-presence portion of their 'complicated relationship.' As Opal put it.

Ignoring the way my heart rate always ratcheted up every time I contemplated my childrearing ineptitude, I opened the fridge and pulled out a large container of milk.

That got the goblin cat's attention.

Another whisper of that malignantly tainted power brushed against my senses as I pulled a pot from the cupboard, set it on the stove, and poured in half the jug of milk.

As I retrieved three mugs—and one saucer—the cat stretched out across the kitchen island, dangling one paw off the edge of the counter. Then the creepy goblin began batting at the top of the lower cupboard.

A cupboard that normally housed Aiden's high-tech coffee maker, but which now also contained a four-year-old boy.

A boy who sought out tight spaces for a variety of reasons. Including segregating himself.

I stirred the milk, not wanting to scald it.

Samantha had been able to confirm Six's date of birth and medical history, from Lindi's records. After he'd taken out the security system to cover my movements, Fish had wiped all the Chemist's systems and hard drives. Just in case sinking the mega yacht hadn't been destructive enough.

And yes, the two of them had ignored Christopher's warnings and snuck into security after I'd gone in for the boy—somehow managing to restrain themselves from going after Lindi. Though, they hadn't known that she'd been fighting off the Gen 4 telepath and telekinetic at the far end of the upper deck at the time.

Aiden wandered into the kitchen, hair completely mussed and yawning widely. He'd thrown on a T-shirt over his boxers. The tag was sticking up at the back of his neck.

My heart did that squelching thing it did at every first sight of him. As if it actually hurt to love him so much. It didn't, though.

My dark sorcerer laid a warm hand on my hip, brushing a kiss across my eager lips before leaning over me to pull another mug out of the cupboard over my shoulder.

Opal appeared next, wearing sleep shorts and a tank top, and dragging her orange floral comforter after her. She pinned her brown-flecked blue eyes on me, as she had every waking moment since I returned, and hopped on a stool on the far side of the island.

Paisley instantly crossed to Opal's side, propping her front legs up on the stool next to the dream walker and leaning against her shoulder.

Swiveling slightly to wrap one arm around Paisley's neck, Opal laid her head on the counter, keeping her gaze still fixed to me. She hummed contentedly.

My heart was in a hard twist now.

Aiden plucked a fifth mug out of the upper cupboard, placing all the mugs beside the goblin cat. The little creep acknowledged the sorcerer just long enough to receive tribute in the form of pets and murmured praise, then went back to batting at the top edge of the lower cupboard.

"Chocolate?" my little witch asked, laying on the sweetness.

Sliding his hand across my back before stepping away, Aiden crossed to the pantry and retrieved some of the expensive chocolate Christopher reserved for baking from the topmost shelf. As if a shelf well out of her physical reach was any real deterrent to a witch.

Opal wrinkled her nose. "Needs sugar too."

Quashing a smile, Aiden retrieved the sugar. Then he took over stirring the now-hot milk from me, working with one hand to add the chocolate. The other hand, he kept around my waist, holding me tucked next to him.

He and I hadn't stopped touching each other since I'd brought Six to him on the yacht, but we also hadn't been alone. No time for restorative sex, or the conversation—the argument—I knew the sorcerer was still holding back.

Swapping the wooden spoon for a whisk, Aiden frothed up the hot chocolate, then poured it unsweetened into three of the five mugs. He added sugar to the remainder in the pot, whisked it some more, and poured two more mugs. Turning off the burner, he then dropped the pot into the sink, pouring some water and a squeeze of soap into it.

I set a sweetened hot chocolate in front of Opal, and one of the unsweetened mugs in front of Paisley. Then I poured a bit of milk from the jug into the saucer, setting it on the floor near the lower cupboard that the little goblin had been batting at. I scooped the cat off the counter and set him down as well. He yowled snottily in protest, of course.

Aiden shut off the water, grabbed his unsweetened mug, and leaned back against the counter.

I set the second sweetened hot chocolate right next to the lower cupboard, close enough to reach from within but not close enough to knock over as the cupboard door opened.

Then I took my own mug and leaned back. Even though hot chocolate wasn't my favorite, I enjoyed the warmth cupped in my hands.

We just looked at each other, Aiden and me gazing at Opal and Paisley, and them gazing back at us. Smiling almost gently, almost… carefully. As if more emotion would destroy the moment.

A moment of all of us together, relatively whole, relatively grounded. And… on the verge of something new.

The goblin cat was purring madly, lapping at the milk in his saucer like a fiend.

Opal giggled quietly, taking a sip from her mug. A single black tentacle whipped out from Paisley's neck to curl around the handle of her own mug. The demon dog raised it almost primly to her mouth—then tried to lap up the entire contents of the mug with her forked blue tongue.

The hot chocolate spilled. Everywhere.

Opal giggled, bright and sweet.

Aiden leaned heavily on my shoulder, relaxed and at peace.

And the cupboard door opened. Just enough for small feet to settle on the floor, and small hands to reach for the waiting mug.

I worried, just for a moment, that the mug would be too heavy. But Aiden hadn't filled it all the way, and Six easily dragged it into his lap, pressing it between his knees. Still not looking up at me, he leaned over to smell the warm drink.

Aiden's hand curled into mine.

Paisley scoured the splattered hot chocolate from the island counter with her tentacles, downing the rest of her mug. Then she began eyeing Opal's mug, still full.

Grinning and giggling at the demon dog's antics, Opal made a show of pivoting away and leaning as far as she could without toppling off the stool. The pure, sleepy joy radiating from the dream walker filled the moonlit kitchen.

And a tiny section of my shredded soul somehow—impossibly so—wove itself back together.

THREE DAYS LATER.

Dressed in black jeans and a formfitting black tank top, Samantha marched into the kitchen, crossing through to the eating area without sparing me a glance. Pushing one chair aside with a touch of her power, she unrolled a large swath of paper across the table. Daniel, in shorts and a T-shirt, barely managed to lift his empty cereal bowl and full coffee mug before losing them.

Six, who had declined clothing in favor of his teddy bear pajamas, slipped into the kitchen in Samantha's wake. Literally. The telekinetic practically streamed power behind her these days. It was possible that I had overamplified... well, everyone... after they'd all been so badly drained.

Six had been playing under the dining room table. Well, his own version of playing, which involved a lot of the picture books he'd carried with him from the yacht being assembled into structures rather than read. New picture books, including any child-friendly magical texts Aiden could source, arrived daily, and we'd made a game of unpacking those new books during afternoon tea.

Six tucked himself around my side of the kitchen island, narrowing his emerald eyes at Samantha past the barrier of my legs. Though he presumably couldn't see much from his low vantage point.

I placed a sugar-rolled ginger snap on a parchment-lined cookie sheet while Daniel grumbled at Samantha. The first batch of cookies was already cooling.

Amanda, wearing a blue-printed sundress pur-loined from my closet—it was slightly too long but not as loose on her petite, curvy frame—appeared at the opening to the hallway, hovering with her gaze flicking around the kitchen.

"Horses!" Samantha declared. Then she stabbed a finger at what appeared to be architectural drawings.

"Jesus," Fish muttered, standing up to peer down at the diagrams she'd unrolled. "I thought you were joking."

"Nope," she said, grabbing his empty bowl to secure one corner of the plans. He dodged her attempt to grab his coffee and secure another corner.

Samantha huffed, then pressed the other three corners down with a touch of her telekinesis, one at a time. That was a new and impressively well-honed application of her notoriously destructive power.

"Did you know," Samantha gushed enthusias-tically, "that you can purchase custom-made plans? Like, see?" She gestured to specific areas of the drawings. "Four-bedroom ranch house, barn, horse paddocks—"

"Seriously, Zans?" Daniel asked. "You want to breed fucking horses?"

Samantha huffed again. "I told you!"

"I thought that was one of those I-almost-died things."

Samantha gave him an indignant look. "How many ranches would I already own if it was tied to near-death experiences?"

"Come on…" Daniel looked to me. "Emma?"

"It's Opal's land," I said neutrally.

"But…" Fish trailed off, then looked at Zans with a completely different unvoiced question.

She nodded. "We're leasing from the baby witch. We're staying."

The nullifier's eyes narrowed on me. But before he could say whatever he was planning to say, Samantha slapped her hand over his mouth and tugged a smaller set of plans out from the other drawings. "I've ordered this already." She pushed the papers at him.

He blinked at them dumbly. "Another house?"

"It's one of those prebuilt units. They had an order fall through. I paid a bonus for quick delivery. It'll be here next week. We just need to find a builder to help us get it together. So we can live on the property while the main house is being built."

Daniel opened his mouth again, but Samantha interrupted him once more. "We're not staying at the farm full time. Bee will live here until we have more room, then she'll take over the prefab house."

"Under continual guard," Amanda muttered, speaking for the first time in days. At least within my hearing.

Samantha acknowledged the telepath—barely—with a shrug of her shoulders, all her attention on the drawings and her mind on her plans. "You'll figure out it's better to have your own space, near me and Daniel, than remaining under Socks's roof. She and her dark sorcerer are exuberant in their affection."

Still hovering in the doorway to the front hall, Amanda folded her arms across her chest and leaned against the wall, not otherwise commenting.

Six pressed his hand to my thigh.

I glanced down at him—surreptitiously, I hoped—trying to get a look at the still-healing botched blood tattoo at the base of his neck. The bruising was still fading, thankfully. No signs of infection.

"Horses?" he asked quietly.

"Do you want to see?"

He nodded tentatively, then he held his hand up to me. "Take."

I crouched in front of him, taking his hand but not pulling out his power. "You know you can't hurt us. Any of us. Unless you really want to."

"Take," he said, his voice thickening with emotion. He pushed his power at me, all of it—the healing and the malignancy as well. It was only the tiniest of trickles, because he'd been making me absorb that power daily since he'd figured out how to ask me to do so.

Blisters rose across the back of my hand as I allowed his magic to touch me, rather than simply absorbing it. Six flinched and tried to pull away. I held onto him as gently as possible. Then I said, "Now heal me."

He shook his head, brow deeply furrowed. "Take. Take, Emma."

I smoothed my free hand down his arm, allowing the blisters to heal on my hand. Then I took the whispers of his power.

He huffed, shifting his feet. "Tickles."

I smiled at him, straightening and retrieving a ginger snap from the cooling rack. I pressed the cookie into his hand.

"Get me one of those, squirt," Daniel said.

Fish, Amanda, and Samantha each had their attention riveted to the boy throughout our exchange.

I gave Six a second cookie, and he hesitantly carried it over to Daniel. The nullifier swept the boy up into his arms without asking. But before Six could react, Fish grabbed his hand and took a bite out of one of the cookies the boy held with a playful growl.

"Mmm," Daniel said, peering at Six in his arms as he made a show of chewing. "Tasty."

Six took a tentative nibble at the other whole cookie, blinking a little at the intense flavor. Then, after squeezing his lips together for a moment, he looked over at Samantha. "Horses?"

"Let me show you where they'll live." Samantha reached for him. And for the first time that I'd witnessed since Aiden had held him on the yacht, Six reached out his arms, willing to be transferred into the telekinetic's grasp. "I have pictures on my iPad, too. We'll look at those next."

Amanda wordlessly crossed farther into the kitchen, slipping onto one of the stools on the other side of the island to watch me hand-roll the next batch of cookies.

"These are pictures—outlines, really—of what the horse stable and paddock will look like," Samantha said. Six leaned way over in her arms, following her hand gestures and getting cookie crumbs all over the drawings.

"Is there a workshop at least?" Daniel asked.

"What do you think the barn is for?" Samantha huffed. "And we can make additions and revisions to the plans before breaking ground."

"Like… space for an additional sorcerer?" Fish narrowed his eyes at Samantha, presumably referring to Khalid.

She shrugged one shoulder. "We'll see how well he follows up first."

"Because two Azars aren't enough," Daniel muttered.

Without warning, Six straightened in Samantha's arms and pressed the previously bitten cookie against the nullifier's lips.

Though it took Daniel a moment to figure out how to react, he grinned, then pretended to eat Six's fingers along with a hunk of cookie.

Six looked at me. For approval, as if I were his… keeper. But actually smiling. Not just mimicking our expressions back to us.

My chest and heart flushed with a heavy emotion that I steadily ignored as I smiled back at him.

Then Six chomped at his own cookie playfully, spewing crumbs everywhere. And… he giggled. That sound that was still just a barely modulated expulsion of air, but it was a giggle.

Samantha ducked her head.

Daniel swallowed harshly.

Amanda tilted her head, gaze steadily trained on Six. And her expression was tinged with… hope.

Then they all looked at me. To me. All with that same bit of open… hopeful… emotion reflected in each of their gazes.

Another tiny section of my shattered soul wove back together.

"ANOTHER FUCKING BLOOD TATTOO IS NOT THE answer," Aiden snarled at his father, pacing the length of the front sitting room. He was in jeans and a T-shirt, despite Kader's continuing presence in our lives.

The elder sorcerer, sitting on the loveseat nearest the front window, made no reaction other than to brush a piece of nonexistent lint from his knee. He was wearing one of his beige linen suits and looked far more rested than he had during our video call.

"Then put a block on his power," Chenda said, not looking up from the hand-painted tarot cards she was gently shuffling. Wearing a black raw-silk sleeveless dress, and with her white-blond hair smoothed back into a complicated bun secured with gold chopsticks, the Mystic of the Golden Peninsula was sitting on the opposite loveseat, facing Kader. Though the two elders rarely acknowledged the other's presence, let alone traded opinions.

I was also fairly certain that the chopsticks were more weapons than hair accessories.

"Absolutely not!" Aiden huffed.

"The boy is scared of his magic," Kader said mildly.

"You've barely been in the same room as him." In black shorts and a T-shirt, Daniel stood in the doorway to the hall, arms crossed and legs spread— and not so subtly blocking one of the sitting room's two exits.

"The amount of the boy's power simmering from Emma tells me enough." Kader's tone was mild, but measured.

"It's you who are blocking our access to the boy," Chenda added.

"It's too much," Christopher said, scrubbing a hand across his face. He had managed to pull on light-washed blue jeans and nothing else after spending all day in the garden, cooking dinner, then showering. "And it would be one thing if Socks could absorb enough of the healing to be able to cast it—"

"My magic doesn't work like that," I interrupted, leaning back in the doorway that opened into the dining room behind me. This was the third time our self-appointed elders had invited themselves into a conversation I wasn't all that interested in having.

Christopher opened his mouth to interject. I cut him off again.

"Six is not a project," I snapped. "He's not an experiment."

"He will grow to trust us," Aiden said, pausing his pacing.

"Opal," Chenda said, setting her tarot deck on the arm of the couch with her hand resting over it.

Kader nodded, actually looking at the mystic in agreement. "Opal."

"Six is not going to hurt…" I trailed off.

They all looked at me, silent but concerned. Even Aiden.

Fish cleared his throat. "He's comfortable with me… getting comfortable with me… he could come with me when—"

"No," I said. "I offered him a choice."

"He's four!"

I pinned my gaze to Daniel. "Like when we were four?" I said quietly.

The nullifier clamped his mouth shut, tension running through his neck and bleeding into his already-stiff shoulders. Then he rounded on Kader and Chenda. "If it were up to me, you'd both be bleeding out in the garden, not sipping tea in the parlor."

"You've made that abundantly clear," Kader said coolly.

Chenda clucked her tongue. "That much blood? It would ruin Christopher's garden."

The clairvoyant barked out a laugh, seemingly surprising himself.

Daniel snarled, then turned on his heel and into the hall. He slammed through the front door, striding out into the night.

"Although," Chenda said, her head tilted slightly, "tea does sound good. Emma?" She glanced over her shoulder at me. "Something that won't keep us awake?"

"That chocolate mint from Christopher's garden was lovely," Kader said. "And… a few cookies?"

Aiden frowned, his lip curling into a vicious sneer. But before he could tear into Chenda and his father for giving me orders, I shook my head at him, pivoting back toward the kitchen. I wasn't interested in the endless chatter anyway. I didn't view anything about Six as a problem that needed solving.

The plague bringer was tucked into the glass-fronted china cabinet. The door was closed, but I could see him clearly through the glass. He had two of his books shoved in the narrow space with him, and was playing with a trio of small, smooth stones. Six had chosen the stones himself during a walk around the property after breakfast. Aiden had chalked a healing rune onto each stone, talking Six, Opal, and Paisley—of course—through the process.

Yes, even drained of his magic, Six could easily sneak around me. And all around the house.

Instead of simply crossing through into the kitchen and hoping that the plague bringer followed, I walked over and tapped gently on the glass of the cabinet. "Come. I'm making some tea."

He blinked up at me, but made no move to exit.

I straightened, then crossed slowly through to the kitchen. Just as my front foot hit tile, I heard the china cabinet door click open behind me.

I smiled. Unable to contain my joy in response to that tiny little… acceptance? At least not without allowing the almost painfully wide expression to etch itself across my face, knowing… knowing that I was changing within even as Six was growing into his new life.

And it had nothing to do with absorbing magic and becoming ever more powerful.

I WASHED MY FACE, THEN RAN A BRUSH THROUGH MY hair. Taking my time, though I normally barely bothered to look at myself in the mirror in the morning. Taking my time because Six was watching me over the lip of the bathtub, mostly tucked behind the shower curtain.

He was dogging my steps more and more as days passed, absorbing everything happening around him from the confines of various hiding places. He always went to bed dutifully in the nest that Opal had built him in her room. But at some point in the night, he curled up next to me, his sharp spine nestled into my back or side. Just as he'd done in the yacht, when I'd inadvertently stolen enough of his magic to stave off death one more time.

That morning, I'd woken curled around Six, with Aiden curled around me. The goblin cat—who was currently in the otherwise empty bathtub with Six—had been sleeping in a tangled nest of my hair. After kicking the cat off the bed, I had ignored Six when he'd snuck into the bathroom after me.

Samantha had joked that the boy had imprinted on me. None of us in the room at the time had found that funny, so she snarled and stomped away to play with her horse ranch plans.

But she wasn't wrong.

Six's continual observation of me felt weighted with too much responsibility. And a pile of frustration at my own inability to help him through his transition. I wanted it to go faster, smoother, with less residual scarring to his psyche.

That observation also made it exceedingly clear that regardless of the circumstances of our creation and subsequent training, someone among the Collective had understood correctly that five of us would function more effectively than a single uber-powerful super soldier.

Given their current clingy behavior, I now suspected that Kader and Chenda had contributed heavily to that specific aspect of their breeding program.

From what I'd witnessed, Lindi had treated the Gen 4s as little more than weapons who could walk and talk. And it seemed unlikely that she'd actually allowed them to talk, or to otherwise express their opinions, all that much.

And with Six… the bedroom on the yacht, the dust-covered toys. That had all been performative somehow. For the benefit of her employees?

We had left Sarah in Oslo. Left her to recover her own magic, and walked away with Six. She had forced her contact information on Daniel, the only one of us who would accept it. But at the last minute, I'd taken a picture of her with Six. Just sitting side by side on a bed. I didn't know if I was ever going to show it to him, but… maybe he would need to see it someday?

Sarah could have walked away with Six years before she'd helped me escape from the stasis chamber. She knew. She'd seen through Lindi's—

I set my hairbrush down and shoved those thoughts out of my head. Rehashing the past was never helpful.

I crossed back out into the bedroom, hearing the rustling of the shower curtain behind me. Aiden was awake but still sprawled across the bed, his sleepy gaze resting on me for a moment before flicking behind me to take in Six.

I pulled on fresh underwear beneath my robe—yes, we were all sleeping at least partially clothed for the time being—then tugged a sundress out of the closet. Facing the closet, I dropped the robe, pulled off my T-shirt, and quickly slipped the sundress over my head. The bodice was stretchy, so I didn't need a bra.

The sound of a drawer being opened drew my attention to my high bureau. The bottom drawer had been empty the last time I'd bothered to look. Six pulled a neatly folded T-shirt and shorts from its depths. He sat down and changed out of his pajamas—folding them and tucking them back in the drawer—with the same efficiency as I had done.

While Six was getting dressed, the goblin cat wandered out of the bathroom, then hopped into the bottom drawer.

"Gus," Six said, making a show of shaking his head at the cat while grinning. The cat was apparently named Gus now, not Sweetness. Or Asshole.

Aiden, fighting a smile, slipped out of bed and crossed into the bathroom, pausing to brush a kiss against my cheek and tousle Six's hair.

The plague bringer didn't flinch away or avoid Aiden's touch.

"What are your plans today?" my dark sorcerer asked, leaving the door to the bathroom open.

Six slipped around the edge of the bureau and snuck a peek into the bathroom, watching Aiden pee. The goblin cat, Gus, jumped cleanly out of the drawer to follow suit.

It was my turn to quash a smile. "We're going to pick out some furniture for Six's room."

Six pivoted back toward the still-open drawer, slowly pulling a long scarf from it.

Lindi's scarf.

I had tucked it into Six's backpack on the helicopter, but he must have hidden it in the house somewhere, because I hadn't been the one to pull it out.

He held the scarf across both of his hands, then lifted his gaze to me.

Aiden leaned against the doorway to the bathroom, brushing his teeth.

"Is it my turn?" I asked Six.

The boy nodded, and I knelt before him.

Aiden frowned. "Emma?"

I just smiled up at him, then returned my attention to Six. "First, you fold it."

Six laid the silk scarf out on the floor. Then, needing to step back and forth to do so, he carefully folded it until it was narrow enough to lie across my eyes.

Even kneeling, I was too tall for him to blindfold me properly, so I lay down, facing up with the back of my head positioned on the scarf. Gus came to investigate, tickling my neck with his whiskers. Remembering I was supposed to be modeling good behavior, I resisted the urge to shove the goblin cat away.

Abandoning his toothbrush, Aiden crouched beside Six, carefully not touching him. "Do you want to wrap it twice?"

Six nodded solemnly, picking up one end of the scarf. I closed my eyes. Offering minimal guidance, Aiden helped Six get the scarf secured across my face.

"Now, Emma," Aiden said pointedly. "Can you see anything?"

I sat up, carefully holding the scarf over my eyes in case it slipped. It didn't. "A little bit of light around the edges," I said.

"What do you think?" Aiden asked Six. "Is a little light okay?"

"Yes," Six said, quiet but decisive.

"Do you have your healing stones?" Aiden asked.

A bit more movement and rustling occurred, then Aiden spoke again. "Put them in your pocket. Good, good. Now if Emma gets scraped up today, you can help heal her."

Six didn't respond. And that was okay. Aiden was just trying to normalize the idea for the boy.

"What?" I gasped playfully. "You aren't going to carry me? I carried you!"

Six giggled. The sound reserved, almost unsure, but it was still a laugh.

Aiden laughed more robustly.

I held my hand out to Six, rising to my feet after he took it. Then I allowed him to lead me around the upper floor of the house, entering each room.

By the time we made it downstairs, I realized what Six was doing, beyond the obvious trust game. He was using me as an excuse to check on or interact with the others, out in the open, rather than just sneaking around and spying on all of us.

Kader was in Aiden's study. I picked up the scent of the chai tea the elder sorcerer favored in the mornings more than his skillfully masked magic.

"Good morning," Kader said as Six tugged me—still blindfolded—a couple of steps into the room. "Emma. Six. And... hello Gus."

Apparently, I was the only one who hadn't gotten the goblin cat's name-change announcement.

"What are your plans for the day?" Six asked the elder sorcerer. Perfectly mimicking Aiden.

The muscles in my chest, centered on my heart, pinched so tightly that I actually pressed my free hand against my ribcage and had to stifle a gasp.

Kader didn't miss a beat. "I'm answering some messages from contacts right now. But then I think I'll work a bit on some spell building. I'm intrigued by Aiden's pentagram in the loft. Have you seen it?"

Six's nod was exuberant enough that he tugged at my hand slightly.

"Well, imagine taking the clever combination of components built into that, but in mobile casting."

Papers shuffled, and Six leaned forward to look at whatever Kader was showing him. Presumably a sketch of the pentagram.

"And what are your plans for the day?" Kader asked politely.

"I'm with Emma," Six declared. "And... furniture."

"Delightful. But perhaps some breakfast as well?"

Six thought about that for a moment, then nodded.

"Let's head to the kitchen, then." Kader stood, moving close enough that I finally picked up the muted tenor of his immense power.

"You... you're Opal's grandpa," Six said.

"Yes."

"And… I'm Opal's… brother."

"Yes."

I stiffened against another explosion of emotion through my chest, struggling to not tense my fingers in Six's grip.

"So… you… my grandpa?"

"Yes." Kader's tone was steady and sure. He touched my elbow lightly, then added, "I would be honored."

"Okay," Six said. Then he was tugging me back out into the hall and toward the kitchen.

Kader followed behind.

A moment after my feet exchanged hardwood flooring for ceramic tile, Six squealed so quietly it was almost a whisper. "Waffles?!"

Christopher laughed from deeper within the kitchen. "That's what you said you wanted."

Seeming to suddenly remember that he still had me blindfolded, Six tugged firmly on my hand. I got the message and crouched before him. He pushed the blindfold up off one of my eyes. "Waffles, Emma. Like in my book."

"Yes," I said, my insides all uselessly mushy. "Shall we help set the table? We can play more after breakfast."

A DAY LATER.

Barefoot, I slipped up the wooden stairs that led to the barn loft. Despite the warmth of the day, I'd closed the main doors of the barn behind me. Aiden hadn't bothered with any of the lights, so the space was currently lit only by the slashes of sunlight pouring in from the upper windows. The dust spiraling within those golden beams seemingly mimicked the anxious churning of my stomach.

Yes, I was nervous.

Idiotically so, I knew. But I'd put off this conversation with my dark sorcerer for so long that I actually didn't know how to broach it anymore. And... I desperately didn't want to fight, didn't want to justify my actions.

I didn't want to be held accountable.

Aiden pinned me with blazing blue eyes the moment I came into sight on the stairs. That gaze, filled with magic, raked down me. And his lips twisted into a tight smile.

The sundress I'd put on that morning was almost identical to the one I'd been wearing the very first time I'd come to him while he'd been in his pentagram, with buttons running up the center. The original dress had been trashed in the demon attack that had interrupted us then, and I was seriously hoping that no such interruption was going to present itself now.

Aiden was sitting cross-legged in the pentagram he'd etched in copper into the wide, white-painted planks of the floor. Since we'd returned home, he'd added another layer to it, another edging around the main pentagram—runes that I couldn't read. And he had a platinum ring set in the center of each point of the main pentagram. The five smaller pentagrams centered on each point, with a carnelian gemstone in the heart of each, weren't currently being fueled or utilized.

He was replacing the copper rings he'd lost on mission. Only five remained.

"Six?" Aiden asked, almost gently.

"He's napping, along with your father, on the front porch. Chenda, Christopher, and Opal went to the farmers' market with Paisley. Samantha, Daniel, and Amanda are at the other property, going over plans."

Aiden raised his eyebrows. "Christopher voluntarily left the property? With Chenda?"

I smiled stiffly. "I think... he didn't want Opal alone with her."

"And you need to be here, with Six." He smiled again. But still tight lipped and twisted.

I leaned back against the railing, hands clasped on the top rail, and feeling like... like... so much distance had spread between us. Even as close as I stood to him now, I could feel this yawning chasm—

Aiden frowned. "Emma?"

"Are you punishing me?" I blurted.

He blinked. The magic dimmed in his eyes. "Punishing—"

"... by withholding sex?"

He stared at me for a moment. A myriad of emotions flickered across his face too quickly for me to read or pick up empathically.

My chest was starting to hurt. He made as if to speak, but cutting him off for the second time, I just kept talking. "Christopher said… he said… at the compound when you were so badly hurt—"

"What did Christopher say?" Aiden's tone was suddenly low, darkly tinted as he rolled to his feet, still within the pentagram. His expression was almost blank, but not in that thoughtful, considering way of his…

More as if he was holding something back.

Masking some terrible truth.

The compression restricting my chest worsened. Logically, I knew that all I had to do was inhale, deeply and fully, to loosen it. But taking that breath suddenly felt beyond me, beyond my abilities.

"If this is what's holding you away from me," Aiden said quietly, "we need to discuss it… I want—" He cleared his throat. "I always want you. Rather desperately."

"But…"

"I thought it was simply that there were too many people in our house."

"It's not like we ever needed a bed before, sorcerer," I snapped. But I felt my cheeks flushing as I realized I'd been acting on an assumption rather than fact.

Aiden prowled toward me. His feet were as bare as my own. He cleared the edge of the pentagram, leaving the fueling spell in place. "What did Christopher say to make you surrender yourself at the compound instead of fighting?"

"That you would survive. That you would live. And I asked him. He didn't just offer it up as an option."

The sorcerer took another step toward me, raking a molten-eyed gaze over me again—then pinning me in place with one of his soul-binding looks. And a sharp smile. "And when you asked him to look into the future..." His tone became clipped, strident. "Before you sacrificed yourself, what did he say of the consequences?"

So much emotion was rolling off Aiden that I was having a hard time feeling my way through it. Anger, yes. But much more utter frustration and... fear...

So much bottled-up fear.

"I almost lost you," I whispered.

"What did he say?"

"I was watching you die!"

He closed the space between us abruptly, grabbing the railing on either side of me and pressing as close as he could without touching me. Looming over me.

"Tell me, Emma, so I can counter it."

"He said you'd be angry. Angry enough to call off the wedding."

Tension ran through Aiden's jaw and neck. His shoulders were stiff. His gaze was unrelenting.

"You are embedded underneath my skin, Emma. Twisted through my heart, imprinted into my brain, woven through my soul. I would have you... want you... love you... through death and beyond."

I breathed. Deeply, fully. The pain across my chest finally loosened. "But... you've been so angry since I returned. And I've been—"

"I'm sorry you felt that any of that was directed at you."

"The… situation? You don't want—"

"I want you. I want this life. I will adapt to my father being part of it."

"But… no sex?"

He flashed me a wide grin. "You haven't been exactly handsy yourself, amplifier. It isn't like you to not simply take what you want."

I huffed. "It's a little difficult with Six following… me… everywhere…"

Understanding, then chagrin, flushed through me. The second emotion was a new and uncomfortable one. "The wards…"

"We can't even close the bedroom door right now, Emma." Aiden leaned close enough to whisper across my lips. "And Six needs to be able to see you, even be within arm's reach, right now. I'm not so selfish to begrudge him that, to take you away from him, even to tear one off."

Grinning at his euphemism, I touched his jaw gently. Aiden hadn't started shaving again. Just as he hadn't gone back to wearing his fortified suits, even with his father still in residence.

A completely different sort of warmth flushed through me. "Remember the first time, sorcerer?" I asked, my hands falling between us to unbutton the middle section of my dress. Just in case he needed a visual reminder.

"We were interrupted." He pouted playfully. But then he lowered himself to his knees, still not touching me.

I let my half-unbuttoned dress hang open, and Aiden caught the edges to peel it back, exposing my lacy, pale-pink panties and the faded scars still slashed across my abdomen.

My dark sorcerer looked up at me. His expression was filled with want and need, though he was careful not to touch me skin to skin. Waiting for permission, as he'd done the first time we'd hovered in this moment together. "Emma…"

I smiled and breathed his name. "Aiden."

He chuckled. "Emma."

I completed the claiming section of our dance. "Aiden."

He tucked my dress behind me, holding it bunched together in one hand at the small of my back. And then he traced the scars Silver Pine's greater demon had scored into my flesh with his fingertips. Not quite touching, but close enough for me to feel the heat of his skin. And a prickle of his magic.

I moaned quietly with knowing… knowing what being with Aiden was like, how it was between us—and anticipating that now.

That first time, I'd had no idea what the bright, sharp attraction between us actually was.

I unbuttoned the rest of my dress.

"What would you have done then, sorcerer?" I asked, husky and teasing. "Had we not been interrupted?"

Aiden flashed me a wicked, playful grin. Then he released my dress, curling the fingers of one hand around my ankle while settling his free hand on my hip.

As he leaned in to brush kisses across my scars, somehow sexy yet reverent at the same time, I threaded my fingers through his thick, silky hair, scratching his skull lightly. He trailed his fingers from my ankle up my leg in an almost painfully slow caress, pausing to swirl his fingertips at the back of my knee.

Sensation shot through me—an aching awareness of how vulnerable that section of my leg was, coupled with a flood of heated, aching desire.

"Too slow, sorcerer," I moaned, on the edge of begging but also not wanting to rush.

He laughed. "You asked what I would have done. If we'd been together the way I ached to be with you even then."

He had my panties around my ankles, then one of my legs over his shoulder before I could work out another response. One hand still pinned my hips back against the railing.

He paused there, just looking at me, at my core, then dipped his nose into the red curls at the apex of my legs and inhaled deeply.

More heat flushed through me, and my grip in his hair tightened.

He teased the backs of his fingers along my inner thigh, his attention still riveted to my exposed pussy. Nerve endings sparking, my muscles clenched, fluttering under his touch.

"Emma," he murmured again. Then he flicked out his tongue and teased my clit with just the tip.

"Aiden!" I groaned.

He flicked twice, three times more, and I was already shaking, quivering.

His hold on my hip and thigh intensified, pinning me back even harder against the railing right before he closed his entire mouth over me, sucking and licking.

I rocked against him, panting small, sharp noises of need as my head fell back.

My feet started tingling almost immediately, pleasure building and building between my legs, throughout my core.

"I need… I need…" I didn't know what I needed, but I needed something—

Aiden reached up and pinched my nipple through my bra. Hard and abrupt.

My orgasm exploded through me, my hips bucking and my stabilizing leg giving out. I tipped over across Aiden, even as he was trying to lick me through the apex of my pleasure.

He grabbed both my hips as I stumbled over him, and we fell back together, already tugging off items of clothing before we'd even settled on the floor.

I freed Aiden's hard length from his boxers with one quick yank—and a slight tearing—of fabric. I stroked him hard and fast. He swore almost violently, kicking off his jeans.

The power still emanating from the pentagram swelled in response to the sorcerer's words.

He grabbed my hips, tugging me forward to settle me on top of him. But I rolled to the side instead, pulling him over me.

I felt a hint of surprise flicker through our empathic connection, but it was immediately overridden by pure, fierce desire. Without any other words or encouragement, Aiden thrust into me, stretching me, filling me.

He settled his hands on either side of my head. Then, visibly straining with the effort of holding himself back, he gazed down at me, fully seated within my core.

"That first time… I would have made you come like that," he whispered. "Then buried myself deeply inside you just like this, and confessed…" He swallowed harshly.

"Confessed?"

"That… it was love at first sight for me, Emma."

He slowly shifted his hips, withdrawing until he was barely inside me at all. "That on one of the worst days of my life…" He slipped back inside me just as slowly—every muscle in his body clenched, held in check. "I saw you and I just knew."

Another stroke, still slow but quicker than the first. His arms were trembling now. And with the feel of his pleasure empathically paired with the physical sensation of him slipping in and out of me, I was already teetering on the edge of my own orgasm.

"I knew I had to be in your life, belong to you."

He leaned over me, brushing a tender kiss to my lips. I settled my feet on the floor, then bucked my hips to meet his next slow stroke.

He half-snarled, half-groaned, then finally lost himself to the moment, picking up the pace and driving into me.

I cried out, quietly at first. But then he reached between us and pressed his thumb to my clit, and

I was falling into my second orgasm, shuddering underneath him as he somehow managed to hold on for a few more measured thrusts.

I lifted my legs and grabbed my ankles, holding them up near his shoulders. Giving him even deeper access.

He swore vibrantly. His rhythm was on the edge of harsh, thrusts erratic, but still somehow not tumbling over the edge.

I wrapped my magic around him, practically coating myself in the pleasure flooding from him. Then I—my core, my very being—was clenched around him in a third orgasm.

Aiden groaned, hips jerking stiffly as he emptied himself in me.

He collapsed over me, still riding his climax. I trailed my fingers up his spine and across his shoulders.

The energy emanating from the pentagram dimmed.

"You used a spell," I teased, speaking into his neck.

He laughed huskily. "I almost lost it on entry, my goddess. I simply tried to distract myself, just a little."

I hummed contentedly.

He pressed up on his elbows to look down at me, still buried deeply within me. "I don't think there is anything to forgive, Emma. You did what you thought was necessary. I… if what you felt was even half of what I felt, not knowing if you were even alive—"

"The other four would have known."

He huffed. "So they kept saying."

"The members of the Collective see me as theirs. Their achievement. I was never in any danger of dying." I would keep the couple of times that Lindi, and then Six, had almost managed to kill me to myself. Knowing that withholding the full truth in this instance was the correct thing to do, for Aiden.

He pressed his forehead against mine. The contact was almost harsh as he held back whatever he really wanted to say, and instead whispered, "You belong to me. To me and Opal. And hopefully to Six. Not the Collective."

"Yes." I ran my hand through his hair and kissed him as gently as I knew how to. "Yes."

Aiden closed the kiss, then opened his mouth slightly, flicking his tongue lightly against my bottom lip—encouraging me to meet his tongue, to thrust into his mouth.

"Oh," I moaned against his lips. "Again?"

He chuckled.

And then we didn't exchange any more words. Not until Six woke up from his nap and Opal returned from the farmers' market with fresh bread and corn on the cob for dinner.

THIRTEEN

Chenda perched on the edge of the couch, leaning over Opal, who was sprawled across the floor near the unlit fireplace. The mystic's straight, white-blond hair fell forward over her face as she gestured to something in Opal's book and pointed out an inaccuracy in the text. Not for the first time.

Kader was deeply engrossed in a handwritten runed spellbook, sitting on the couch he'd apparently claimed for himself. He made the occasional note in the notebook he had splayed open on the arm of the couch.

With books and multiple notebooks scattered across the coffee table before him, Aiden was leaning against the front of the couch I was inadvertently sharing with Chenda, though she was mostly half out of her seat.

I was reading a romance novel that had been forced upon me by Lani. The part-time intuitive, full-time mechanic had given it to me for our trip to

Tofino, claiming it was 'exactly like *Downton Abbey*, but with magic and more sex.' I wasn't particularly enjoying it, though there'd been some sword fighting in the last chapter that had been somewhat titillating. Enough so that I might contrive a way to get a sword into my dark sorcerer's hand. Soon.

Christopher was cooking dinner—roasting a chicken on the rotisserie that had come with the new barbecue he'd purchased, and making salads. Bee was holed up in the attic, as she had been for the past few days. Sulking over what she saw as her incarceration, I presumed. Even with a fan blowing, it had to be far too hot up there.

Samantha had taken over the dining room after finding another table somewhere. A table that she'd proceeded to cover in revisions and other plans. Fish was hanging out with her—none of the other three were comfortable around Kader or Chenda for more than a few minutes. I was certain that it was only the names of the former members of the Collective on Opal's adoption papers that continued to dissuade Zans, Fish, and Bee from murdering the pair outright.

The thought of the adoption papers made me remember that I still hadn't heard back from Ember Pine, my witch lawyer, about how we were going to handle Six's official... well, everything. Sighing internally, I gave up on my book, reaching for my iPad to check for recent emails.

Six was grinning up at me from just under the edge of the coffee table. He had three of his picture books open before him on the floor, but was currently running a fire truck up Aiden's leg.

While the sorcerer pretended not to notice.

I grinned back at Six, abandoning my iPad. But before I could ask if he wanted to grab one of his books and join me on the couch, Opal let out a sharp hiss.

"Ow! Ow!" The little witch held up her finger, displaying a rather nasty paper cut.

"Ouch, my darling," Chenda said, reaching for her. "Here, let me—"

Six got to Opal first, crawling out from under the coffee table and reaching for the dream walker's hand.

Every adult in the room held their breath. But Opal just grinned at the plague bringer and offered him her bleeding finger.

He wrapped his hand around that finger. And with barely a whisper of magic, he healed the wound.

Opal peered down as if inspecting his work, then sucked the remaining blood off her finger before she presented it to Six. "Perfect. Thank you, bro."

Six bobbed his head, then seemed to realize that we were all watching him. He turned wide emerald eyes on me, lifting his chin almost defiantly. "I heal Opal."

It was the first time any of us had seen him voluntarily use his magic. And he'd done so despite having insisted on me draining him again just that morning.

"Yes," I said, smiling at him so hard that the expression hurt my face. "You are a healer."

His breath became shaky. His chin quivered, and one large tear rolled down his face.

I reached out for him, offering the embrace even though I really just wanted to scoop him up. He reached back for me, his face screwed up as he desperately tried not to cry.

Leaning over Aiden, I pulled Six into my lap. He pressed his wet face to my neck, and I rubbed his back soothingly. "Such a good job," I murmured. "Such a good job, my boy."

Aiden wrapped his hand around my ankle, leaning into me.

"And this one?" Opal asked brightly, deliberately pulling Chenda and Kader's attention to her. "Calming, right? That's one of Christopher's oracle cards."

"When dried, yes," Chenda said. "But the oil can be… coercive with the right application of magic."

"You mean 'corrosive,' right?" Opal asked. "Because the Academy frowns upon mind control."

Kader laughed quietly.

Chenda huffed.

Tuning out the rest of their conversation, I loosened my grip on Six, wiping the tears from his face. He reached up and ran his palms across my own cheeks, then looked at his wet hands. "Sad?"

"Happy." I brushed my hand over his head. His hair was growing quickly and looked as though it was going to be as thick as Opal's. "What about you?"

He looked at me for a long while, sucking on his bottom lip. "Cookie?"

I laughed. "We just had tea."

He tilted his head, blinking his eyes at me—and totally mimicking Opal. "Cookie is happy."

Aiden chuckled.

"It totally is," Opal said, jumping to her feet. "Come on, Six, let's check the freezer."

The dream walker skirted the back of the couch, holding her hand out to Six. The same hand he'd healed. He looked at her for a moment, and she just smiled gently back at him. Then he climbed off my lap and took her hand.

"Come, Gus," he commanded.

The goblin cat appeared out of nowhere, popping up right in the middle of the living room, then sauntering after Six and Opal.

Chenda gasped lightly, pressing her hand to her chest. "That damn cat," she muttered to herself.

Aiden threw his head back, laughing.

And though I loathed to stopper his joy, I leaned over and offered him a lingering upside-down kiss.

When I finally looked back up, Kader was watching us with the slightest of smiles. I could clearly see the pride in his gaze now. Still possessive, yes. But... also threaded through with contentment. Even happiness.

I WOKE, FEELING SIX CURLED UP NEXT TO ME ALONG the edge of the bed. Though his own bed had arrived— he had helped Christopher and Aiden set it up in my former upstairs sitting room—he still crawled into our bed at some point, early each morning.

But that wasn't what had woken me. I turned my head to find Bee lingering in the open bedroom doorway, hesitating.

Then, having apparently made up her mind, she crossed to the bed and attempted to climb in next to Six. There wasn't enough room, but she disturbed the little healer enough that he crawled over me, grumbling to himself, and promptly sprawled across Aiden's bare chest. He fell asleep again the moment after Aiden's arm closed over him.

I took a moment to absorb the burst of utter joy that followed that not-as-simple-as-it-appeared cuddle. Except in rare moments, Six still wasn't touching anyone but me voluntarily. Initiating the embrace with Aiden was something different. Something new.

Bee shimmied into the bed, trying to steal a portion of the top sheet. Unfortunately for her, one half of it was pinned under Aiden.

"Socks," she complained, hushed but grumpy.

I sighed, then slid farther into the middle of the bed.

Bee lined herself up next to me, not touching me but sharing the corner of my pillow. It was dark enough that I couldn't discern the color of her eyes, but I could still see that the wound on her neck had almost completely healed over.

"You need to forgive me," she said.

I didn't answer. Mostly because I didn't take orders from anyone. But also because it wasn't my forgiveness she needed to be begging for.

"Forgive me, Socks," she whispered. "I feel… more balanced with you near. I should have…" Her voice cracked. "I should have known… if I had told you…"

"I was never going to go after Gen 4 for you," I said.

"But the boy," she whispered. "I know you would have gone after the boy. And…" She rolled over onto her back to stare up at the darkened ceiling. "Gen 4 would still be alive, if not for me."

"They made their own choices," I said stiffly. "Now you'll live with the consequences of your choices."

"If you forgive me, the others will forgive me."

"No," I murmured. "I'm not their leader. You'll have to repair what you've broken with each of them."

"I thought… that Knox would still… that he could… but he loves you."

"He loves his family."

"And I… I nearly destroyed it."

"Go to sleep, Bee." I rolled into Aiden and Six, laying my hand on Aiden's shoulder. Magic glinted from my dark sorcerer's eyes as he peered at me, then he smiled and closed them again.

Bee hovered her hand over the blood tattoos etched into my upper spine, presumably sensing, even taking comfort in, the simmering magic in each, but she didn't otherwise touch me.

At some point, we all fell asleep again.

Two weeks later.

I had retreated to my room, alone for the first time in weeks. Opal was due back at school in three days. We wanted to get married before the dream walker was forced to leave us again.

And I still definitely wanted to get married.

But things had gotten way, way too out of hand.

As Aiden had warned me, Kader and Chenda had gotten involved. At first, their doing so was to keep Opal occupied while we rescued Samantha and Daniel. And then when I'd needed rescuing, and when we brought Six home. But somewhere during all that, a competition between the former architects-of-the-Collective-turned-enemies-turned-co-grandparents was sparked.

While my attention had been rather necessarily diverted.

And now, chairs and tables were being delivered and set up in the backyard. The back patio was strewn with delicately woven flower garlands and dotted with unlit candles, each of which held some different magical significance.

There was a guest list. It included people I'd never even met, most of whom had the Azar surname, including a young sorcerer who Opal had befriended at school. But there were also Myers coven witches, including Sky and Ocean, who had returned to the house two days before, and Godfrey witches, including Pearl and Scarlett. Plus Aiden's brothers and cousins, and Becca and Calhoun, both fully recuperated from our mission.

A teleportation pad with a ridiculous amount of security surrounding it was now radiating immense power from the northeast corner of the property.

A silky, ivory-colored dress emanating witch magic had been gently laid across the bed behind me. Along with jewelry. So. Much. Jewelry. In velvet boxes. Including an emerald circlet I was supposed to wear across my forehead, tucked back into my hair. And a massive cut emerald—easily the size of a small egg—strung on triple strands of white, rose, and yellow gold that was supposed to dangle just above and between my breasts.

So I had retreated.

Retreated from a battlefield that had nothing to do with blood or death. The power plays and strategic moves were still prevalent, however. Far too prevalent.

I had managed to shower, then slip on a shiny silk sheath that fell all the way to my ankles. I assumed it must have been an underlayer for the dress.

Then I'd made the mistake of peeking out the window into the backyard, and just stopped moving.

I was having some sort of anxiety attack.

It had been subtle at first. A slight tightness in my chest as I'd gotten breakfast into Six while the first of the deliveries arrived. Then, after Daniel had distracted Six, and with Lani and Jenni Raymond arriving to help with final touches, I'd become sort of disconnected. As if I might just float through the rest of the morning.

Then I started feeling light-headed.

And now I was all but immobilized, my hair not even fully dry.

Watching the chairs get set up in the backyard.

Too many chairs.

Way, way too many chairs.

It was possible I should have been paying more attention to Chenda and Kader's preparations.

Out in the yard, Six was riding on Daniel's shoulders. The little healer had really taken to the nullifier over the past few days, giggling whenever he begged Fish to use his power on him. Chenda had started teaching Opal some basic healing spells, though she herself wasn't a healer, knowing that Six was listening in on every lesson. And I'd been working at distinguishing the different tenors of the plague bringer's power and siphoning off only what felt malicious.

But we would eventually need to find a teacher who could guide Six to use all his magic. Because if he didn't learn to wield it, he could someday be triggered again, just as he had been on the yacht. There, it was fortunate that his power had been somewhat contained by the confined environment. But if the same thing happened somewhere else…

Outside, Daniel tilted his head as if listening to something. Then he headed off toward the barn with Six clutching at his hair and smiling broadly.

"Mom?"

Opal's sweet voice freed my limbs from their anxiety-induced immobility just enough for me to turn my head.

She was peering in from behind the bedroom door, looking around as if she expected me to have company. When she saw I was alone, she entered with Paisley at her heels.

"Are you okay?" she asked, stepping over to brush her fingers across the circlet still nestled in the velvet confines of its box.

"Fine," I said, completely lying.

Outside and directly below me, Lani and Jenni stepped out from the house, with Lani immediately engaging Chenda and waving a hand toward… the patio? The floral arrangements?

Jenni was striding over to engage Kader, who was already in discussion with Khalid and Isa. Both of Aiden's brothers had arrived only an hour before.

I frowned.

Something was going on. Something other than the wedding prep.

Opal slipped her hand into mine, and I almost flinched. I hadn't felt her cross around the bed. "I've got a surprise." She grinned up at me. "But we have to move now."

Paisley lumbered around to press her shoulder to my leg, giving me a shove.

"I'm supposed to be…" I didn't finish the thought, my gaze sweeping around the room while my mind skipped through and over the myriad of little tasks that were now somehow expected of me.

"You look beautiful like this…" Opal tugged on my hand. She had black roses and pea shoots woven into her hair in a half crown, but was still dressed in torn jeans and an orange-and-pink T-shirt.

And I discovered I could move.

For Opal.

I smiled at my little witch as she grinned back at me, blue magic glinting mischievously in her eyes. She tugged me, barefoot and naked under the long silk sheath, out into the hall and down the stairs. Paisley escorted me on my other side.

Opal paused midway down the stairs, pressing a finger to her lips and cocking her head to the side. I couldn't feel anyone in the house, but I indulged whatever the dream walker had planned.

Then, with a stronger tug on my hand, Opal dashed through the already open front door and made a break for the barn.

Paisley loped alongside us.

Only one of the main doors of the barn was open, and just wide enough for Opal to slip through and pull me after her.

We stepped around the Mustang, and I picked up an intense well of magic emanating from the loft. But I couldn't see anything unusual when I glanced upward.

I opened my mouth to question Opal, but she dropped my hand, skipping excitedly toward the base of the stairs.

"I got her!"

Paisley grumbled, giving me another nudge forward with her shoulder.

"We got her," Opal corrected.

And then she completely disappeared.

I lunged forward on pure instinct, all my residual anxiety burned away between one step and the other. My summoned black blade settled into my outstretched hand, and a step later I had it against the throat of the person who'd been hiding behind one of the most powerful obfuscation spells I'd ever *not* seen.

"Trust you to bring a blade to a wedding, Fox in Socks," Christopher said wryly. The white of his magic ringed his light-gray eyes but didn't obscure them.

Opal was standing at the bottom of the stairs leading up to the loft, one hand clasped over her mouth and her eyes wide as she watched me nearly decapitate the clairvoyant. She was carrying a small bouquet of black roses and pea shoots in her other hand now.

His hair still wet from a shower, Christopher flashed me a grin, then placed two fingers to the pommel of the blade and directed it away from his throat. He was clad in light-blue jeans, leaving his chest and feet bare.

I let my blade drop to my side, narrowing my eyes. "What is going on?"

Christopher simply grinned at me, then slipped a simple half crown of flowers on my head—woven out of more black roses and pea shoots, though it was slightly more intricate than Opal's crown. He carefully secured the three tiny combs hidden underneath it into my hair.

"Time to get married the way you want to be," he murmured, brushing a kiss across my lips. "But… maybe leave the blade?"

I huffed, still not quite following what was going on. But Paisley curled one of her tentacles around my sword, so I released it. She absorbed the weapon into her otherwise invisible mane.

"I'm going to need that back," I said sternly.

Paisley dropped her mouth open in a wide, toothy smile, then flicked her forked blue tongue at me.

"Here." Opal pressed the bouquet into my hand. "And…" She spun back to a white box set on the stairs and pulled out another half crown of black roses. This one she placed on Paisley's head. "You go first."

Chuffing happily, Paisley started up the stairs.

Then, grinning back at me, Opal followed.

Christopher took my hand and laid it over his arm… as if he was going to… escort me? I glanced up the stairs, watching as Paisley and then Opal disappeared at the top, crossing through what appeared to be another obfuscation spell.

Christopher whispered against my ear, "Last chance to run away with me, Socks."

Finally putting together what my family had done for me, was in the process of doing for me, I simply met his gaze for a long moment. Then I whispered back, "We already tried running away."

"That we did."

"Let's make a different choice this time."

He flashed me a grin. "Together."

Magic punctuated that word, his vow.

"Always," I vowed back.

Then I took the steps up into the loft, with one of my blood-bonded siblings at my side.

Aiden was waiting in his copper-edged pentagram, with Six peeking at me from around the sorcerer's jeans-clad legs. Aiden was also barefoot, and his chest was covered in inked runes that I didn't take the time to decipher. He ensnared me in his gaze, and I couldn't look away.

I stepped away from Christopher, crossing to join Aiden in the pentagram. Samantha, wearing jeans and a tank top, plucked my bouquet out of my hands as I passed her.

Aiden touched Six on the shoulder, directing him to stand to the side but between us. Opal took up the opposite side, so that the four of us were tucked tightly together in the center of the pentagram.

Paisley settled into the main point between Opal and me. Then Daniel, Bee, Knox, and Samantha arrayed themselves the same way. Bee swept my hair over one of my shoulders as she stepped into place, exposing the blood tattoos on my back.

Which explained why she and Samantha were in low tank tops, and why Daniel and Christopher were bare chested.

Aiden was…

Aiden had designed a…

I swallowed the utter happiness threatening to choke me, and reached for my dark haired-sorcerer's hands. Because I apparently couldn't respond verbally.

Aiden took Opal's hand in one of his, grasping me with the same hand, so I was holding them both. Understanding, I took Six's hand—he had to lift up on his tiptoes and press himself against my leg for balance—and placed it in Aiden's free hand covered with my own. So the four of us were clasping all of our hands together.

Paisley wrapped a tentacle around my ankle.

The other four stretched their arms over our shoulders, each just managing to touch the blood tattoo where their magic resided on my upper spine.

Aiden's pentagram ignited around us, humming gently.

And I understood what we were doing, what Aiden had set up for me.

My wedding present.

I had been created for this moment. Designed from inception, tied to the others, and trained to implement it.

The Amplifier Protocol.

Except when the Collective created the protocol, they hadn't factored in... this feeling.

This genuine attachment.

This love.

I released my power. All of it.

My magic met Aiden's unleashed, then Opal's. Not quite understanding the sharing part, Six tried to push his power into my hand, but I didn't pull any more from the healer.

Christopher's power flooded from him. Then Samantha, Daniel, and finally Bee joined their magic with ours.

It should have been suffocating, standing there surrounded by all of them. All that intense energy.

But I just breathed it in. My heart rate slowed, my stance firmed.

I gazed into Aiden's eyes and knew I had everything I'd never known I wanted. Never known I needed.

Yowling indignantly, Gus leaped onto Paisley's back, then prowled forward to perch on her head. Paisley gnashed her teeth threateningly.

"We looked for you," Opal said to the cat.

Six threw his head back and giggled, his power now instinctively threading through all of ours.

Fully unleashed and accepting of each other, we could have crushed any army of far more powerful magic users. We could have decimated cities. We could literally rule the world.

But I would settle for this life.

"Emma. You told me that I could have you in my life," Aiden murmured. "But that you came with four others who were bound to you by blood and magic, for life. And I wanted any part of you that I could have, even if it meant sharing. Then you brought Opal and Six into our lives, and I never thought I would have the capacity to... love so unselfishly, yet so completely selfishly. I would do anything for you. For our family. I am... so very blessed, Emma. That you've given me so much. Not only a family who will walk into death for each other and back out again. But two incredible children, who I get to see blossom alongside you every day in our home."

He squeezed my hands, and I somehow found I could speak.

"It wasn't really a home, Aiden, until you. Until you showed me I could... love. That I had that capacity, and that it wasn't a weakness. And... I got to choose. You, and Opal, and now Six."

I flashed him a smile.

And whatever was etched across my face had him respond with a wickedly dark gaze of his own.

"No one comes between us," I vowed. "Not ever again. I won't allow it. Forever."

"Always."

All our power, unified and overwhelmingly intense, churned around us as Aiden pressed his forehead against mine.

Pressing a kiss filled with all the power at my command against his lips, I murmured, "Home."

"Yes." Aiden kissed me back. "Home."

EPILOGUE

Sometime later.

The blood wards simmering around the French-paned windows of the bakery known as Cake in a Cup were a sharp contrast—almost viciously so—to the eclectic wind chimes hanging in those windows, and the colorfully topped cupcakes filling the display case just beyond the seating area.

I had felt the wards from a block away. Aiden hadn't bothered even glancing at the directions Scarlett Godfrey had sent, along with her invitation to visit. Or, rather, the charming witch's exuberant but explicit it's-time-we-see-you-all-in-Vancouver command, delivered to our doorstep via a delicately calligraphed note and wrapped in a wallop of boundary-ward-defying magic. Aiden swore he'd been steadily compelled in the direction of the bakery all the way from the boutique hotel in downtown Vancouver, where we were staying for the weekend.

We had timed our arrival perfectly for after-noon tea.

Aiden smoothed a hand down his already pris-tinely pressed navy suit, eyeing the magic coating the entire building like others might eye beautiful people or expensive jewelry or sports cars.

Opal bounced on her toes next to me. "I told you!" she said. "They have every flavor!"

"Marshmallow?" Six asked suspiciously.

According to Kader, the plague bringer was going through his questioning phase. To the delight of the elder sorcerer, of course. But that meant he was questioning everything, with most of those questions asked with narrowed eyes. Of course, when asked anything himself, Six's immediate response was a disgruntled no. Except for anything involving marsh-mallows. His new favorite thing.

Interior doors that led back into the bakery kitchen swung open to reveal a curvy blond woman wearing a thick gold-chain necklace that heavily contrasted her jeans and T-shirt. Her curly hair was pulled back in a high bun, and her sun-kissed skin set off her indigo eyes.

As I stepped toward the bakery storefront, the blond met my gaze through the paned glass and didn't look away. Didn't even bother glancing at the dark sorcerer at my side or the children.

I stared back at her steadily.

Her rose-glossed lips quirked. Then a blazing smile overtook her face. She beckoned with fuchsia-tipped nails, and the wards… shifted. Not opening, but offering passage.

I spotted the resemblance then.

The buxom blond was Pearl Godfrey's grand-daughter. Scarlett's daughter.

I transferred Six's hand into Aiden's hold, stepping through the wards as I opened and crossed through the bakery doorway—feeling a robust, almost edgy power tasting my own magic as I did so. I offered my hand to the blond as I closed the space between us.

She reached for me in turn.

I knew she wasn't only a witch the moment I touched her.

She grinned at me.

We were the same height, with her in low heels.

"I'm Emma," I said.

"Jade," she gushed. "So lovely to finally meet you, Emma."

Jade Godfrey carried almost as much cha-risma as her mother, Scarlett. But the weapon of mass destruction disguised as a piece of pretty jewelry wound around her neck seethed with unfettered, deadly power.

I pivoted slightly, still holding Jade's hand but looking back at Aiden, Opal, and Six as they too stepped through the wards and into the bakery.

"This is my family."

ACKNOWLEDGEMENTS

With thanks to:

MY STORY & LINE EDITOR
Scott Fitzgerald Gray

MY PROOFREADER
Pauline Nolet

MY BETA READERS
Anteia Consorto, Terry Daigle, Gael Fleming,
and Megan Gayeski Pirajno.

**FOR THEIR CONTINUAL ENCOURAGEMENT,
FEEDBACK, & GENERAL ADVICE**
SFWA (esp. the Discord crew)
FAROFEB (esp. the Discord crew)
Hailey Edwards
Carrie Ann Ryan
Elizabeth Mackey – for her oracle cards

Meghan Ciana Doidge is an award-winning writer based out of Salt Spring Island, British Columbia, Canada. She has a penchant for bloody love stories, superheroes, and the supernatural. She also has a thing for chocolate, potatoes, and cashmere.

The Amplifier Protocol (Amplifier 0)
Close to Home (Amplifier 0.5)
The Music Box (Amplifier 4.5)
Moments of the Adept Universe 1
Recon Mission: Bee (Amplifier 5.5)

For recipes giveaways, and a glimpse of her upcoming stories
please connect with Meghan on her:
Personal blog, www.madebymeghan.ca
Email, info@madebymeghan.ca

Please also consider leaving an honest review at your point of sale outlet.

DOWSER SERIES ● BOOK 1

CUPCAKES, TRINKETS,
and other
DEADLY MAGIC

MEGHAN CIANA DOIDGE

DOWSER SERIES ● BOOK 2

TRINKETS, TREASURES,
and other
BLOODY MAGIC

MEGHAN CIANA DOIDGE

DOWSER SERIES ● BOOK 3

TREASURES, DEMONS,
and other
BLACK MAGIC

MEGHAN CIANA DOIDGE

ORACLE SERIES ● BOOK 1

I SEE ME

MEGHAN CIANA DOIDGE

ORACLE SERIES ● BOOK 2

I SEE YOU

MEGHAN CIANA DOIDGE

ORACLE SERIES ● BOOK 3

I SEE US

MEGHAN CIANA DOIDGE

RECONSTRUCTIONIST SERIES ● BOOK 1

Catching Echoes

MEGHAN CIANA DOIDGE

RECONSTRUCTIONIST SERIES ● BOOK 2

Tangled Echoes

MEGHAN CIANA DOIDGE

RECONSTRUCTIONIST SERIES ● BOOK 3

Unleashing Echoes

MEGHAN CIANA DOIDGE

THE AMPLIFIER SERIES: BOOK 0

THE AMPLIFIER PROTOCOL

MEGHAN CIANA DOIDGE

THE AMPLIFIER SERIES: BOOK 1

DEMONS & DNA

MEGHAN CIANA DOIDGE

THE AMPLIFIER SERIES: BOOK 2

BONDS & BROKEN DREAMS

MEGHAN CIANA DOIDGE

www.ingramcontent.com/pod-product-compliance
Lightning Source LLC
Chambersburg PA
CBHW072110250626
47159CB00007B/2384